DISCARD
Peabody Public Library
Columbia City, IN

D1525253

Angel Dreams

By

Chris Schneider and Michael Phillips

FICTION C SCHNEIDER
Schneider, Chris,
Angel Dreams / by Chris
Schneider and Michael
Phillips.

NOV 2 9 2014

CHRIS SCHNEIDER is a well-known sportscast journalist and public speaker in Dallas, Texas. Author of the best-selling *Starting Your Career in Broadcasting*. He has worked on the air from London to Los Angeles and his broadcasts have been heard on the BBC, ESPN, CBS, and Armed Forces Radio. As well as working for the legendary Gene Autry in Los Angeles, he hosted pre and post-game shows for the Angels, Rams, Clippers and UCLA Bruins. From there he hosted a nationally syndicated talk show based in Chicago, followed by a stint in London working for ESPN and the BBC. He has now been with CBS in Dallas for the past fourteen years. He is the Sports Director and Morning show sports anchor at KRLD, 1053 The Fan, and the Texas State Networks. Schneider has won several broadcasting awards and is considered one of the top sportscasters in the country. He has also done multiple video Bible studies and Tele Award winning interviews for the Lutheran Hour Men's Networks (http://www.lhmmen.com/studyvideofull.asp?id=19297.) Schneider also enjoys public speaking, talking to audiences in the United States and England. He looks forward to doing as many radio and television interviews, and public speaking engagements as possible to promote this book. More information can be found at www.RadioActiveSpeaking.com.

MICHAEL PHILLIPS has been writing in the Christian marketplace for thirty-five years. He is the man responsible for the resurgence of interest in Victorian author George MacDonald, C.S. Lewis's spiritual mentor, through his edited and republished editions of MacDonald's work. Phillips is also a best-selling novelist in his own right, recognized as one of this generation's gifted storytellers. Phillips also possesses a gift for working with other writers, helping elevate shared vision to the maximum of its potential by the collaboration of talent. His partnership with Judith Pella in the 1980s and 1990s produced fourteen Phillips/Pella bestsellers. Phillips is excited now to link his authorial skill with the imaginative vision of Chris Schneider. In his long and distinguished career, Phillips has written and co-written over sixty original novels, with numerous appearances on CBA best-seller lists. Combined sales for his work tops seven million books. More information can be found at www.FatherOfTheInklings.com.

Angel Dreams
Copyright © 2014 by Chris Schneider and Michael Phillips
Published 2014 by Big Friend Books

All rights reserved. No part of this book may be used or reproduced in any form or by any electronic or mechanical means, including information storage and retrieval systems, without permission in writing from the publisher, except by a reviewer who may quote brief passages in a review.

ISBN: 978-1500820046

Contents

Dreams are illustrations from the book your soul is writing about you.
—Marsha Norman

ONE

VALENTINE'S PLANS

New Mexico, Sunday, February 2, 1947

Jack Holiday followed his friend from the private terminal outside to the tarmac of the Santa Fe airport. An icy gust of wind nearly sent him sprawling to the ground.

"Whoa — it's really kicking up!" he shouted, recovering himself. But Manny bent into the wind toward the plane without turning back. Casting a quick glance at the black clouds hanging over the Rockies to the north, Jack shivered and hurried after him.

Manny kicked away the tire guards and climbed into the pilot side of the two-seater Cessna. Jack jogged around the propeller, opened the opposite door, threw up his bag, then hauled himself into the passenger seat.

"That's some wind!" he said as he yanked his door shut. "Are you sure this is a good idea, Manny? That storm looks to be heading this way."

"We'll be okay," replied Manny, cinching up his seat belt and adjusting his headset. "But I want to get up and ahead of it pronto. No time to lose. Strap yourself in."

He leaned forward and turned the ignition key. The engine fired. Quickly the prop began revving up to speed.

"Cesna 8XGK Niner requesting clearance," Manny barked into his mouthpiece as he eased the small craft into motion.

Seven minutes later, after being bumped by two TWA flights, at last they were cleared. Manny turned his small craft north, directly into the increasing headwind and bore down on the controls to full throttle. Twelve seconds later the tires

1   Peabody Public Library
Columbia City, IN

eased off the runway and the Cessna's nose arced up steeply. The moment he was up to speed, Manny banked sharply to the right until he had achieved a southeasterly heading.

The black clouds off the left wing, visibly closer than just a few minutes ago, reminded Jack of the Valentine's Day he and Janet had spent in Hawaii, watching surfers negotiating the terrifying Pipeline of Waikiki. Now he and Manny were trying to stay ahead of a ferocious storm wave bearing down on central New Mexico. Unfortunately, they had no surfboard. It if caught them, this wave would pummel their small plane to bits.

"Okay...we're on our way to Dallas!" said Manny. "Sit back and relax and enjoy the ride!"

"I don't know if I *can* relax," replied Jack. He tried to laugh but the anxiety was obvious in his voice. "That storm looks nasty. Are you sure we shouldn't wait it out and go back to the airport?"

"Naw. Look...we're already up to a hundred five knots with nothing but sunny blue ahead. We'll outrun it. By the time we're looking down on Clovis and crossing the border, we'll be surrounded by clear skies."

Jack drew in a deep breath, leaned his head back, and closed his eyes.

He loved Manny like a brother. Manny was his best friend ever since they had shipped out together in early forty-two. They were buddies even before their transport plane landed in England. It was a natural—they were the two oldest soldiers on the ship. Uncle Sam was taking anyone he could get and wasn't about to turn down two WWI vets. Both native Texans, they lived in Dallas after the war and had been close ever since. But if Manny had a fault, he could be *too* sure of himself. Downright cocky sometimes. He didn't know when to back off from a fight. You never won an argument with Manny. Jack learned a long time ago just to keep his mouth shut.

With his cockiness came a sense of invincibility. After surviving action in two world wars a little stormy weather was nothing to Armando Ramsay. He'd flown his Cessna all around the country, landing in snow, taking off in lightning, fearing nothing. If Jack didn't know better, he'd think his friend had a death wish. But Manny was just sure of himself.

His confidence in his abilities knew no limits.

That was the reason Jack didn't often fly with him. Manny was a cracker jack pilot. But Jack was never quite sure when he might play a little fast and loose with good sense. He would never have come with him to Santa Fe three days ago if the weather report hadn't called for fair weather through Wednesday. The predicted storm slicing down from the Pacific Northwest wasn't due to hit until the early hours of Tuesday morning. Now here it was chasing them across eastern New Mexico on Sunday afternoon.

Manny's voice interrupted Jack's reflections.

"Does Janet know what you were doing in Albuquerque?" he asked.

"No," replied Jack. "I told her you had meetings and asked me if I wanted to come along. She probably suspects though."

"Why would she suspect?"

"She's always suspicious this time of year, wondering if I'm up to something."

"You mean about Valentine's Day?"

"Yeah. Usually we plan our Valentine's adventures together. But since this is our first one since coming back from the war I want to give her something really special. Surprise her, you know. Our Hawaiian trip was that way. I showed her the tickets a week before Valentine's Day and we were on our way driving from Dallas to L.A. the next morning."

"Why do you guys get away on Valentine's Day and not Christmas? Didn't she leave on Christmas?"

Jack was quiet for a moment. He didn't really want to talk about the wound so old and yet still so fresh. "I don't know," he said. "I guess we kind of mourn her loss over the holidays and by Valentine's Day Janet and I need to reconnect, spend some special time together to know we will always have each other."

Only the drone of the plane engine could be heard for a few minutes while memories played through Jack's mind.

"You never forget, of course," he went on. "It will always be a painful time. Suddenly finding yourself alone as parents at Christmas—it's a shock. I mean...we had lots of good years when Leslie was young. We just weren't prepared for it to end so abruptly. I suppose we should have seen the handwriting on the wall sooner. But we didn't. That made it all the harder when she left. I tell you, I hated that young man for years."

"You never met him?"

"Nope. But it took me a long time to get over him stealing our daughter. Not that I *am* over it. If I met him now, I'd probably have a go at him. But life goes on. Somehow you've got to deal with it. When the Christmas card came, suddenly we hoped she might be coming home...then that was dashed too. That's when we started our cycle, I guess, mourning at Christmas and getting away on Valentine's. The war has kept me away from her the last four years—I want to make this trip special for Janet."

"And for *you*?" queried Manny.

"Men and women deal with their pain differently, I suppose. It's always done us both good to try to get away, do something unusual after suffering through the holidays. But you never forget."

Jack drew in a long sigh. Manny said no more. They'd talked about all this before. Talking helped...but it didn't help. Nothing could help. Miracles were for fairy tales. He had long given up hoping for a miracle to come to him and Janet.

So, like he had said to Manny—life went on. Now that he was back from the war they would continue their yearly challenge to suffer through Christmas and recover their emotions enough by mid-February to find diversions and create new memories to replace the painful memory that always sought to intrude. They had ice skated in both Minnesota and Rockefeller Center on past trips. They'd swum in the balmy Pacific of Honolulu. They had opened their Valentine's cards to one another in a first class cabin of the Trans Canadian Railway on a five day excursion from Vancouver to Montreal. They had taken cruises in the Caribbean and up through the Alaskan inland channel. It wasn't that he made that much money. Bankers were well paid in Texas, but he and Janet had to budget carefully to make their yearly Valentines possible. Yet it was a priority, so they made it work.

Of course, the pain would always be there. They still had trouble talking about it. He would get silent. What was there to say? But having something new to look forward to every year helped them look ahead rather than back. They had each other, thought Jack. That counted for a lot.

This year he hoped to pull off a surprise that would surpass any possible expectation Janet could have. The place he'd booked yesterday was perfect—a hunting chalet in the southernmost expanse of the Sangre de Christo mountains between Santa Fe and Albuquerque. The view of Mt. Sandia and the surrounding mountains—now laden with white—was spectacular. Dry oak was abundantly stocked in for the huge fireplace. The *piece de resistance* would be an authentic horse-drawn sleigh ride up from the tiny town of Placitas up to the chalet. He'd seen the advertisement in a hunting magazine and had flown to Santa Fe with Manny. While Manny was busy with his meetings, he'd made all the arrangements. Nothing was left to chance. He'd even brought in a supply of romantic record albums for the Hi-Fi—Bing Crosby, Dean Martin, Frank Sinatra. In a little over a week, he and Janet would be on their way by train from Dallas to Albuquerque for Valentine's Day in the mountains.

A sudden lurch of the plane brought Jack quickly back to reality.

He glanced out the windows. He hadn't noticed, but the sun had disappeared. The plane was swallowed in swirling black clouds.

"Looks like that front was moving faster than we were," said Manny. "I think I'll take it up to thirteen thousand and see if I can find some smoother air."

Jack felt himself pushed down into the cushion below him as Manny pulled back on the controls. Now that they were engulfed in the thing, the ride was bumpy, and worsening every second. At thirteen thousand it felt like they were being pummeled like a pinball.

"This isn't good," said Manny. For one of the rare times in his life, Jack detected anxiety in his friend's voice. If he didn't know better, it sounded like a tinge of fear.

"No good going higher…that's where the real weather is…I'm taking her back down."

A flash of light to their left was followed almost instantly by a deafening blast. The plane shook mightily from side to side.

"That was too close!" cried Manny. He bent the stick forward and jammed the wheel to the right, hoping to arc quickly away from the center of the electrical activity. "We'll head down low, way low…try to make a run for Lubbock…we'll set down there."

Jack had been in the Air Corps too. He'd never flown himself but had been on plenty of harrowing missions. He wasn't easily frightened. But Manny's little Cessna was no match for a storm of this ferocity. He didn't mind admitting it—he was scared now. Everything in the small cockpit was rattling as they bounced up and down and from side to side. How Manny could keep his hands on the controls was a miracle in itself. Jack glanced about, wondering where he kept the parachutes.

Another flash…then another…thunder echoed all around them. Whatever Manny's plan might have been, he had taken them straight into the eye of the tumult.

A great blast shook the plane dangerously. An explosion off the left wing sent them careening suddenly to ninety degrees.

"D—!" shouted Manny.

Jack's eyes were already closed. He tried to pray. All he could think of was Janet. A thousand fleeting thoughts raced through his brain…*how cute Janet was when they were both young with pig-tails and freckles…how beautiful she was when he fell in love with her, glad I bought that life insurance after we were married…how she beamed after giving birth to Leslie…getting sitters and going out dancing the Charleston and Jitterbug in the 20s…the Fred Astaire movies of the 30s—they never missed a one…dancing to Glenn Miller…dear Leslie, where did you go…come back, little girl…come back to your mother…I love you, Janet…give her a miracle, God, so that her life won't be full of more heartache…Lord, take care of her…Oh, God…Lord Jesus…Janet…Janet—*

Two

DESOLATION

"Mrs. Holiday...yes, hello, my name is Bill Slayton. I'm sheriff in Bailey County over here in west Texas. I've been working with Search and Rescue...I'm afraid I have some bad news..."

The words changed Janet Holiday's life in an instant.

The message was unreal. Dreamlike. From a nightmare that would remain for the rest of her life. The words had been constantly reverberating off the hollow walls of her brain ever since that terrible moment. Expecting Jack's call from the airport to say that he and Manny had landed, the last thing she had expected was a stranger's voice.

"...fierce storm came through...trees down...terrific electrical storm...hundred mile an hour winds..."

How ironic, Janet thought, to be holding Jack's Valentine's gift when the dreadful news came. She hated gift shopping — at least ever since Leslie left. She and Jack had stopped giving each other Christmas presents, it just did not seem right after their daughter was gone, so now they exchanged a gift on Valentine's Day. Yesterday she'd bought a new Buck hunting knife to add to Jack's collection — elk horn encased handle, three blades. She had just cut the wrapping paper when the telephone rang.

"...think the wing was hit by lightning...wreckage mostly intact...went down...thick forest north of town...wanted to call as soon as the identifications were made..."

Phone, paper, and scissors fell from her hand and clattered on the floor. She staggered across the room in a stupor, her brain seared of all thought and feeling.

Her best friend Anne Brodie found her hours later, asleep on the couch, a blanket pulled over her shoulders, huddled in a ball like a baby in a crib.

"Janet...Janet," said Annie softly, easing onto the edge of the couch and gently laying a hand on her friend's shoulder. "Janet...are you okay?" A stirring under the blanket told her that at least Janet was alive.

"I've been calling for two hours. The line's been busy. We were supposed to meet for lunch, remember? I thought something was wrong."

Slowly Janet came awake. She glanced up at her friend with wide eyes, swollen and red from crying herself to sleep. They were filled with the most forlorn expression imaginable.

"Janet, dear...what *is* it?"

"Oh Annie..." she whimpered at last, " —Jack's dead!"

"What! Surely, Janet...are you sure you weren't dreaming or —"

"He and Manny were coming back from Santa Fe. They got caught in the storm. The plane was hit by lightning."

"My God...oh, Janet!"

A blast of wind against the windowpanes and a distant rumble of thunder gave all the evidence needed to confirm Janet's words. It was not just a dream, or a nightmare. All day the news had been full of warnings that after dumping several feet of snow on the Rockies, the biggest storm of the winter was heading across the southern plains and northern Texas with a force likely to produce dozens of unseasonable winter tornados.

Annie bent down and took her friend in her arms. Janet burst into fresh sobs. Annie wept with her. But even the shared tears of a friend could do little to console the desolation of one who suddenly found herself alone.

THREE

GOOD BYE

Dallas, Texas, Friday, February 7, 1947

A raw gust of wintry air sent a shiver into the depths of Janet Holiday's bones. The terrible chill came not from the thirty-nine degree temperature, but from the sight in front of her.

She stood stoically, silently, solemnly. Every eye was on her. She knew it, but didn't care. It was hard to care about anything. This was a time for going through the motions, for doing what you had to do, doing what was expected, doing what you needed to do.

Slowly she removed her glove, then reached out and laid her right hand on the top of the wooden coffin. Her hand nearly recoiled at the touch. Ice shot through her fingers and into her soul. Beneath the coffin, a black empty hole yawned into the earth. What could be colder than a grave...the coldness of death?

"Good bye, Jack..." she whispered, blinking hard to keep the tears at bay. With slow determination she drew her hand back from her husband's final lonely resting place.

Behind her, tall oaks with their bare branches made her think of a skeleton. Faded leaves long since fallen from the oaks blew about from the final remnants of the storm that had passed through Texas with such fury. The storm that had taken Jack.

Two black-suited men from the funeral home came forward. Moments later the coffin began its solitary descent into the unknown.

It reached the bottom. They released the straps.

Slowly and silently the crowd of twenty-five or thirty came forward, clustered close, and filed by, tossing flowers on top of the coffin, then stepping away. Some greeted Janet, exchanging hugs and tears.

Manny's six children were fidgety. The rest of his clan— wife, sisters, aunts, uncles—wept freely with all the emotion of a Mexican family. They were weeping more for their own loss than Janet's. The outpouring of their grief would be even greater at Manny's funeral tomorrow.

Suddenly through the chilly afternoon, the piercing notes of a single bugle split the air. Everyone stilled. A few hands went to hearts and foreheads. The slow military rendition of *Taps* proceeded with its lonely tribute to a fallen comrade. Since neither Janet nor Manny's wife had served, the two men had made prior arrangements to opt out of burial at the military cemetery. The bugler and flag presentation were sent by the military to honor both veterans of two wars.

Tears fell in earnest as the final note died away in the wind. A uniformed Air Force captain came forward, stood before Janet, saluted, and handed her a folded American flag. Janet acknowledged the tradition with a nod.

The officer spun on his heels and returned to join the bugler. Slowly the crowd disbursed. More greetings...a few words of sympathy...hugs...tears...and the ordeal of the funeral was over.

"Are you ready, dear?" whispered Annie, stretching her arm around Janet's waist.

Janet nodded. They walked to the funeral car where Annie's daughter and sons were already waiting. Annie opened the back door. She and Janet climbed into the back seat together. As they drove away, the damp wintry cemetery faded into a blur in Janet's mind. She was hardly aware of Annie in the seat beside her. She saw nothing out the windows, scarcely knew what had happened as she walked into the Brodie home, and remembered nothing of the rest of the day. Annie did her best to mitigate the pain. People came by in ones and twos. There was food, conversation, a blazing fire in Annie's fireplace. Organizer that she was, Annie had invited people to come by in stages through the afternoon.

With Manny's funeral tomorrow and a full-scale Mexican gathering planned, it would have been silly to do the same thing two days in succession.

Janet was oblivious to most of what took place the rest of the day. The last thing she knew was getting home and being put to bed, Annie kissing her good-night on the cheek, then tip-toeing down the hall to spend the night in what had once been Leslie's room and for the past dozen or so years had been their guest room.

Thankfully, exhaustion took over the moment Janet's head hit the pillow. She slept soundlessly, and without unsettling dreams of storms and crashing planes disturbing the peacefulness of her oblivion.

FOUR

THE FIRST DREAM—THE MOUNTAIN AND THE ANGEL

Christmas Eve, 1936

A boy of six soared through a bright sky of blue, over and under cotton candy clouds floating in the expanse of the universe.

Bright and alive, he was filled with energy and health. Gone was the deadness he had always known below his waist. He felt his legs just like he felt his arms. They were moving and kicking. Was this how swimming felt! How could he know? But he wasn't swimming – he was flying!

He saw himself coming to a mountain ahead covered to its very peak with green. He swooped down toward it and came to rest, standing barefoot on the thickest, most luxurious grass imaginable. He was standing! He felt the grass between his toes, as if it were growing and tickling the underside of his feet. In disbelief, he broke into a run across the expanse of green.

He ran and ran and ran. His legs were strong and powerful. He saw a figure dancing down from the top of the mountain ahead of him. She had flowing blond hair so she must be a girl...or a woman. She was older than him, though he couldn't tell how old. She seemed to be gliding down the slope on a cushion of air.

He ran gaily to meet her.

"Are you an angel?" he asked as he ran up. He hardly noticed that he had spoken for the first time in his life.

The tinkling laugh that met his ears was like the music of a choir, running water over pebbles, and the vibration of the strings of a harp all at once.

"I don't know," she replied.

The moment he heard her voice, he recognized her.

"Mommy, it's you!"

"Of course. Who else would I be?"

"So are you an angel?"

"I told you – I don't know," she said with a smile.

"Then what are those tiny wings growing out of your back?"

"I don't know. I suppose I shall find out all I am supposed to know. Maybe I am growing into an angel. Do you want to dance with me? This grass feel so good on my feet, I can't help dancing."

The boy followed his mother-angel in this wonderful dream, as they danced and skipped around one another, both leaping ten feet off the ground with every step.

"I've never danced in my life!" he said. "In fact, I've never been able to talk before now. You know that I can't talk."

"I always knew that you would be able to talk one day. You are talking now and you sound so wonderful!"

"I haven't had so much fun in my whole life. You haven't forgotten that this is my birthday?"

"Of course not, my little boy!" she said, giggling with childlike laughter. "I would never forget that."

"Can you fly too, Mommy?"

"I don't know. I saw you flying a minute ago. You were flying in those clouds up there. But I think maybe I am dreaming."

"Me too! But isn't it a happy dream!"

Soon the mother-angel with the tiny wings growing on her back was skipping away from him back toward the high mountain.

"Mommy, don't go," he called after her. "I'm not ready for the dream to end."

"It won't end," she said, though her voice was becoming faint. "It will never end. The Dream-Maker turns all our dreams into life."

"Come back…please don't leave me."

"I will send another to visit you while you sleep."

"Please don't leave me, Mommy."

You will dream and you will live. Because you live, you will dream. Your dreams will become real, and I will always be with you."

"Don't leave me…don't leave me…"

Already the wings on the woman's back had grown. She was flying high and soon disappeared above the mountains into the white clouds and the sky of blue.

Five

MEMORIES

Dallas, Saturday, February 8, 1947

Janet drifted dreamily back to consciousness with the sounds of a love song on the radio floating up from downstairs. It was accompanied by the faint aroma of bacon and coffee.

Jack, she thought, *it's not Valentine's Day yet...what are you doing? But the coffee smells so wonderful I could —*

With full wakefulness she was seized with the horrifying reminder of the truth.

Jack...oh, Jack, she whispered as her eyes filled, *what am I going to do without you?*

She allowed herself to weep softly for a few minutes. She lifted back the covers, and forced herself to rise. After a good dousing of her face with cold water, she wrapped her robe around her and started downstairs.

"Annie, you are a dear," she said walking into the kitchen. "There are no two more intoxicating morning smells than bacon and coffee."

Annie turned and went to her. The two friends embraced warmly.

"How did you sleep?" asked Annie.

"Pretty well," said Janet, forcing a smile. "No nightmares. I feel rested. Now that the funeral is over, I guess I will have to start thinking again."

"I'm glad you are feeling better."

"It was good of you to stay. Thank you." Again Janet drew in a deep breath forcing a show of strength she really

14

did not possess. "I think I will be okay now. I mean, I *won't* be okay. But I'm not the only woman in the world who's been widowed at forty-nine. You of all people know that. Jack and I had a good life together...well, except for Leslie, after...you know."

"Sit down and have some coffee."

Annie poured out two cups and the friends sat down at the table.

"Is there anything I can do for you today?" asked Annie.

"You've got your own family and responsibilities at the store to think of. I'll manage."

"What will you do?"

"I don't know. Maybe I will sit down with our photo albums. I need to remember Jack as he was, his smile, his laughter. And Leslie. Maybe I need to remember her now too, and draw some comfort from that. I'm sure I'll cry. But it's time for me to cry alone, and let the tears do their work."

She paused and a wistful expression came over her face. "I want to remember the happy times," she said after a moment. "It will be sad to see the pictures. Funny, isn't it, how happy memories make you sad? But Jack and I had so much fun together back in those days. He was so full of life. We went to movies and dances, even after Leslie was born we got out as much as we could. You remember the 20s — everything was full of life. And Jack loved his little daughter! He would play with her and roll on the floor and crawl around giving her horsey rides on his back for hours. I think he read to her more than I did. He was such a devoted father. I think that's why it was so devastating for him when Leslie left. He poured his whole life into that girl. He wanted nothing more than to be a good father as she grew into adulthood. He wanted to be the shoulder she cried on, the listening ear, the compassionate daddy she came to with her troubles. Then suddenly all that was taken away from him. We went on with our lives, I suppose. But in a way, Jack never completely recovered."

The kitchen fell silent. Both women sipped at their cups.

"How did you and Jack meet?" asked Annie. "As long as I've known you, I don't think you've ever told me."

Janet was quiet for a few moments trying to decide if she should tell the truth. She and Jack had always skirted the issue when it came up, embarrassed really. With her heart breaking Janet hoped maybe telling the truth would bring some magical balm of healing to the pain she was feeling. Maybe she was being punished for the mistakes she had made as a young woman.

Finally Janet spoke in scarcely more than a whisper. "It was scandalous really," she said.

Annie's eyes grew wide with surprise as Janet took a deep breath.

"Jack and I grew up together in Abilene," she continued softly. "He was a few months older than me but we were in the same grade. Our families lived across the street from each other and there was not a time in my life I don't remember Jack. We went to school together, we played together, and sometimes we had terrible fights and said we would never speak to the other again. But, of course, we always did."

Silent tears began to stream from Janet's eyes as she continued. Her best friend listened in amazement.

"Something happened when we were fourteen," said Janet. "I guess we were maturing too fast for our own good. We thought we were so grown up, you know. What had always been friendship turned into something else—love I guess. I mean, we were too young to know what love was, but then we were sure we were in love. We would hold hands when nobody was looking. We carved our initials into trees. We would even sneak down to the creek and kiss sometimes," Janet added, blushing.

She was silent for the next few moments, too embarrassed to make eye contact with her friend. At length, Annie prompted her to continue. "So? What happened?" she said

"Well, we were just dumb kids I suppose," Janet said. Her words almost seemed to carry the tone of an apology. "We ran away and got married. I was only fifteen."

"You didn't!" Annie exclaimed.

"It's true—we did," Janet nodded. "When they found out, at first our parents each blamed the other and would not speak to each other. We were both still living at home. For a while they refused to let Jack and me see one another.."

"Seriously...you were only fifteen?" said Annie, still incredulous

Again Janet nodded.

"So what happened?"

"There was talk of an annulment and threats and accusations back and forth. But as all that gradually died down from the scandal and our folks realized that Jack and I really did love each other, everyone came to accept it. We had hurt our parents deeply, but all four of them tried to help us make it work. Eventually we moved in with Jack's parents. Leslie came along. Our moms helped us raise her. Our parents insisted we both finish high school, which we did. I guess being married and having Leslie made us grow up real fast. Maybe because of what we had done, we were determined to work hard in school and prove that we could make a success of our lives. Leslie was two years old and as cute as a button when Jack and I were starting college. Our parents both babysat and helped take care of her. Jack was so smart. He was the valedictorian of our class and was given a full scholarship to study to be an engineer. That's when he started to fly. The banker in Abilene was Mr. Roberts — he was the richest man in town. He was a plane fanatic and had his own bi-plane that he learned to fly. Mr. Roberts had a special place in his heart for Jack. Jack worked for him all through high school and college — and he even taught Jack how to fly. They did some crop dusting for the farmers once in a while."

"This is amazing" Annie exclaimed. "How could I not know this?"

"It's not something I advertise, or even that I am particularly proud of," Janet answered. "We made it work, and I am thankful for that. But we learned quickly that our youthful marriage was not something to be talked about openly. We were ostracized. I still remember some of the ugly looks the women at church gave me when they found out. I guess Jack and I just carried that tight-lipped reluctance with us as we got older"

Annie nodded her head in understanding.

"We both graduated a year early from both high school and then college. My dad," Janet continued, "was a pretty progressive thinker. He wanted me to go to college. After he had forgiven me for getting married, which took a while, we became close again and when I graduated from high school he knew that I wanted to go to college, and insisted that I do so. My mom and Jack's mother took care of Leslie when needed while Jack and I went to school."

"So what happened after college?" Annie prompted.

"We both graduated a year ahead of schedule from Abilene Christian University in 1917, Jack at the top of his class with an engineering degree and me with my teacher's degree. Mr. Roberts promoted Jack at the bank—he was making pretty good money. We had been living with his parents and were ready to buy our first house, everything was going well. We were happy—and then America became involved in World War I."

"And?" Annie asked, riveted to Janet's story.

"Jack decided he needed to be a hero and enlisted in the Army." Janet replied. "I remember it like it was yesterday. We have a little five year old girl, we are just out of college, he's got a great job, we are about ready to buy our first house, and he decides he needs to go off to war. Annie, I was so mad I didn't talk to him for days. I refused to talk to him until the day he was scheduled to ship out. Finally I broke down and cried like a baby. I was so afraid. I didn't think I would ever see him again."

The two women were quiet amidst their thoughts. Annie refilled their coffee cups.

Annie was the first to speak again. "So what happened in the war?"

"Typical Jack," Janet gave her friend a wry smile. "He was in the Army Corps of Engineers—they were desperately needed over there. He was promoted to be a Captain after a while. Since he was one of the few who knew how to fly a plane, he even flew a few reconnaissance missions. Just as he said he would, Jack came back a war hero in 1918 and he was the toast of Abilene. Everyone knew who he was. He went back to work at the bank. We bought our new house. Leslie was starting school and I was teaching."

"How did you end up moving to Dallas?" Annie asked.

"Jack's folks were both killed in a car accident in 1920 just outside of Abilene. They had gone out dancing for their anniversary and were hit coming home. A few months after the accident an Army friend offered Jack a position at Texas

First National Bank in Dallas. Jack felt like he needed the change. By early 1921 we were living here in Dallas. We bought this house and have been here ever since." Janet looked around. Memories of Leslie and Jack flooded back into her mind.

"Did you go back to teaching right away?" asked Annie.

"No. Jack didn't want me to go back to work. I think he felt that he ought to be able to support his family himself — you know how men are. It was hard for me at first, but I accepted it. Leslie was nine when we moved to Dallas. I stayed home with her."

Janet paused — trying to summon the strength to say what came next. "Leslie and I were close, wonderfully close for the next seven years," she finally went on. "But I guess what they say about the sins of the fathers is right. Jack and I had gone against our parents' wishes and married far younger than we should have. When Leslie was sixteen she met a cowboy who swept her off her feet. Before we knew it she had run away in the middle of the night."

Annie was quiet, lost for words.

"Leslie left in '28. I didn't know what to do with myself. I was going crazy just staying here at home, alone. So I went back to work teaching. I had to get out of the house and Jack knew it. I enjoyed teaching, trying to influence young lives."

"Why did you stop?" Annie asked.

"Jack volunteered to fight again after they bombed Pearl Harbor. I just laughed. I didn't think there was any way they would accept a forty-four year old banker into the Army — but I was wrong. He was reinstated as an Army Corps of Engineer Captain. I figured I needed to do something to help out too. I resigned my teaching job and helped sell war bonds and volunteered with the Red Cross at the Veterans Hospital. I really felt like I was helping. Not like Jack and the rest of the men who were over there fighting, but at least I was doing what I could, right?"

Janet sighed reflectively. "I can't help but feel that there's not much left for me to live for anymore," she said after a minute. "My daughter is gone. My husband is gone. We won the war and saved the world. But what am I supposed to do now?"

"You could teach again."

"Who's going to hire a forty-nine, soon to be fifty year old?"

"I bet there are dozens of schools who would love to have you. If you don't find anything, there will be a place for you at the Hay and Feed. I can always use another clerk."

Janet chuckled. "I'm not sure I want to spend the rest of my life selling Dog Chow and hay seed."

"It's not so bad," laughed Annie.

"Maybe not for you. You're the boss."

"Half the boss. Don't forget Jim's cousin Hank. All I am saying is that there are opportunities out there. When life throws you a curve, sometimes you have to explore directions you wouldn't have thought of before. I never intended to be a businesswoman. But when Jim was killed in the war and suddenly I found myself half-owner of a supply house for farmers and with a house full of kids, I had to adjust. Now I love it. The kids all help after school and in the summer. It's a family business. There's something fulfilling about that."

The word *family* sent Janet's thoughts back toward her own. Unconsciously her gaze drifted through the open kitchen door into the living room, where a framed photograph of her daughter at fifteen stood on the mantel above the fireplace. The sight brought her back to the reality of the present. Everything Annie said was well and good. But Annie had her children. Who did *she* have?

Janet finished the lukewarm coffee in the cup in front of her, then let out a long sigh.

"Manny's funeral is this afternoon," she said. "I hate to ask, after all you've already done...I know you didn't know him, but would you go with me? I just don't want to go alone."

"I'd be happy to," replied Annie.

"Then I promise...I'll let your house of teen-agers have you back!"

"They understand. You will come for supper tonight?"

"I don't know, maybe," answered Janet. "But I need to start figuring out what it feels like to be alone. After Manny's funeral and the gathering afterwards, I won't need anything to eat. Women never know what to do after someone dies, so they bake and cook."

"The invitation is open, even if you just come for the company."

"I know that. Thank you, Annie."

SIX

THE CHRISTMAS CARD

Dallas, Sunday, February 9, 1947

Janet did not go to the Brodie's for supper. As well as she'd slept after the funeral, the following day, if possible, was even more tiring. The emotional drain of the past several days finally caught up with her. She could hardly keep her legs beneath her through Manny's funeral, then the graveside service, then the interminable visiting at the Ramsay home. She and Annie paid their respects one last time to Manny's wife as soon as they felt propriety would allow, and slipped away.

It was five o'clock and Janet was exhausted. She walked into the house, thanked Annie for accompanying her, said she didn't think she would make it back over to her house for supper, then staggered up the stairs and flopped face down on her bed. She did not move for two hours.

When Janet awoke, night had descended. The house was dark, silent, and cold. After a hot bath, she was back in bed by eight-thirty. She did not awaken until she saw sunlight streaming through her bedroom window.

The storm had passed. The day dawned bright and clear. No aroma of coffee or bacon wafted up from the kitchen. No love songs sounded from the radio. At last Janet Holiday was alone. And she knew it.

Today truly was, as the saying went, the first day of the rest of her life. What would she do with it? What would she do with this day...*every* day?

She sat down on the couch with her cup of coffee half an

hour later. She lifted the photo album from the coffee table where she had left it yesterday.

She was ready now, she thought. She was ready to look at Jack's face...and Leslie's. She glanced up at the mantel again. Maybe they were both gone. But they were the only family she had. Did she or did she not believe that they were still alive...somewhere...with God...Jack in heaven, and Leslie *somewhere* in the world? They always said they believed. They prayed with Leslie when she was young. They taught her that God was a good Father who loved them, and would always love them no matter what.

Did she believe it or not, Janet wondered. Sure, she believed in God. But Jack was really the one who had insisted they go to church all those years. Janet doubted she would have gone every week if he hadn't wanted to. Memories filled her mind of the looks of the women back in Abilene when news of their secret marriage had swept through the church like a brushfire. Those women were Christians but all she was aware of was their whispering behind her back. She knew then that if that was what it meant to be a Christian, she wanted no part of it. She had always attended church for Jack. But today, the first Sunday after his death, she could not face the thought of it. What did it all mean...now? Death suddenly brought many new things into focus.

Like *doubt*. Did all people doubt at times like this? Was doubt a sin? Was it wrong to wonder such things?

So many quick and easy answers sprang to mind. But at a time like this, clichés didn't work very well. It was hard not to blame God. *Why?* was the great question on Janet's lips. *Why, God...why me...why Jack...why now...why grief...why suffering... why death? Hadn't we been through enough when Leslie left? Haven't I been through enough? God, why did you – "*

But was it really *God's* fault that Jack was dead? It was more likely Manny's.

What about Leslie? Was it *God's* fault that Leslie was gone...or theirs? Or was it *nobody's* fault? Was it just part of life?

Life was hard, they said—harder for some people than others. Well, they were right. Life *was* hard...and painful.

What was the purpose of it all? Was there *any* purpose?

Could good come out of death? She was alone, Janet thought. Her husband and daughter were both gone. How could that be good? Or might good come from it?

Maybe that was up to her.

Slowly Janet began thumbing through the photo album — she and Jack dancing the Charleston at the Ritz ballroom...Leslie's baby pictures. Gosh, she had put on so much weight after Leslie was born! It had taken her two years to shed those thirty pounds! Jack standing with Manny. They were just back from the war and happy to be alive. Leslie's birthday party at seven when they had invited her class to the park in Abilene. It had been almost more than she and Jack could handle! Janet quickly turned the pages back to the beginning of the album, how quickly the years had sped by. Leslie had been a baby and then suddenly she was a teen-ager. Overnight, it seemed, she turned into a gorgeous young lady...fifteen...then sixteen then —

From between the oversized sheets of the photo album an envelope fell to the floor.

Not recognizing it at first, Janet reached down and picked it up. Sight of the familiar handwriting, and the hastily torn envelope, immediately flooded her mind with memories. Suddenly even the loss of Jack receded briefly. The image of Leslie's face — no baby now, no ten year old, but a headstrong sixteen year old with a life of her own to live — filled her mind's eye.

Slowly Janet removed the card, opened it, and read again the last words she had heard from her daughter.

Dear Mom and Dad,

I have been thinking of you more than ever lately. I am sorry for the pain I've caused. I hope with all my heart you can forgive me for what I did. I know Christmas is coming up soon. I wish I could be there with you. But I am planning to visit you soon after Christmas. I will be in touch.

Your loving daughter,

Leslie.

Janet could not prevent the tears flowing again. Such hope had filled her when the card appeared in the mail nearly a decade ago. She had been so keyed up in the weeks following the card. She had baked and decorated in anticipation for their daughter's visit. She and Jack had done their best to prepare themselves to meet the young man, her husband now they assumed, who had taken their daughter away from them.

But Christmas and New Year's and Valentine's day all came and went. The eagerly hoped-for visit never arrived. Eventually the Christmas tree and decorations came down and were boxed up for another year.

Days and weeks…then months…and finally years continued to pass. Not another word ever followed. No letter. No visit. No card the next year, or ever again.

Only silence.

SEVEN

THE SECOND DREAM—A PARTING

Christmas Eve, 1937

A young mother eased her son, his legs hanging limp over her arms, into her bed. "There, my little man, how does that feel? It's Christmas Eve. Happy birthday again! You are seven now. You will sleep with me tonight.

She lay down next to him, stretched her arm around him, pulled him close, and began softly to sing. *Joy to the world, the Lord is come...*

Luke snuggled close, a smile of contentment on his face, He wished he could sing along. But being close to his mother was the next best thing. She was a lifeline in the midst of his helplessness. She was his mouth. She was his legs. Her eyes were the sun that lit his days.

The wonderful holiday feeling made the boy remember something he had completely forgotten. "Oh, Mommy," he exclaimed as she sang. "I've been wanting to tell you...last year on Christmas Eve I had the most wonderful dream. I want to tell it to you. I could walk and fly and talk! And I met an angel, Mommy, and it was *you*. You were in my dream! You were a real angel. But you were part of the dream too, and—"

Suddenly Luke remembered. He couldn't talk. His mother couldn't understand him. Whenever he opened his mouth, only babbles came out.

She paused, looked at him a moment, and smiled.

"I know, Luke," she said. "I know it's hard. You're trying to sing along, aren't you? You just lay there and sing in your mind, and dream of the day God will give you your voice. Then you will sing with the angels. Sing with me now in your mind. We'll start again— *Joy to the world, the Lord is come. Let earth receive her king...*

He would always have his mother's smile to comfort him, thought Luke. He would have to satisfy himself to speak to her through his own smiles.

And heaven and nature sing...and heaven and nature sing...and heaven and heaven and nature sing.

Luke smiled as broadly as he could. But his mind was no longer on Christmas carols. All at once he couldn't wait to go to sleep. If his wonderful dream had come on Christmas Eve a year ago...maybe it would come again! Gradually he felt himself getting drowsy.

"I've got a surprise for you Luke. We are going to turn over a new leaf this coming year. I sent your grandma and grandpa in Dallas a letter letting them know we would be coming to see them. I've been saving up for months. In a couple of weeks we will have enough to buy bus tickets to go see them. Does that sound fun?"

Luke had seen other children playing with grandparents and they always looked like they were having great fun. "Yes!" he hollered joyfully in response. Again, his mother heard only gurgling noises but she knew exactly what he had said.

"Good! I'm excited about it too. You will like your grandma and grandpa. Let's say a prayer before you go to sleep?" said his mother, happier than Luke thought he had ever seen her.

He looked into her eyes with a smile and nodded.

"Dear Lord," she began, "thank you for this day and the wonderful gifts in life you give us. Thank you for the blessing of my beautiful son. I love him so much." She pulled Luke closer as she prayed. "Tomorrow is Christmas and we are going to make a new start of it. Please watch over Luke, Lord. Protect him and may he always know you and love you as he grows. In Jesus name, amen."

And, God, Luke added silently, *could you please let me have the happy dream again? I won't ask you for anything else if I could just walk and talk and live the dream again.*

His mother kissed him, then sat up. "Good night, Luke. Sleep well. I love you."

She rose, turned out the light, and left the room.

The moment she was certain her son was asleep, the mother slipped on her coat and hurried from the house. She had never left Luke alone in his young life. But it was Christmas Eve. He would be safe for fifteen or twenty minutes. There was a special gift she wanted to get for his stocking in the morning. She hurried through the chilly night air. Downtown was a walk of only four or five minutes and she knew that several of the stores were still open for last minute shoppers.

Her errand did not take long. She knew exactly where she was bound. Fifteen minutes later she was on her way home with a small bag under her arm.

Ahead in the distance, the headlights of an approaching car caught her attention swerving back and forth across the street. The car was coming toward her faster now — she moved off the sidewalk onto the lawn at her left, continuing to eye the oncoming lights warily.

The dreamer came awake, or seemed to come awake. He felt himself pulled up...up out of the bed...up into the sky through a tunnel of purest light. He was weightless...floating higher still. He felt his legs! He flapped as he had before, pretending to be swimming in a weightless sea of air.

His Christmas dream had come again!

In an ecstasy of happiness, the boy kicked and flew in the liquidy vibrant air until he felt himself descending. He looked beneath him. He was coming down into the middle of an expansive field of grass. He felt his bare feet settling onto the luxurious carpet of green.

His legs were strong! As if it were the most natural thing in the world, he broke into a run. He ran and ran, as fast as the wind. He could not stop running for pure delight. He ran a mile...maybe it was a hundred miles! The grassy field went on forever.

Finally he stopped. His chest was moving in and out. He felt a strange sensation in his lungs. Was this what people meant when they said they were tired? He had never been able to move fast enough to get tired. It was an odd but exhilarating sensation. He loved it. He was actually tired from running!

He lay down in the grass, breathing heavily. But he was restless to run. As soon as he was able, he jumped up and darted off across the field again.

In the distance two figures walked toward him. They weren't running but were walking slowly side by side. He stopped and waited for them.

A tall lady with hair flowing down over her shoulders to her waist walked calmly across the grass. At her side was a girl about the boy's own age. As they came closer he recognized the woman. It was his mother!

He began to run excitedly toward her. This time her face wore a somber expression. She was not happy, and laughing as in the dream before. It scared Luke so he stopped and waited.

The two approached and stood before the boy.

"Hi, Mommy," he said. "You are in my dream again. But you are taller now – and sad. Why are you sad? It's my dream mommy, so you can be happy too."

She did not reply, only gazed down upon him with eyes of love. Tears began to flow from her eyes.

"Why are you crying, Mommy?" he said. "Are you mad at me?"

"No, son. I have never been happier."

"Then why do you have tears in your eyes?"

"Because I will not see you for some time, until your own wings begin to grow."

"Oh, I forgot! Let me see your wings now!"

He hurried around behind her.

"Oh, Mommy!" he exclaimed. "Your wings are big and long! They have grown since the last dream! Are you a real angel now?"

"I do not know. I think I may be closer to becoming one than before. But now I must leave you."

"Why? I don't want you to go."

"It is my time, son. I have been called. It is time for you to be strong. It is time for you to see what you can become."

The boy's gaze drifted to the little girl-angel beside her. The smaller girl's expression was blank.

"I have been sent to bring a friend to be with you now," his mother said. "I will not be in your dreams again."

"Who sent you, Mommy?"

"The One who is watching over you. You will not see me again for a long time, until you are called. But you will have a friend, because He is caring for you both. Now it is time for you to start growing into a man."

As she spoke, she began to move away. He watched her go, feeling sorrow but not sadness. In the distance he saw a man. He was older than his mother. He appeared to be waiting for her. He was standing surrounded by light and his arms opened to receive her. In an instant both were swallowed in whiteness and he saw them no more.

The boy turned. The girl-angel still stood beside him, waiting patiently. Unlike the mother angel, the girl-angel had no wings that he could see.

Before either could speak, suddenly the boy felt himself pulled up and into the sky again. He was flying and spinning as if he was in the middle of a perfect sunset with all the colors of the rainbow shooting out in every direction.

Faster and faster the clouds and colors swirled around him until they became a spinning tunnel of color. He began to feel heavier...so heavy that he was falling...down...down...out of the clouds, out of the wonderful air of light...until all finally went black and he was in his own bed and sleeping dreamlessly once more.

EIGHT

DYING FOR ANSWERS

Dallas, Easter, April 25th, 1947

Janet had not been to church since Jack's death. Almost three months had passed. She had no more answers now than when the sheriff from west Texas had phoned. Recurring nightmares had plagued her ever since. Haunting her in the aloneness of the nighttime hours, the man's voice and words were as clear as they had been then...*I'm afraid I have some bad news... wanted to call as soon as the identifications were made..."*

Today was Easter. Something told her she needed to be in church on this day. Not that she expected any more solace than had come in recent weeks from any other source. But where else was she going to go on Easter Sunday?

Janet slipped into the back of the sanctuary at two minutes before eleven. Familiar hymns from the organ greeted her as she found a seat in the last row. She could think of nothing but the question that plagued her day and night: Why was God doing this to her? First Leslie, now Jack...both taken from her in the prime of their lives. How could she not feel bitter? She was angry at God, and she knew it.

Worse than that, in her present frame of mind Janet knew that her growing bitterness was wearing on her relationships. Most of her friends had stopped calling and coming by to visit. Only Annie had not given up on her. Just a few days ago Annie had invited her to join their family for Easter service and dinner afterward of baked ham and sweet potatoes. Janet had declined, just as she had declined dozens of other invitations these last two months. It was too hard to play nice—acting like everything was okay. She had only come to church today because she felt God owed her some answers. In the midst of her anger, she was also heartbroken. Sometimes she hardly knew whether God existed at all. Yet where else could she turn? If God couldn't help her, no one could. In the end she had decided to find a church this morning where no one knew her or would recognize her. She knew nothing about this place. But for some reason this was where she decided to come, and here she was.

In a fog of renewed grief, Janet was hardly aware as the service proceeded around her. The joy of this most joyous of Christian days found no entrance into her lonely heart.

"Lord, you have to help me," she said silently, more to herself than because she felt any Presence beside her. "Please help me. I don't think I can make it through another day like this. If you are for real, you have to help me…please."

Hymns, a Scripture reading, a special number from the choir, happy Easter greetings and various announcements… Janet's subconscious could hardly focus as the service progressed. She was too distracted, too consumed by thoughts of Jack and the unanswered perplexities of her swirling brain, she did not even realize when the pastor's sermon began. As was expected on this day, he was speaking about Jesus' resurrection. For a few fleeting moments she considered standing up, beating a hasty retreat, and leaving as unceremoniously as she had come. Maybe this had all been a mistake.

Then without warning, suddenly a handful of simple words plunged straight to the depths of Janet's heart.

"Death is never the end, it is always a beginning," the man had just said.

Janet sat bolt upright in the pew and glanced about. None of the strangers around her could realize what thoughts filled her mind, or why her attention was suddenly riveted on the man standing in front of the small sanctuary. For the first time since her arrival, Janet now took in the man who was speaking. He certainly did not look like a preacher—no robes as she might have expected on this day. He had come out from behind the pulpit and had no notes. He seemed speaking from his heart, not a prepared sermon. He wasn't even wearing a tie!

Yet all at once this preacher who didn't look like a preacher was speaking directly to *her*. Were the prayers she had just been praying suddenly being answered by this man in front of her?

Janet continued to gaze straight into his earnest face. Not only were her *ears* newly attuned to his words, but her *heart* was suddenly open to receive their life-giving truth as well.

"Death is never the end, it is always the beginning," the pastor repeated. "All physical life is temporary, fleeting, momentary, transitory. Everything that is part of the physical world around us will eventually fade. We might as well think to cling to a wisp of smoke as to base our lives on the things of this world. Even the intangibles we value so highly fade with the rest. Beauty, happiness, power, influence...how long do they last?

"Physical reality is a passing reality. So what lasts? Only the *spiritual* will endure. Will relationships last? Will our hopes and dreams last? Will our choices and desires last? Will character last? Yes, but only those aspects of them that have combined to make us the *spiritual* beings we are. We are *spiritual* men and women, you and I—not mere physical creatures. What kind of people are we becoming? That can only be answered as a *spiritual* question.

"That is why death is but a beginning. Death is the beginning of an eternity that will reveal what kind of spiritual men and women we made of ourselves. Will it be an eternity with God, or an eternity separated from him? That is why Jesus died. His death was a beginning, a door God gave us to walk through from one life to another. From a temporary, physical world into the spiritual world, the world beyond, the world of eternity, the world where God dwells, a world where spiritual not physical men and women live with him forever."

The man paused. Janet drew in a deep breath as she waited.

"We speak often of Jesus' death," he went on. "His death on the cross, of course, is the central event of our faith. But greater than his death is the Lord's resurrection. That's why God urges us not to get stuck at the foot of the cross. He urges us to leave the hill of Golgotha and move on to the garden of

Peabody Public Library
Columbia City, IN

the resurrection. It is there where the Son of God was brought back from the dead to live and reign with God his Father. It is because the door of the tomb stands open wide, flooded with light and empty, that makes this day the most remarkable in all the history of the universe. That open empty tomb shouts a great truth for all to hear. It reminds us of that resurrection door, and reaffirms the great truth of creation, that we too can walk through it—out of the tomb of this fleeting physical world around us into the light of God's kingdom, there to dwell, not amid the *passing* but amid the *eternal*, no more grasping after fading wisps of smoke but holding firm to eternal truths that will endure."

As Janet listened intently to the remainder of the sermon, she sensed faint seeds of hope sprouting in her heart. Had God begun to answer her prayers and give her the answers she was looking for?

NINE

THE THIRD DREAM—A MEETING

Christmas Eve, 1938

A kindly man of thirty-five, tall, muscular, and with a rugged look that belied the tenderness in his heart, wheeled a boy who had just turned eight down a sterile hallway strung with a few Christmas lights toward the small room the boy now called home.

Carl Elkin knew what it was like to adjust to these surroundings. He had grown up in an orphanage himself. It wasn't easy. No lonelier place existed on earth than an orphanage at Christmas. That's the reason he was here. His had been a rough life. From the time he was old enough to begin thinking about a career — he knew he wanted to dedicate his life to easing the suffering of boys and young men who felt the same pain he had felt in his early years.

His present charge had gone straight to Carl's heart the moment the boy arrived at the orphanage almost a year before. The poor boy suffered from a rare form of MS, rendering him both crippled and speechless. Not only was an orphanage a lonely place to grow up, it was also a cruel place for any child with an abnormality. As much as the staff tried to guard against it, they could not prevent the heartless treatment meted out upon those the others perceived as black sheep in their midst. A cripple bound to a wheelchair, without the wherewithal even to defend himself, was a defenseless target for their abuse. It had been a rough year for the newest member of what they called their "family," but which they all knew was no substitute for the real thing.

"Well, here you are, young man," said Carl, trying to sound cheerful as he wheeled the boy into the room. "It's Christmas Eve and I can say *Happy birthday* and *Merry Christmas* all at once! How old are you today, Luke...eight, isn't it?"

From his chair Luke nodded and blinked twice. He had been trying not to think about his birthday, or Christmas. It was too painful without his mother to share the special day with him. She had always made him feel that his birthday was just as important as Christmas itself. They always had a big Christmas tree and she decorated his room with blinking lights, with a second tiny Christmas tree for his room on the table. This year his room seemed dark and cold and empty. He missed his mother more than ever.

Carl stooped over, slid one of his strong arms under Luke's legs and wrapped the other around his back and shoulders then lifted him out of his wheelchair and into his bed. "There's your buzzer if you need me or need to go to the bathroom," said Carl. "Otherwise, you have a good night's sleep. You'll be fine?"

Luke smiled and blinked again. It was his way of saying yes.

"Good. Then I'll see you in the morning. Good night, Luke."

Carl walked out of the room, leaving the door slightly ajar. Luke could faintly hear the Christmas music coming up from downstairs where the older children were enjoying the Christmas Eve party later than he and the other ones. A few blinking lights from the hallway reflected through the door onto one of the walls of his room. They reminded him of his mother. He felt a tear burning his eyes as it squeezed out and slid down his cheek.

He lay back on the pillow and closed his eyes. He drifted to sleep every night thinking of his mother. But tonight was especially sad. Last Christmas Eve was the night—

He blinked hard as the tears flowed in earnest. Luke struggled to turn away from the door and buried his face in the pillow, and began to cry.

Gradually he felt himself getting sleepy. It was just a year ago when she had put him to sleep and prayed with him and had sung Christmas carols to him as he lay in bed. He tried to pretend that she was with him again, singing to him just like last year. He couldn't quite remember the words. It was something about heaven singing. Were there angels too...angels singing?

*And heaven and angels sing...*That was it, Luke thought.

And heaven and angels sing...and heaven and heaven and angels sing.

Gradually his mother's voice faded away as sleep engulfed him.

Luke awoke in a spinning tunnel of light. In the heartache of losing his mother, he had completely forgotten his Christmas Eve dream! The orphanage...the sadness...the tears...the loneliness all faded away. He was happy again, weightless and free, floating upward, all his body strong and alive! Maybe he would see his mother again! He had already forgotten what she told him in his last dream.

Just like before, he felt himself descending. He was coming down in the midst of a lifeless city. There were no cars, no people, no sounds. Everything was deathly quiet. Disappointed at first, the moment he felt the sidewalk beneath him, he remembered the most wonderful thing about his dreams – he could walk and run and talk and feel his whole body full of health. How wonderfully free he felt, with a magnificent awareness that he could go anywhere and do anything. He took a tentative first step, fearing the magical dream would disappear and he would find himself waking up in his bed or his wheelchair.

But the moment he felt the strength of his legs beneath him, a rush of joy overwhelmed him. Adrenalin pounded through his veins. For a few seconds he could hardly breathe from the excitement of realizing that he was living in his wonderful dream for a third time. He was walking again...then running through the strange empty town.

"I'm running, I'm running!" he cried, as thrilled to hear his own voice and to have such command of his legs. "Look at me – I can run like the wind!"

He slowed. Ahead rose a large forbidding building. It was an unfriendly looking place. He didn't want to go closer. But something compelled him to continue. He walked toward it, then through the large glass doors and inside.

There were no people. His own footsteps were the only sounds. Somehow he knew where to go. He did not stop to think how. Things happen in dreams and you are pulled along in the world of the dream without asking why. Luke did not ask why he was in the building, he merely obeyed where his feet took him.

He climbed up several flights of stairs. He came out in another long corridor. It reminded him of the hallway in the orphanage. A pang shot through him that he was going back to his own room and that the dream was about to end. But instead he turned and walked into a room with a bed in the middle of it. Around the bed stood several people, silent and stoic, staring down at the bed. He could not see their faces. They had faces but they looked plastic and unreal and unalive. They stood unmoving, making no sounds. Great rivers of tears ran from their eyes, down their faces and necks and chests and legs and ran off like tiny streams across the floor of the room. But there were no sounds from their weeping.

Slowly Luke walked into the room. No one turned to face him or noticed that he was there. They did not seem to see him at all. Luke approached the bed. A girl lay upon it, her eyes closed, a peaceful expression on her face. He could see the features of her face clearly. He thought he knew her, but he did not know why. She was the only one in the room besides him who was not silently crying.

Suddenly a voice sounded from somewhere. "Why are you weeping?" it said. "The girl is not dead, but sleeping. Little girl, I say to you arise."

Gazing upon the girl's face, Luke reached out and took her hand where it lay outside the blanket. The girl's eyes fluttered, then opened. She saw Luke beside her bed staring down at her. She smiled at him. Still holding her hand, Luke pulled her gently up. She sat up, then climbed out of the bed. All around, none of the weepers seemed to notice. Hand in hand, the two left the room. Luke led the way back along the corridor, down the stairs, and outside. Immediately the great building disappeared behind them.

"Was it your voice that woke me into my dream?" said the girl.

"I don't know," replied Luke. "I don't remember saying anything."

"When I felt your hand, I woke up. When I saw you, I remembered you from my dream and I was happy to see you again."

"Now I remember!" exclaimed Luke. "You were in my dream before too. You were with my mother."

"Was that lady your mother? I thought she was an angel. She

had big angel wings growing out of her back."

"I think she was becoming an angel. But she was my mother too. I called her my Mommy-angel. My name is Luke."

"I am Vanessa. How old are you?"

"I was seven…no, I think I'm eight now."

"What do you mean?"

"My birthday is on Christmas Eve. So I just turned eight – I remember now."

"I don't know anything about what day it is. I think I have been asleep for a long time."

"How old are you?"

"I don't know. I might be seven or eight too. Or maybe only six. I can't remember. I have been asleep a long time."

They came to a shopping area with stores and bright lights all colorfully decorated for Christmas. At last they began to hear something – it was the sound of Christmas carols. They stopped in front of a huge store. In the window was an enormous Christmas tree. Beneath it were dozens of presents with bows attached. But they were not wrapped. He could see every present – toys of unimaginable variety…cars and trucks, a great red fire engine, airplanes, trains, dolls, models, building blocks, games, tinker toys, picture books, a record player, and behind the tree even more presents they could not see.

They stopped and stared in wonder.

"I wonder who all those are for!" said Vanessa.

"I don't know, but the store looks open," said Luke. "Let's go inside?"

They went through the doors beside the window. Walking toward them came a man whose eyes sparkled and with a great smile of welcome on his face. Both Luke and Vanessa thought immediately of Santa Claus, because he had a white beard, though he was not dressed in red like Santa Claus.

As if he had read her mind, the man looked down at Vanessa.

"So you would like to know who all those presents under the tree are for, is that it, young lady?" he asked.

"Yes, sir," she answered a little timidly.

"Haven't you yet guessed?" he said. "They are for the two of you. I have been expecting you. Every toy and gift must be played with on Christmas morning. All the shoppers have left and are at home nestled all snug in their beds with visions of sugar plums dancing in their heads. Only the two of you are awake to enjoy

39

them."

"Are they really...for us!" exclaimed Luke.

"Christmas is for all children," replied the man, laughing with delight. "Its meaning is for all men and women. Children learn to love Christmas first by receiving gifts. As they grow, they learn its deeper meaning from the joy of giving. Every parent loves nothing more than to see his son and daughter happy. So come – enjoy these gifts and you will make me happy."

Luke and Vanessa needed no more persuasion. They rushed to the Christmas tree laughing and talking excitedly between themselves. Luke tried to play with the fire engine and the airplanes and the tinker toys all at once. Vanessa tried to dress two or three paper dolls while she held the large doll with one hand, and also looked at the picture books. They were also trying to show each other everything at once. Behind them the man who had invited them chuckled as he watched. He gazed down upon them with eyes that seemed filled with all the love that made Christmas special.

How long Luke and Vanessa played and talked and scurried about exploring every gift under the tree neither of them had any idea. They were not thinking of time, for in this world time did not even seem to exist. But no dream lasts forever.

Eventually they began to feel a change. They both knew it. They glanced toward one another and tried to speak. But they could not. Their voices had grown too soft for the other to hear. They looked around. The man who had invited them into the store had disappeared. The tree and decorations now began to fade as the light around them grew thin and pale.

Luke looked down at the toy fire engine in his hands. It too now disappeared. Again he was alone, light spinning about him as he flew through a void of white...down...down...down...until he felt himself settling into his own bed, and that instant he knew no more.

TEN

JULY FOURTH

Dallas, Saturday, July 5th, 1947

Janet sat up in bed and listened. Had she just heard the phone ring, or had she imagined it?

Another ring confirmed that it was no dream. Quickly Janet slipped out of bed and downstairs to the phone. Who would be calling on a Saturday morning. Nobody called anymore.

"Hello," she said sleepily into the mouthpiece.

The chipper voice of her friend brought a smile to Janet's lips. "Hi sweetie," said Annie. "Did I wake you?"

"Who is this?" Janet deadpanned.

"Yeah, right!" rejoined Annie. "Like you've got a million *other* friends left who would call you and invite you to a July fourth picnic tomorrow!"

Janet knew her friend was joking. Somehow the words still stung. She *didn't* have any other friends anymore. A lot of acquaintances, but not many she would call friends. Yet the pain of that fact was deepest because she knew it was her own fault. Wallowing in her grief and bitterness during the last five months, she had driven them all away—all but Annie.

"What kind of fourth of July picnic do they have on July sixth?" asked Janet.

"A picnic after tomorrow's service at our church. Our whole family is going. You are part of the family, so I thought if you would like that I could swing by and pick you up on the way."

"Hmm...well, yeah—maybe I would like to at that." The words surprised even Janet when she heard them coming out

41

of her mouth. "Okay," she added more decisively.

The phone was silent a few seconds .

"*Okay!*" Annie exclaimed after a moment. "Fantastic — and I must say it's about time!"

"I know...I know — I've been a bit of a recluse."

"A hermit is more like it!"

"Don't make me feel guilty or I may change my mind! — But I'll drive myself, if that's all right. I'll meet you there. What time?"

"Service starts at eleven," replied Annie. "We'll save you a seat. The picnic is right after service outside on the lawn. You don't have to bring a thing...except yourself."

"Thank you, Annie," said Janet. "I will see you there."

Wondering what had prompted her to accept Annie's invitation, Janet made herself some coffee and turned on the radio to a Perry Como song. She had planned to go to church tomorrow anyway. She had been slipping anonymously in and out of services on most Sundays ever since Easter. She still felt like a hermit, but she had been hungry to hear more of the simple preacher's common sense approach to the Christian faith and living the life that Jesus taught. She even occasionally pulled out pad and paper to take notes as she listened. She supposed going to church with Annie and her family tomorrow wasn't really as great a stretch as Annie probably thought.

The church parking lot was nearly full when Janet pulled in at ten-fifty the following morning. Even as she closed the car door and began walking across the parking lot, she saw Annie's fifteen year old daughter Judy making a beeline toward her.

"Hi, Mrs. Holiday!" she said, greeting her with a warm smile. "Mama told me to watch for you and show you where we're sitting."

"Thank you Judy," said Janet. The two walked toward the building together and inside. Judy was a beautiful young woman, thought Janet. She reminded her of Leslie at the same age. Inside the sanctuary, Judy led her to the rest of the Brodie family. Annie's older two children were already seated beside her. Nineteen year old John Jr. had just started college. He was the spitting image of the father who had been killed on the beaches of Normandy on D-Day three years earlier. Joshua was seventeen and a junior in high school. Judy was the baby. Janet eased onto the pew beside Judy as Annie, John and Josh all smiled and whispered friendly greetings.

"I wondered if you were going to show," said Annie, leaning across her daughter with a smile.

"I wasn't so sure myself," rejoined Janet truthfully. Janet watched as Joshua teased Judy about a boy she had a crush on two rows further toward the front. She had to smile when John Jr. elbowed his brother. Suddenly a realization struck her. These children had tragically lost their father just three years before. Yet they were handling it. They seemed happy and well-adjusted. Most people would consider their loss greater than hers. Yet she, supposedly a mature woman, was moping about like she had nothing to live for. Meanwhile, they were getting on with their lives.

The thought was convicting. A strange sensation came over her as the service began—she could not help feeling ashamed.

The patriotic sermon that followed did nothing to mitigate Janet's chagrin. The sobering reminder of the men and women who had given their lives to save the country, including a number from this very congregation, brought obvious pain to the faces of all four Brodies. Janet was not alone in having suffered the loss of a loved one. If other people could get over it, maybe it was time she did too.

When the service was over, Annie led Janet outside to a heavily shaded expansive lawn behind the church where rows of tables and chairs had been set. Women were scurrying back and forth from the church kitchen carrying baskets and platters of food. Soon coffee and tea and soft drinks were added to the long serving table in front. Twenty minutes later, the entire congregation had made its way outside and begun the festive potluck ritual—everyone filling their plates, making their way to tables, trying to keep the boisterous children from crowding in line or knocking over the punch bowl, and laughing and talking as a great happy family.

Annie introduced Janet to so many women it was hopeless even to remember half their names. She was surrounded by men and women who really seemed to care for each other She could not help noticing several mothers with young children without fathers. So many had been lost in the war. Yet they too, like the Brodies, were managing to go on with life.

How could they be so strong and she so weak? At last Janet knew the answer. It had taken a long time. But she was finally ready to let her bitterness go and begin to heal.

ELEVEN

A CHAT BETWEEN FRIENDS

Dallas, Saturday, August 9, 1947

"Janet, good morning…it's Annie," said the familiar voice at the other end of the phone.

Janet rolled over and sat up in bed and tried to gather her wits. 'Hi, Annie…I'm afraid I'm still in bed."

"I didn't wake you up!"

"That's okay—what time is it…" said Janet, glancing toward the clock on her nightstand, "—gosh, nine-thirty! I had no idea."

"Sorry—what happened to my friend, the early riser?"

"I was up late last night reading," Janet answered.

"Got hooked in a good whodunit, eh?"

"No," said Janet. She yawned and let out a deep sigh. "At the Bible Study I've been going to," she continued without thinking, "we had been talking about the Last Supper. It's pretty amazing—"

Suddenly she stopped herself. The phone went silent for a second or two.

"You've been attending…a *Bible study*?" said Annie in surprise.

"I guess I should have told you."

"No, that's okay. It's fine…where?"

"At a little church I stumbled onto last Easter."

"That's great."

"And going to church with you in July helped too. I realized maybe I wanted to find some spiritual foundations for my life. But I needed to do it where no one knew me, where I could make a fresh start. I hope you understand."

45

"Of course. I understand completely."

"It's helped me put things in perspective. And last night, weird as it sounds to say it, I fell asleep reading in my Bible the account of the Last Supper from the book of John. It's really amazing, everything Jesus said that night about what heaven is like."

"Gosh, Janet, sounds like you're really getting a lot out of it. Then you are totally excused for sleeping in late!" laughed Annie. "I can't remember the last time I fell asleep reading *my* Bible! I'm eager to hear all about it. But I called to see if you want to get together today. I know your birthday is Tuesday but I'm going to be tied up at the store. I thought maybe we could go out and do a little window shopping, and then I could take you to lunch somewhere."

"I would like that," replied Janet. "A *light* lunch – I haven't even had breakfast yet! What time?"

"Eleven-thirty...twelve – whatever suits you."

"I'll put on the coffee and take a bath. I'll be ready whenever you come by."

Three hours later, Janet Holiday and Annie Brodie sat beside one another at the Woolworths lunch counter in downtown Dallas.

"It feels good to be out," sighed Janet. "Stores and people and bustle and shopping and traffic, I guess I forgot how much I enjoy being around other people sometimes."

"What about.the Bible study?"

"That's different. It's just once a week, and I still haven't allowed myself the luxury of seeing anyone from the group socially. They invite me for coffee, but I haven't felt ready to laugh and chat and that kind of thing. It's a slow process."

"How are you feeling, then?" asked Annie.

Janet smiled and reached over and placed her hand on Annie's arm. "I know you will always be there Annie," she said. "You are the best friend I could have. In fact, you are the only friend who has been patient enough to stick with me the last six months. The ladies in the Bible study are great too. I haven't shared everything with them. I just can't...not yet. My emotions are still tender. I know it's been six months. I suppose I'm a slow healer. But I think I'm getting better. Some days I feel like I'm stronger and ready to look life in the eye and say, 'Give me your best shot.' On other days I still just feel like curling up in a ball and staying in bed."

Janet took a bite of her ham and cheese sandwich. "Thursday, for instance, I felt good, " she went on. "Then yesterday I felt terrible. I looked at pictures and cried and puttered around the house. Maybe you need to do those things to put it behind you. I mean you never put it behind you, but...you know what I mean — you have to figure out a way to go on. At least I think so. This isn't really the sort of thing you plan for."

Annie nodded.

"And there are still a million questions — Why did God let this happen...how will I manage alone...what will I do? The biggest question of all — Is God really there at all? Because, you know...if God is good and all that, why do things like this happen? I'd never admit such thoughts in the group I've been going to. But you can't help it sometimes."

"I understand," said Annie. "Everyone has doubts."

"And I wonder about Jack, where he is now, you know."

"You don't...I mean, what are you saying, Janet? You don't think — "

"No, I'm not talking about hell or anything like that. I saw Jack baptized myself. But is that enough? You knew Jack — he had his tough side. He liked to hunt and he loved his guns. He and Manny would have a beer together from time to time when he was sure no one from church would see him. I don't know...I just can't see Jack and Jesus together with Jack wearing a long white robe. I mean, Jesus isn't the kind of person you sit down and have a beer with, is he? So what happens with men like Jack? Maybe it's crazy to think thoughts like that. But I can't help it. I want to know. Or maybe he is that kind of man. I guess he turned water into wine. Everyone talks about heaven. But then when you lose someone you want to know what it's *really* like. Angels and harps and gold...I'm not sure Jack would fit in very well. Of course I can't help thinking about Leslie now too."

"You've still heard nothing from her?"

"No," replied Janet shaking her head. "Not since the Christmas card she sent me. That was ten years ago."

"It seems she ought to know about Jack."

"I've been thinking the same thing. But how would I contact her? I have no idea where she is."

"Didn't you say the town where the card was sent was a small place?"

Janet nodded. "I looked the town up in an atlas. But there was no return address on the card. That was a long time ago. What's to say she's even still there?"

"Why didn't you and Jack try to locate her then?" asked Annie.

"We thought she was coming home. So we just planned for her visit, though I was nervous what would happen when Jack saw Joe. But then she never came. We kept waiting to hear something, but we never did. We had to go through the whole process of losing her all over again just like when she left the first time—the anger, the grief, the sadness."

"Didn't you think about trying to find her?"

"Sure we thought about it."

"Why didn't you?"

"We'd heard a sermon at church—it wasn't long after Leslie left. It was about the Prodigal Son parable. The sermon was about the parents of the prodigal, and how they were willing to wait patiently at home, praying and hoping for their son's return, but not trying to force him to return too soon. Can you imagine the tears that poor mother must have shed during those years of her son's absence? I *can* imagine because I cried for Leslie. I cried myself to sleep more times than I can remember. I wanted with all my heart to go after her and bring her home. But though Jack was both hurt and angry, he grieved differently than I did. I shudder to think what would have happened if we had gone after Leslie and if he and Joe had confronted each other. He talked about hiring an investigator to find Leslie. Sometimes his anger would get the better of him. But when we heard that sermon, it really got into Jack. He realized that nothing *we* did would bring Leslie home. If we tried to force her to come back, it would only deepen her resentment toward us. Jack said that it had to happen at the right time, when *she* was ready. Trying to force it would only make the situation worse. It was the hardest thing in the world. But that's what we did."

"Didn't the Christmas card make it seem like she *was*

48

ready?"

"That's what we hoped. But then she didn't come. Jack said we had to keep waiting."

"Maybe that was just his pride talking," said Annie. "I don't mean to speak disrespectfully, Janet—I hope you know that. But Jack did have a temper."

"I know," smiled Janet fondly. "You don't have to tell me. But he never got angry with me in my life. He was a good husband and a good father, Annie."

"I know that, Janet. I was only wondering...I don't know what I'm saying exactly...but how long does a mother wait before she says, 'It's been long enough. I want to see my daughter.'"

Janet was silent. The idea was sobering.

"That's a hard question," she answered at length. Her voice was soft and reflective. She let out a long sigh. "I hadn't thought of it like that before," Janet went on after a moment. "I suppose I just accepted the fact that we were waiting for Leslie to come to us—like the prodigal in the story."

"But isn't every prodigal story different? What if there are times when it *is* up to the parents to go find their son or daughter?"

"Maybe you're right. When do you say, *It's been long enough*?"

"I have to tell you, I think there are times when a parent has to take the initiative. Waiting is all well and good. But what if a son or daughter isn't strong enough to swallow his pride and come home? What if Leslie isn't strong enough on her own? What if her heart is yearning for you just as much as you are yearning for her? What if she needs you to go to *her*?"

The words stung Janet's heart. Memories of Leslie as a young girl flooded her mind. With them came fresh tears, this time not for her husband but for her daughter.

The two friends finished their sandwiches and salad. Suddenly Janet's mind was filled with tender thoughts of Leslie, wondering where she was, what she was doing, if she and Joe were still together, and whether the years had softened Joe's heart.

They left the lunch counter and wandered through Macy's for an hour. The huge department store was gearing up for the

49

back to school season and the place was crowded. Janet had retired from teaching to help out the war effort five years ago but she missed the feeling she used to get this time of the year. Excitement for the new school year and the bright young minds she would have the opportunity to help mold. Jack's life insurance made it so that she did not have to work, but suddenly she wanted to. The realization made her smile. Maybe this was another step forward in her healing process, she thought.

"Would you like to join the Brodie clan for dinner on Tuesday?" Annie said as they pulled up in front of Janet's house. "I'll make you a birthday cake, candles and all."

"Thanks," said Janet, smiling. "I appreciate that. I'll let you know."

"Come on," rejoined Annie good naturedly. "You can't stay home alone, and I won't have you eating your birthday dinner at Woolworths!"

Janet laughed lightly. "I promise I will not go to Woolworths. I just have lots of things to think about. I'll let you know."

TWELVE

CHANGE OF PLANS

Dallas, Monday, August 11, 1947

Janet awoke suddenly. Everything was black. It was the middle of the night.

She glanced at the clock on her dresser. Two-forty-seven.

What had disturbed her sleep?

Jack...she had seen Jack! He had been saying something.

She remembered now. Yes, Jack had come to her in a dream. *It is time,* he said. *The time for healing is at hand.*

What did it mean? Then she remembered Annie's words from lunch on Saturday — *When does a time come when you say, It's been long enough?* Maybe Annie's words had prompted the dream. But it had been so real! It was as if Jack had actually appeared to her.

Was it a dream...a vision...or was her subconscious just remembering what Annie had said at lunch?

It is time...it is time...time for healing...it's been long enough.

As she lay in the darkness, the rest of the conversation from the previous day returned to her, and more of Annie's forceful words.

I think there are times when a parent has to take the initiative...what if Leslie isn't strong enough...what if her heart is yearning for you...what if she needs you to go to her?

Janet did not sleep again. By the time the sun began to stream through her window, she realized that sometime during the night she had reached a turning point. She didn't know exactly when that moment had come. But by morning she knew the decision was already behind her. She would make the arrangements this morning.

The minute she got up she sensed that something was different. It was not because she was turning fifty tomorrow. Suddenly she had a purpose again.

While she was waiting for her coffee, she began picking up a few things around the house. The place was a mess. She started to pick up the phone then hesitated as a wave of fear swept through her. Minutes later the mail arrived. Absently she went through the ritual of sifting through it. There was nothing she cared about—bills, ads, flyers, magazines. It was all so entirely uninteresting that it woke her again to her resolution of a few minutes earlier.

She walked to the telephone again. *Do I really want to do this?* she thought. The answer was instant and emphatic.

Yes!

Janet spent the rest of the morning on the phone making the arrangements.

As soon as that was done she bathed, dressed and packed, and then drove to see Annie at the Hay and Feed store.

"I appreciate the invitation for birthday dinner, Annie," she said. "But I am going to decline."

"What...why?" replied Annie. "I told you, I won't have you spending your fiftieth birthday alone."

Janet laughed. It was one of the first times she had laughed, really laughed, since Jack's death. It felt good.

"I cannot promise that I won't be alone," rejoined Janet. "But I do promise I will not eat my birthday dinner at Woolworths."

"What then?"

"It's actually your fault," said Janet.

"Me—what do you mean?"

"Something you said Saturday. I woke up in the middle of the night thinking about it. I decided to do it."

"Do what?"

"I am going to go try to find Leslie."

"Oh, Janet—that's wonderful!" exclaimed Annie. She ran forward and embraced her friend affectionately. "What will you do?"

"I'm not really sure," replied Janet. "I suppose I'll have to figure that out as I go."

She paused thoughtfully. "I remembered something you

said right after Jack died," Janet went on, "about life taking directions you don't expect. I prayed half the night about what I should do. Only one thing came to me. So I guess that's what I will do and see what happens."

"What is that?"

"Go to that town in Wyoming where her Christmas card was postmarked. It's the only thing I know to try."

"Wyoming — that's a long way!"

"I know," nodded Janet. "But I'm determined to do it. I'm leaving on the Greyhound for Cheyenne this afternoon! The bus leaves at five!"

Thirteen

A LONELY BIRTHDAY

Cheyenne, Wyoming, Tuesday August 12, 1947

Other than being exhausting, Janet's long overnight trip was uneventful. The buses were full with people traveling back home for last minute get-a-ways before school started again. The weather was stifling hot, but got a little cooler the further north and west she went.

Once she settled into the long journey, the folly of her madcap decision began to dawn on Janet. What would come of it she had no idea. But for the first time in six months she felt a sense of purpose. She felt life returning to her limbs and veins and brain. When she thought about Jack, the sadness was still too painful for words. A renewal of despair was always just one reminder or memory away. But she no longer felt dead . She had something to live for. She had a mission to accomplish.

Granted, that hope hung by the slenderest of threads — a faded postmark more than ten years old from a town in Wyoming she had never heard of. *Eaglescliff, Wyoming*. Not much evidence on which to base a future. But it was all she had and she intended to make the most of it. It was her birthday — a time for families to be together. What better time than her fiftieth birthday to embark on trying to find the only family she had left, even if it meant spending the day alone. If she was successful, perhaps she would be spending future birthdays with Leslie in the years to come.

She pulled out the envelope, scanned the postmark again for the hundredth time, as if one more look might somehow reveal what she hadn't noticed before, then opened it. She had placed another brief letter inside the card. Slowly she unfolded the single sheet. She had not read it in almost twenty years. The two communications — the note and the card — were completely linked in her mind. The one had brought deeper pain to her mother's heart than anything she had ever known. The Christmas card from a few years later had brought fleeting and temporary hope, only to have it dashed again.

Drawing in a deep breath, Janet closed her eyes for a moment, then opened them and stared down at the brief words that had exploded apart the world she and Jack had always dreamed of.

Dear Mom and Dad, she read in Leslie's sixteen year old hand.

I'm very sorry to have to tell you like this, but Joe and I are going to get married. I know you don't approve of him, but I love him. I knew you wouldn't let me go or consent to what we want to do. I know you warned me not to become involved with him. Because of that, Joe is very angry. It hurt him that you weren't willing to get to know him. I think you will like him too once you know him as I do. I hope that will be possible in the future. But right now Joe is too angry with you and does not want me to see you again or say good bye in person. I'll write when we get settled. I love you. Please don't worry.

Leslie.

They found the letter on the kitchen table and Leslie's room empty. Jack had stormed about all day alternating between bouts of silence and rage. Janet knew that he was more hurt than angry, broken hearted to realize that his only daughter had run off with a wild cowboy she had only known for two months. Later that day he called the police. Their only answer was that they would look into it and do what they could do. She was sixteen. In the eyes of the law she was almost an adult. They felt helpless — they didn't even know Joe's last name. He was just a rodeo rider who had come through town and caught their daughter up in his rough and tumble world. They could do nothing but wait to hear from Leslie again.

Day after day went by. They kept hoping to hear something. Eagerly Janet rifled through the mail every morning. Somehow she knew that Leslie would come to her senses, that she would write an apologetic letter and say she was ready to come home. But no letter came. Weeks went by and turned into months. Gradually they realized that Leslie was not coming back. Their daughter was gone.

Nine years of silence followed before the appearance of the Christmas card. Then their sudden joy and renewed hope were dashed again

Ten more years of silence, now Jack was gone. At last it was time. If Leslie was not going to come to *her*, she would do all that lay in her power to go to her daughter.

Janet blinked hard and tried to pull herself out of the painful memories. She stared out the window and did her best to enjoy the drive. But the scenery through north Texas was as dry as her thoughts. After changing buses in Amarillo in the middle of the night, for the rest of the night and most of Tuesday she tried to convince herself she wasn't crazy. Sight of the Rockies was spectacular as they drove through Colorado. Another bus change in Denver finally brought her to Cheyenne a little after five in the afternoon, just under twenty four hours after leaving Dallas.

With suitcase in hand, Janet wandered out of the bus station and looked up and down the street. A lonelier and more desolate city she could hardly imagine. By Texas standards it wasn't even a *city* at all. A town...a cow town...a rodeo town. Who could tell, it might even be Joe's home town. Right now she didn't want to think about Joe. She just wanted to find someplace to get in out of the August heat and take a cool bath.

She'd got the name of Cheyenne's three main hotels from the attendant in the station. He said they were all reputable and clean. She struck out walking the three blocks toward the center of the city. A hot wind from the southwest burned her face. If there were clouds anywhere in the vicinity, she thought, she could sure use the shade.

Perspiring from the dry heat, ten minutes later Janet walked into the lobby of the Buffalo Bill Hotel. The place looked deserted. She walked to the counter and set down her suitcase as if it weighed a hundred pounds. A pleasant looking man came through the open door of an office behind the counter.

"I would like a room for the night," said Janet. "I assume you have some rooms available?"

"Of course, ma'am," replied the man, "you will have a wonderful selection to choose from. You're alone, I take it?"

Janet nodded.

"Well then, we will try to make your stay as comfortable as we can. Just sign here, ma'am. Where have you come from, if you don't mind my asking?"

"Dallas," replied Janet, signing the registry.

"A long trip. Did you drive all the way?"

"No—the Greyhound."

"Ah, yes…I see. Well then, here is your key. It's room 205, just at the top of the stairs there and to the right. Since we have plenty of space this week, except for our regulars, I've given you one of our large deluxe rooms at no extra charge."

"Thank you. That is very kind of you."

"So then," added the man, coming out from behind the counter, "just let me take that suitcase for you, ma'am, and I will show you the way to your room."

Janet followed the man up the stairs. Three minutes later she sat down on the bed as the door closed and breathed a sigh of relief. She was worn out from the trip. She would sleep well tonight.

She laid down on the bed, still with her suitcase unopened. She was drowsy. She shook her head awake and sat back up. She couldn't let herself go to sleep yet. She rose, hoisted the suitcase onto the bed and opened it, then went into the bathroom and turned on the water in the tub.

Two hours later, as evening was falling over Cheyenne, feeling clean and refreshed, though still tired, Janet returned downstairs to the lobby.

"Hello again," she said to the man at the counter.

"How is your room?" he asked.

"Very nice and spacious. Thank you again. I had a bath and I feel much better now. I wonder if you might recommend a nice place to eat."

"There are a couple cafes up the street, and an all you can eat buffet. The nicest place in town is Jossie's Steak House. It's a more family atmosphere than it sounds. They've got more than just steak and potatoes. A little pricy, but the folks are friendly. There'll probably be lots of people having their dinner there."

"That sounds perfect. Is it within walking distance?"

"A block back toward the bus station where you came from, then two blocks west—that'd be to your right."

"Thank you very much. I'm sure I shall find it."

Janet left the hotel. The temperature had dropped several degrees and felt quite comfortable now. She caught the scent of pine on the breeze blowing from the purple colored Rocky Mountains easy to see on the western horizon. Janet took in a deep breath of the fresh mountain air and set off along the sidewalk. A couple minutes later she saw the lights of the steak house sign ahead. The moment she walked through the door, she was heartened to see the place nearly full. Laughter and cheery talk came from the tables scattered through the expansive room. The unmistakable aroma of sizzling steak pervaded the atmosphere.

A waiter came forward, greeted her with a friendly smile. Moments later she was seated at a table out of the way at the back of the room. Once her order was placed, she asked where she might find a pay phone. She rose and the waiter led her to a phone booth adjacent to the kitchen.

A minute later she heard her friend's voice on the other end of the line.

"Annie, hi…it's Janet."

"Janet—happy birthday! Where are you?"

"Believe it or not, I'm in Wyoming."

"Wow—you made it!"

"I'm calling from a steak house in Cheyenne."

"A steak house!"

"I've just ordered my birthday dinner—steak, baked potatoes, and green beans. Happy fiftieth to me! You see, I promised I wouldn't eat at Woolworths."

Annie laughed. "Well, I'm thankful for that! How was the bus ride?"

"Long and exhausting. But I am checked into a nice hotel here. The people are friendly. They gave me a nice big room. I took a long cool bath and then came here for dinner."

"It sounds like you are enjoying yourself, though I don't

like your being alone."

"This is something I have to do."

"I know, Janet. And I admire you for it. How long will you be there?"

"I don't know. I'll see how I feel after a night's sleep. I may stay in Cheyenne an extra day just to get my bearings and get rested. I also have to check the bus schedule to Eaglescliff."

"I am praying for you, that you will find Leslie and that it will be everything you hope it will be."

"Thank you, Annie. I appreciate that. I suppose I had better get back to my table. I just wanted to let you know where I was and that I'm fine."

"You be sure to call the minute you find out something."

"I will. I promise."

FOURTEEN

THE FOURTH DREAM—AN UNEXPECTED FEAST

Christmas Eve, 1939

Luke had been at the orphanage now for nearly two years. He was in third grade at the orphanage school. His teacher, Mrs. Warpole, was nice enough. But she couldn't stop the other children from making fun of him at recess or when she wasn't paying attention. And she didn't know what to do with a boy who couldn't walk or talk. So he mostly sat in his wheelchair all day with whatever papers and activities she gave him. He tried to pay attention, but sometimes it was hard to keep his mind from wandering. His favorite times came when she read stories. Then he could imagine himself in another place or another time, or even in another body than his own.

Luke sometimes worried that he might be starting to forget his mother. After two years, the pain of knowing she was gone was not as bad as at first. He rarely cried himself to sleep anymore, though occasionally he couldn't help it when the older boys were especially mean to him and called him dreadful names. Every once in a while he had trouble remembering his mother's face. But he determined not to forget. Even though she was dead, his mother was still his lifeline. He thought about her every day.

As another Christmas approached, Luke knew that his birthday was just around the corner too. That helped his memory of his mother to grow vivid again. Many things she said came back to him. He comforted himself with the memory of her words, her smile, her gentle touch, her arms around him, how she played peek-a-boo with him at bedtime, pulling the covers on and off his face, making him smile and giggle. Even if he couldn't talk, he could laugh. He loved his mother's laughter, her touch, her magical voice.

"Where's my good boy...there you are!" she would say, sweeping back the covers again.

After the game, she always sat down beside him and read him a story or just talked to him. Nobody at the orphanage really talked to him like she had. Carl tried, but Carl was a man and could never be like his mother.

"You are my little man, aren't you," he could hear her voice as clearly as if it were yesterday. "Do you know why your name is Luke?"

He let her know he was listening by blinking and nodding.

"It is because you were born on Christmas Eve. You were such a beautiful baby. You were the most perfect Christmas present I could imagine. I had just been reading the Christmas story about the baby Jesus written by a man named Luke. So I named you after him, so that your name would always remind me of Bethlehem and the night the star shone bright over the manger. Every year when I light the candles on your birthday cake, I think of the Christmas star, and I imagine that God placed a star in the sky just for you on the night you were born too, though it might be a star that no one in all the world can see but you."

Then she hugged him so tight it felt like she had squeezed all the air out of his lungs. He loved it when she did that! He cherished the smell of her clothes and her hair in his memory, the softness of her skin, and most of all her love.

"Good night, my little man," his mother's words echoed from out of the past in Luke's mind.

The last thing he remembered before falling asleep was a faint aroma of the turkeys cooking for tomorrow's Christmas dinner at the orphanage drifting upstairs from the kitchen below.

With the smell of food still in his head, Luke found himself again flying through weightless clouds, filled with joy that his amazing miracle dream had swept him once more up into it. He stretched and kicked his legs, as if limbering them up after the passage of another year. Soon he was walking. His limbs felt stronger than ever. He broke into a run. He ran and ran in sheer exhilaration at being able to move with strength and abandon.

He hardly noticed his surroundings. All was white, as if he were in the midst of a great cloud, though solid ground was beneath his feet. There were no buildings or streets or mountains or trees.

Ahead he saw something long stretching out into the distance. He ran toward it and then slowed. It was a table – a great table longer than the eye could see, laid with a luxurious tablecloth of purest linen. Spread out on both sides were platters and pots and plates and kettles filled with every kind of food imaginable. At the sight, suddenly Luke realized that he was hungry. In fact, he was famished! But with so many things to choose from, he had to be selective. He couldn't possibly eat everything.

He walked along the table trying to keep from drooling at the abundance of good things to eat. There were hot dogs and hamburgers, dozens of varieties of pizza, French fries, fried chicken, barbequed beef, tacos, steak, spaghetti, ravioli, hams turkeys and much more. Then he came to a section of the table spread with vegetables and salads and soups, but he hurried on past these. Then fruits – more fruits than he dreamed even existed, beautiful and fragrant fruits. Then came the best section of the table of all – the desserts...pies, cakes, donuts, chocolates, candy, ice cream, éclairs, puddings, custards.

Luke was just about to grab a plate and start loading it with desserts, for whatever lay beyond could hardly top what he had just seen, when in the distance he saw a figure approaching along the other side of the table. He paused and waited for her.

"It's you!" he said as the girl drew near. "I remember you from before. You're Vanessa and you're in my dream again."

"I was just about to say the same thing," the girl replied. "You're in my dream again. But I think I'm still a little sleepy – I forgot your name."

"Luke."

"Oh yes, now I remember. Maybe we're both dreaming at the same time."

"How could that be if we're both in each others' dreams?"

"I don't know. It is a mystery. But you look older."

"I am older – a year older. Today's my birthday."

"How old are you?"

"I'm nine today."

"Then that must be your birthday cake I saw on the table back there. It was a huge cake, with chocolate frosting and vanilla pudding between the layers. It had nine candles on top of it."

"Really! Then it must be for me. Show me!"

"Okay – come on!"

Vanessa turned around and ran back the way she had come. Luke hurried after her on his side of the table. They ran for two or three minutes. The table was so long it seemed to have no end.

Finally Luke saw a huge cake of five or six layers sitting at the end of the table. It was as tall as he was! Eagerly he ran toward it. Now he saw a man standing at the end of the table, all dressed in white, with a white chef's hat perched on the top of his head. The man held a candle in his hand. He was lighting the nine candles of the birthday cake.

Luke and Vanessa came forward and stood before him.

"So, young man," said the man, glancing down at Luke, "today is your birthday."

"Yes, sir. Did you make my birthday cake?"

"Of course. I am the Steward of the Feast. I am in charge of birthdays here – all kinds of birthdays. I see that you have brought your friend."

"I didn't really bring her. She was already here."

The hint of a smile crossed the man's lips. "I invited her," he said. "I thought you would like to share your birthday cake with her."

"This is way too big a cake just for the two of us."

"It's not just for you. This cake, and the whole feast spread out on this table, is for all your friends."

"But there is no one else here."

"They will come."

"Who will come?"

"Your friends."

"I don't have any friends. She is my only friend. Well, except for Carl – but no one else my own age. They all make fun of me."

"You will have friends. You will have friends too numerous to count. They will come to the feast with you. There will be so many they will fill every inch of this whole table."

Luke shook his head in disbelief, "I don't think I will ever have so many friends. They think I'm weird."

"All things are possible if you believe. You must believe in the power of goodness. Whenever you are kind to others, you invite a new friend to your feast."

"Are we allowed to have cake now?" asked Luke, "even though no one else is here yet?"

"You are allowed to do whatever you choose to do. But take care how you choose, because you must eat wisely to become a man of character."

"But I am not a man, I am just a boy."

"Boys become men. Every year you are growing more a man and less a boy. The man you become will be determined by the choices you make. Now come and stand beside me. The candles are lit. It is time for you to blow them out."

Luke walked toward the cake, drew in a deep breath, and blew at the candles with all his might. Instead of going out, the candles ignited and went straight up to the sky and pulled Luke up with them.

High above him, as if the flames were pointing up to it, a star brighter than imagining shone above him. Gazing at the star, a great happiness surged in Luke's heart. "It's my birthday star," he said, "just like my mama told me."

The next instant, the light of the star began to fade. Around him the swirling flickering colors of orange and yellow and red from the candle flames also grew pale...and finally disappeared.

Fifteen

EAGLESCLIFF

More tired from the bus ride than she had expected Janet did not wake the next morning until nearly nine o'clock. Even then she did not feel rested. She knew it was more than the bus ride, however. The emotional stakes of this adventure could not be measured. Maybe she would find her daughter, maybe she would learn something she didn't want to know. Despite what Janet had said to Annie about spending an extra day in Cheyenne to get rested up, Janet knew that wasn't the real reason. She was afraid.

She bathed and dressed slowly and took a leisurely walk around town, had a light lunch, and by mid-afternoon had run out of things to keep her mind off of what she might find in Eaglescliff. She woke up early Thursday morning and was ready to go.

Janet boarded the Greyhound north just after eleven-thirty.

A wave of loneliness swept through her as the bus picked up speed, then headed north on Route 85. Even if Cheyenne didn't rate city status by Dallas standards, it had been a friendly and bustling place. Leaving Wyoming's largest town *or* city behind, the terrain out the window was hot, dry and barren. A more forlorn place she could not imagine. Yet somewhere out in this unknown world she hoped to find her daughter.

Her spirit calmed gradually and the stark landscape penetrated her soul. There was no sound other than the drone of the bus engine. The handful of other passengers seemed to feel it too. No one spoke. Silence intensified the beauty of the wild western landscape. She saw no houses, no people, only cattle grazing lazily behind barbed wire fencing, cluttered with tumbleweeds that paralleled the highway for miles. In the distance, sage covered gently rolling hills. Behind them, the Rockies loomed on the horizon to the west.

This was probably just how it had looked five hundred years ago, thought Janet, except for the road and barbed wire. She could imagine a band of Indians riding over the next ridge behind a herd of stampeding buffalo. It was beautiful in a desolate, solitary way.

The final leg of her journey was broken by a handful of stops, in towns boasting populations ranging between eight and eight hundred, sometimes at run-down filling stations, occasionally to pick up or deposit a passenger alongside the road in what seemed the middle of nowhere.

After a few of hours, the Greyhound crested a ridge and began its descent into the Platte River Valley. Fields of tall ripening stalks of corn dominated the foreground as the town of Eaglescliff came into view. It was a scene, thought Janet, that Norman Rockwell might easily have used for a cover of *The Saturday Evening Post*. Janet noted the population sign as they passed the edge of town: *Eaglescliff, Population 3,897*. A second line read: *Elevation, 4,104 feet*.

Three white towers, the tallest buildings for miles, slid by the window to Janet's left. A sign outside the large industrial plant read "Holly Sugar Corporation." A short bridge over what was called Cherry Creek led the bus a minute later across the North Platte, bringing them finally onto Main Street and into the center of town. Janet was immediately charmed by the quaint look of the place. The bus slowed. After two turns the driver pulled to a stop in front of the Greyhound station.

Janet took a deep breath. *Well, this is it*, she thought. *Here I am!*

She rose from her seat and followed two or three other passengers outside. Janet hadn't appreciated the new high tech air conditioning on the bus until she stepped outside. The hot and thin mountain air jolted her as if she had walked into an oven. She was a little surprised at the heat. Growing up in

Texas she had thought it was cooler in the mountains. Granted, it wasn't as hot as back in Dallas, but it was still hot!

Unconsciously Janet glanced up and down the main street, as if expecting to see Leslie walking toward her. But she had not seen her for seventeen years. Would she even recognize her?

She turned and walked into the station. A few minutes later, with suitcase in hand, Janet was ready to see where this adventure would lead next.

Where it led her was across the street and along the sidewalk to an inauspicious diner whose neon sign, one letter burned out, emblazoned "Eaglescliff Café." The place looked cool and inviting. It was either that or the drug store on the corner boasting a "Soda Fountain." Soda sounded good but she went with more practical thinking of getting something to eat.

It wasn't so easy to slip into the café unnoticed lugging a suitcase. But it was the middle of the afternoon and the place was mostly empty. Janet glanced around, then shoved her suitcase underneath a table and slid across the amply-patched orange vinyl cushion of a small booth next to the window. She looked around and took in her surroundings. It was like any of a thousand small town cafes scattered from coast to coast throughout America, years out of style, faded wood paneling on the walls, with short-cropped orange and brown carpet that looked like it had been installed before the War, WWI that is. Several local ranchers in cowboy hats and baseball caps sat at the counter chatting with the waitress behind it, a platinum blonde with make-up and eye-shadow too thick for any purpose other than to hide the signs of age, with red painted lips to match. A man and woman with two young children occupied a booth at the far end. A man in a business suit and a smartly dressed professional woman sat in another booth in subdued conversation. Faded sports pictures and rodeo photographs — two of them signed — hung about on the walls. Vases of plastic flowers sat at every table. Behind the counter a chalkboard made customers aware of the day's specials. Today's was "Beef stew," though the men at the counter knew that nearly *every* day's special was beef stew, and that Harv, the owner and cook, didn't rustle up a new batch until the old one was gone, even if that took a week. It was usually only strangers passing through town who bit on Harv's blackboard offerings.

"Come on, Madge, quit yaking with Milt," called a voice from the kitchen. "Got your burgers and fries up. Don't let 'em get cold."

"Keep your hat on, Harv," the blond shot back good-naturedly. "I'm coming!"

Two minutes later the two children across the cafe were diving into their plate of French fries. The waitress left them and approached the booth where Janet sat.

"Howdy, ma'am," she said, chewing without a pause on the gum in her mouth. She withdrew an order tablet from the pocket of her pink uniform and pulled a pencil from her blond thatch where it rested on her ear.

"Could I get an ice tea, please," said Janet. "and those fries smell good! I'll have a cheeseburger and an order of French fries too."

"Coming right up."

The woman returned a moment later with the iced tea. While she sipped at her tall glass and waited for the burger and fries, Janet gazed outside at the main street of Eaglescliff. The most notable building for this particular visitor sat almost directly across the street. A U.S. flag flew from a white flagpole. In front of the building a small sign read, *United States Post Office, Eaglescliff, Wyoming*. The sight sent a new thrill of hope through Janet's frame. Leslie had sent the Christmas card from right there, she thought. It was the closest she had been to her daughter in seventeen years. Leslie might be closer than she knew at this very moment. Janet could not help staring intently at every face, at every woman going in or coming out of the shops along Main Street, thinking that one of them might actually be Leslie. It was with great effort that Janet forced herself to remember that she would be much changed. She would be thirty-three now. She might have gained weight, she might have a family. She also tried to think what Joe might look like. She had spent the years trying to forget him.

On the orange seat across from her, a previous customer had left a local newspaper. Janet leaned over, picked it up, and absently looked through the first few pages. She smiled as she scanned the headings. *These are stories you wouldn't see in Dallas,* she thought.

> *Governor meets with local bean farmers.*
> *Ranchers agree on water rights dispute.*
> *Coma girl approaches ten years – doctors pessimistic.*
> *Plans for Fair and Rodeo parade in full swing.*

On the second page a "Community Calendar" was full of homey sounding activities.

> *Goshen County Fair and Rodeo opens Friday at the Fairgrounds.*
> *Fair and Rodeo Queen finalists.*
> *Women's sewing circle meets Wednesday mornings at ten at Baptist Church.*
> *Catholic Church welcomes new priest this Sunday, soup and sweets hour after mass, everyone welcome.*

Below it were a list of local "Job Openings."

> *English teacher K-12 needed, see Principal Pratt at Wyoming Children's Home.*
> *Qualified truck drivers needed – apply at Holly Sugar plant.*
> *Pharmacist needed at Rafferty Drug.*
> *Hiring cosmetics clerk at Daly's Department Store.*

An hour later, full and prepared at last to find a place to spend the night, she again set out along the sidewalk in the direction the waitress told her the two best hotels were located. Already the town had begun to exercise a hold on her. Maybe it was because she knew that Leslie had once lived here, and hopefully still did. For whatever reason, thought Janet, she liked it.

Fifteen minutes later she was climbing the stairs to room 211 of the Eaglescliff Hotel. The stairway and corridor were dimly lit and could have done with a fresh coat of paint. But the room as she walked in seemed promising, though sparsely furnished with a table and chair, an easy chair, and a double bed with a nightstand and lamp beside it. The bed was spread with a multi-colored quilt of what appeared an Indian design. Heavy drapes hung over the window on the far wall matching the pattern of the quilt. She spread the drapes and beheld the view of an asphalt parking lot with a bursting corn field beyond.

It wasn't the Ritz. But it would be her home for a few days at least. It appeared clean, and the air conditioner worked. That may have been the most important thing of all!

She hoisted her suitcase up on the bed, then looked at her watch and thought better of it. She could unpack later. It was a little before three on a Thursday afternoon. She had two hours to get more familiar with the area. She ought to make the most of them.

After washing her face in the bathroom, combing her hair, and putting on a fresh blouse, she left the room and set out to begin the next leg of her adventure.

Sixteen

Initial Inquiries

Eaglescliff, Wyoming, Friday August 15, 1947

Janet was up early Friday morning to begin her search for Leslie in earnest. Directions to the Police Station from the lady who had registered her into the hotel were easy enough to follow. The Rocky Mountain air had cooled into the fifties overnight. Janet found breathing the pine scented morning air refreshing as she made the three block walk. She entered the station. A uniformed officer sat at a desk behind a glass half-wall. He rose when she entered and came to the counter.

"Morning, ma'am," he said. "How can I help you?"

"I'm looking for someone," Janet replied, pulling out a manila envelope. "It's my daughter. I haven't seen her in many years and I have reason to believe she may live in Eaglescliff."

"Is she a minor…is she in trouble?" asked the policeman.

"No — she's thirty-three. She's not in trouble. I just want to find her."

"She's not a missing person?"

"No, nothing like that."

"I don't know that there's much I can do to help. I can look to see if she's in our files. But if she's had no trouble with the law, we wouldn't have anything on her. I can check if you like."

"I would appreciate it very much."

"What's your daughter's name, ma'am."

"Leslie Holiday," replied Janet. "I have an old picture of her here."

She took a picture of Leslie out of her purse and handed it

to the man. He looked it over briefly.

"Can't say as I recognize her, ma'am. This is an old picture, you say?"

"I'm afraid so. It was taken eighteen years ago."

"That's a long time. Is your daughter married?"

"I think so...actually, I don't know that for certain."

"The name you gave me — is that her married name?"

"That would be her maiden name. I'm Janet Holiday."

"What's her married name?"

"Actually...I don't know. When she left home she was still Leslie Holiday, though she was involved with a man whose last name I never even knew."

"It's not much to go on," the man said. "But I'll check our files."

He turned and disappeared into another room, leaving Janet at the counter. He returned twenty minutes later.

He shook his head as he approached. "Sorry, Mrs. Holiday. I didn't find a thing. There is no police record of anyone named Leslie Holiday."

"I suppose I should consider that good news," said Janet with an attempt at a smile.

"The only thing I can suggest might be the courthouse across the street...or —" he added, then paused.

"What?" said Janet.

"I was also going to suggest you try the hospital."

"Thank you...yes, I will do that. And where is the hospital?"

"Just as you're leaving town north, past the Home, about a mile."

"That sounds like a taxi ride, not a walk. I usually don't do this much walking around back at home."

"Where are you from, ma'am?"

"Dallas."

"I see what you mean. If you're from down south you probably don't want to stay through the winter. We get about two weeks of summer," the officer said joking, "then autumn comes and soon it'll get colder than anything you've probably seen down there in Texas. Well, best of luck to you. I hope you find what you're looking for."

Janet thanked him again and left.

Unfortunately, over two hours at the courthouse ended with the same result, as did a visit to the hospital. When the taxi deposited her again in front of the hotel later that afternoon, Janet was mentally and physically exhausted, and wondering if she had made a big mistake coming here. Leslie had probably mailed the Christmas card on her way through town. For all she knew, she might never have spent more than five minutes in Eaglescliff. What was she thinking—that she would just show up here and, after seventeen years, see Leslie walking down the sidewalk…they would embrace in laughter and tears…and live happily ever after? How naïve could she have possibly been!

Dejected, Janet slowly climbed the stairs to her room.

SEVENTEEN

THE FIFTH DREAM—A SOCCER GAME

Christmas Eve, 1940

As it gradually came to be known that Luke's birthday was on Christmas Eve, the orphanage staff planned a birthday cake to be included in the normal Christmas Eve supper. It was nice that they cared, Luke thought to himself. But he would rather not be the center of attention. He knew what the older boys thought as they snickered their way through the singing of *Happy Birthday*, and whispered wisecracks of *Spastic* and *Retard* when he tried to lean forward from his wheelchair to blow out the candles. He would give all the birthday cakes in the world for the chance just once to run out on a soccer field and give the ball a good solid whack into the net.

Today had been an unseasonably warm day for December. The boys had gone out to the playing field in the afternoon, with several snowdrifts piled around the edges, for a game of soccer. His fate, as always, was to be wheeled out by Carl, there to sit on the sidelines and watch, while Carl ran out amongst the boys to make sure the teams were fairly selected and then officiate the game.

Luke watched absently. His thoughts were not on the game but rather on whether he would have another Christmas Eve dream tonight. Suddenly he glanced up to see two of the older boys named Stuart and Marco racing along the sideline toward him kicking the ball back and forth. They were two of his worst tormentors. He did not like the mischievous looks on their faces.

Quickly Luke grabbed at his wheels and tried to wheel himself backwards. But just then Stuart gave the ball a vicious kick straight toward him. He was not fast enough to get out of the way.

Carl's whistle sounded and he came racing forward trying to intercept the ball. But he was too late. Luke threw up his hands to shield himself. The ball hit him squarely in the shoulder and the wheelchair toppled over. Luke sprawled onto the slushy ground.

Laughter erupted over the field as Carl knelt down to see if Luke was hurt. He slipped his arms under Luke's body as one of the boys hurried up and righted the wheelchair. He held it steady as Carl set Luke back into it.

"Thanks, Gary," said Carl. He stood and turned as the rest of the boys came running. "You need to be more careful, Stuart."

"Just an accident, Carl. I was trying to get it down the sideline to Marco."

"I don't know whether to believe you or not. But we're through. Come on, Luke," he said, turning the wheelchair around, "let's go get you cleaned up."

"Aw, Carl, why do we have to go in?" complained several of the boys.

"Because I'm taking Luke in, that's why. You've had enough soccer for today."

"It's all Luke's fault," said a boy named Reuben.

"Why don't you just stay inside, you cripple. You just get in the way!"

"That's enough," said Carl. "Marco, Reuben...don't you know, this is Luke's birthday?

"Yeah, I know. Gotta keep the stupid birthday boy happy."

"What would you think if the other boys made fun of you, Marco?"

"None of them would dare make fun of me. They know what would happen if they did."

The boys wandered back to the main building, muttering comments about Luke spoiling their soccer game. Luke sometimes wondered if they thought he couldn't *hear* either! His face was still red and his knuckles white in anger as he gripped the arms of his wheelchair.

Carl tried to make him feel better the rest of the day. He knew that the incident had not merely hurt Luke but had angered him. Carl did what he could to make the rest of his holiday special, and gradually Luke calmed down. It was times like this that Luke missed his mother most of all.

He was anxious to get to his room after supper and be alone. No birthday cake or *Happy Birthday* could make up for the sting of Marco's words.

As he lay in bed that night, Luke knew what his mother would say. He could remember her very words. She had always encouraged him not to think of being mute and crippled as handicaps.

"Being crippled isn't the worst pain you will have to suffer, Luke," she had told him many times. "You will have to endure in silence the ridicule of people not understanding you, not knowing who you really are. Always remember that the wheelchair isn't who you are. Who you are is the person inside. Never forget that, my little man. As you grow, you won't grow like other boys. You won't be a great athlete. You will grow *inside*. You will become bigger on the inside than you are on the outside. Don't worry if people don't see it. I will see it, and God will see it. No matter how unkind people may be to you, you can still be a good person on the inside. You can be nice to them, even if you are just being nice in your thoughts. That's the most important place to be nice — inside, where God sees who you are."

It wasn't so easy, thought Luke as he drifted to sleep. Remembering the day's incident roused his feelings toward Stuart and Marco back to life again. No, it wasn't easy to swallow their insults without a word. But it comforted him to remember that his mother was still with him, even if only by the memory of her words.

As sleep came, Luke fell into a spinning tunnel. He was twisting and somersaulting until his feet landed solidly on a soft green surface. He looked down and saw that he was in the middle of a huge grassy field. But unlike the last time when he had dreamed of grass, he wasn't barefoot. He was wearing a beautiful pair of blue and white athletic shoes. He had never seen anything like them in his life!

Before he had time to think, he saw a white and black soccer ball speeding toward him over the field. It was coming so fast he had no time to think. He took two quick steps toward it and gave the ball a great kick with the instep of his right foot. His leg trembled from the impact. It was a sensation he had never felt. It felt good! He watched the ball leave his foot and soar back across the field, amazed that he had been able to kick it so far.

Even before it landed, from several directions shouts and cheers went up. Suddenly he was not alone. Twenty or thirty boys his own age and older came running up.

"Did you see that!" yelled one. "Luke kicked it a mile!"

"He's on our team!" shouted several boys at once.

The crowd soon sorted itself into two teams, everyone hoping to be on Luke's team. Now Luke saw the goals and nets at both ends, and the white-chalked boundaries and goal lines. In the middle of the field, a tall man wearing the uniform of referee stood at the center of the pitch. He blew his whistle, and the game was on.

Luke tore around in every direction, not only faster than he had ever been able to run, but faster than anyone else on the field. As he ran, he occasionally tumbled about, flipped somersaults in the air and landed back on his feet, then sprinted off again after the ball. It wasn't just like a dream come true…it WAS a dream come true. He was moving so fast, everything around him, the other boys, the ball, the grass, the goals…everything was a fast-moving blur of color, and he was whacking the ball left and right with both his feet and effortless ease. He loved the feel when his foot met the ball. Before he had time to think what was happening, the score was six to zero. And he had scored all six goals! He must be in heaven, Luke thought.

Into Luke's ear came the sound of clapping and cheering from the sideline. He turned and saw Vanessa standing cheering him on. He ran over to join her.

"You're here again!" he said.

"Yes and you're really good," she exclaimed. "You're the star of the whole game. How did you learn to play so well?"

"I don't know. Actually, I've never played before."

"You'd better get back out there," said Vanessa. "The other team is moving toward the goal."

"Don't worry – I'll stop them!"

Luke darted off in a blur. Within seconds he had intercepted the ball and was streaking back in the opposite direction toward his own goal. Seconds later it was seven to zero!

Luke waved at Vanessa with a big grin across his face. Now for the first time he saw a boy walking toward the sideline a little ways from her. He was walking with a limp. When he reached the line he stopped and stood watching the game. Luke ran toward him.

"Hey, you want to play?" he called.

The boy shook his head. Luke could see the disappointment in his face. He stopped and walked over.

"Are you sure?" he said. "Come on, you'll have fun."

"I can't," said the boy. "I'm crippled. The others never let me play. They make fun of me and call me names."

"I won't make fun of you, and I would like you to play. You can be on my team. What's your name?"

"Stuart. But they won't let me play."

"Hey, Luke – come on," called one of the boys from the field. "Get back out here."

"Stuart's going to join us," Luke called back. "He can be on our team."

"No way…he's no good…he's just a cripple!" called out several of his teammates.

"Besides," said another. "The teams are already even."

"Then he will take my place."

"Aw, come on, Luke – he's no good!"

"He's still taking my place."

Luke turned back to the boy on the sidelines and sat down beside him. He began untying his shoes. "Come on now, Stuart," he said. "You're in the game now. You're taking my place. Sit down and put these shoes on. I think they might be magic shoes. I've never played soccer before, but with these on I could run like the wind."

"I don't even know how to kick a ball," said Stuart as he put the first shoe on one of his feet. "Oh, it feels good – it makes my feet tingle."

"There – see what I mean. Now when you see the ball coming toward you, just focus your eyes on the ball…and believe. You have to believe that you're going to kick it. And you will. I know you will."

A minute later Stuart was trying to run out onto the field, hobbling a little as he went, but gaining strength in his bad leg with every step. Behind him, Luke shouted out encouragement.

The game went on a little more slowly without Luke in it. The other team scored three goals in a row and Luke's former teammates pleaded with him to come back in the game. But he continued to shout instructions and encouragement to Stuart, who by now was running almost without a limp, though he was still slower than the others.

Then as he stood some distance apart from the others, suddenly the ball came straight toward him. No one else was near it.

"Focus on the ball, Stuart!" cried Luke. "Believe you can do it...believe...believe!"

Stuart hesitated a moment, then took a step toward the ball as it rolled toward him, and gave it a great whack. Up it soared in a perfect arc, over the field, over all the other boys, and descended straight into the goal where it fell into the back of the net.

A great cheer went up from Luke's teammates and Vanessa. But the loudest cheers came from Luke himself. He was the happiest player on the field. His heart seemed to explode and grow ten times bigger.

Suddenly all around him went quiet. He could see the boys running this way and that on the field. Stuart was now in the thick of the action. Luke saw Vanessa's mouth moving, yelling for the players. But for him a great silence descended.

From somewhere a voice sounded – soft, as if coming from in the midst of the air around, but clear as crystal, and meant only for him.

"You are growing bigger on the inside, Luke. Your heart grows larger when you give joy to others. You have just given a priceless gift. I see your growth. Don't worry if people don't see it. I will see it, and God will see it."

His mother's words faded. Again the excited sounds of the game filled his ears. When it was over, Stuart ran over to where Luke still stood. His limp was scarcely noticeable now. His face was radiant.

"That was the most fun I've ever had in my life!" he exclaimed. "Thank you, Luke. I don't know why you let me take your place, but that was the nicest thing anyone's ever done for me."

He fell to the ground and began untying the shoes.

"What are you doing?" asked Luke.

"Giving you your shoes back."

"They're not mine," smiled Luke. "They're your shoes now. Merry Christmas, Stuart."

Stuart stared back at him with wide eyes of disbelief. Already his face, and the field, and the other boys, and Vanessa, were fading from Luke's view.

As he felt himself drifting into unconsciousness, he had never felt such happiness as he felt in that moment, he had learned that giving happiness is the greatest happiness of all.

EIGHTEEN

THE SODA FOUNTAIN

Eaglescliff, Saturday, August 16, 1947

The weekend passed slowly for Janet. An impressive thunderstorm came in from the northwest with a crackling show of lightning the likes she had never seen before late Friday night. The heavy winds and rain left puddles of water everywhere the next morning, and even some downed tree limbs. No one else seemed concerned about it. Cars sped along the streets unconcerned. As Janet walked around the downtown area there weren't many stores open to choose from. By day's end she had browsed briefly inside them all. At the department store she bought a couple more light blouses and a wide brimmed straw hat to shade her face from the sun. She had not come prepared for the surprising mountain heat!

With the courthouse closed for the weekend, there wasn't much of an official nature she could do. She upbraided herself for not thinking to ask about Leslie in the Post Office yesterday. She would have to wait until Monday. But she walked about town and enjoyed familiarizing herself with its charms. She was reminded how she and Jack visited a different place every Valentine's Day. She continued to scan the face of every person she met…just in case! If Leslie indeed still lived here, it seemed logical that she would run into her eventually.

On Sunday she walked to the Baptist church for the morning service. No stores were open. There wasn't much to do, and it was too hot to walk too far from the hotel. She ate a Sunday dinner of rubbery chicken with stale bread dressing in the hotel dining room. The breakfasts weren't too bad, but she would definitely have to find someplace else for dinner. Neither the hotel dining room nor the Eaglescliff Café were likely to be featured in Wyoming's travel guides for recommended cuisine.

Later that afternoon, tired of sitting around her room, Janet ventured out again. One establishment that was open was the drug store. Heat or no heat, she would try it. She left the hotel, walked along the sidewalk and crossed the street. She noticed a black sporty hot rod painted with orange flames in front of the door and continued inside the corner shop called Rafferty's Drug. She walked to the soda fountain. Several teenagers were seated at the counter. A boy of seventeen or eighteen, dressed in white from head to foot, with a white cap on his head, came toward her with a bright smile.

"Afternoon, ma'am," he said. "Finally decided to give us a try?"

"Yes, I guess so," replied Janet with a puzzled expression. "But I'm not sure what you mean."

"Just that I've seen you out walking up and down the street both yesterday and today. I take it you're new to town."

"Actually yes. I'm staying at the hotel and haven't quite known what to do with myself."

"Well you'll always get a warm welcome here. My name's Gary."

"Hello, Gary," said Janet with a smile, charmed by the boy's friendly spirit. "I am Janet Holiday."

"Where are you from, Mrs. Holiday?"

"Dallas."

"Oh, wow — you've come a long way! Do you have family here?"

"I *think* so. I don't know for certain. It's a long story."

"I didn't mean to pry, Mrs. Holiday. What can I get for you?"

"I don't know — what do you think? It's pretty hot out so maybe I'll get something cool. Is it normal for it to be this hot?"

"No way! We're having a record setting heat wave. But don't worry — it'll cool off soon enough."

"I think I'm in the mood for a root beer float." Janet said with a smile.

"You couldn't do better—a black cow, one of my specialties!"

"Then a root beer float it is."

Janet's eyes followed the boy named Gary as he turned toward the ice-cream bins. *What a pleasant young man,* she thought. *His parents must be very proud.*

Gary returned a couple minutes later.

"Did you see my car outside?" he said as he set down the tall frothing glass on the counter.

"I couldn't help noticing. It's quite a car!"

"It's a '35 Chrysler Airstream coupe. I painted the flames on it myself. Don't you love the white walls!"

"It sounds like you have a way with cars."

"I've only had it a year. A man where I live has been helping me fix it up. He loaned me some of the money to buy it too. But with my job here, I'll have him paid back in a year."

"May I ask you a question," said Janet, lowering her voice. "I don't mean to offend anyone, but is there a better place to eat than the hotel and the Eaglescliff Cafe?"

Gary roared with the exuberant laughter of a teenager. "You've noticed!" he said. "Yes, actually there is. It's called the Kings Inn."

"Where is it?"

"Just along Main Street...two more blocks north. Toward the orphanage."

"The orphanage? There's an orphanage in a small town like Eaglescliff?"

"It's the state orphanage. I don't know why it's here instead of Cheyenne. It's called the Wyoming Children's Home, but we stay there till we graduate from high school. Everyone just calls it the home. Some of the kids are even older than eighteen. That's where I live."

"*You* live at the orphanage?" said Janet in surprise.

"Yep."

"Are you...you're an orphan?"

He nodded.

"I'm sorry to hear that, Gary."

"Aw, it's all right. You get used to it. When life throws

you lemons, make lemonade—that's what they're always telling us. I'm going to, too. I'm going to make something of my life."

"I'm sure you will."

NINETEEN

THE SIXTH DREAM—A CHRISTMAS PAGEANT

Christmas Eve, 1941

All day Carl made a great fuss about this being Luke's eleventh birthday. He did what he could to make the day special. In the afternoon he loaded Luke and his wheelchair into the orphanage van. One of the other orphans who was a year older than Luke, joined them on a drive through town. Carl invited anyone else to come along that wanted to. But no one else wanted to spend the day with a cripple.

They planned to look at the Christmas lights and decorations and maybe walk through Daly's Department Store where Carl said they had a collection of car replicas in the toy department, then stop by for an ice-cream soda at Rafferty's Drug. The other boy, Gary, was twelve and was a walking encyclopedia about cars. He was always talking about learning to drive and getting his license and finding a job and buying a car of his own when he was old enough. Carl loved all the kids at the orphanage and did everything he could to encourage them to fulfill their dreams.

The result was that after their visit to the Soda Fountain, the three spent most of the afternoon visiting the Ford, Chrysler and Chevrolet dealerships in town, as well as Clint Sanders Studebaker. As Carl pushed Luke up and down between the rows of shiny new cars, and other rows of used cars, explaining some of the differences between the various models, Gary talked excitedly and was full of more questions than even a car buff like Carl was able to answer.

"Don't you love the Packard 'shovel' nose grille, Carl!" said Gary excitedly.

Carl laughed as Gary ran around examining every inch of the bright black car. "I don't know, Gary," Carl replied. "It looks funny to me—like they couldn't decide whether they were designing a car or a rocket ship."

"If you could have any car on the lot, then, what would you want?"

"I'm afraid it wouldn't be a Packard. To tell you the truth, Gary, I'm partial to Fords, Chevy's and Chryslers."

"What is your favorite then?"

Carl thought a moment. "If I could have any car in the world," he said, "I think it would be either a '32 Model B two door coupe, or a '35 Chrysler Airstream." He paused, still thinking, "—with white walls of course."

"Yeah, I really like the Ford Model B two doors, both the roadsters and the coupes. I'm going to have a car of my own as soon as I turn sixteen."

Carl laughed again at Gary's enthusiasm. "I'm sure you will! But how will you pay for it?"

"I don't know. I'll get a job. I just have to have a car of my own!"

Luke listened, enjoying the conversation between Carl and Gary. The cars were pretty. But he didn't share Gary's excitement. He knew he would never own a car. He would never even be able to drive one.

They left the Studebaker lot. Gary helped Carl get Luke into the front passenger seat of the van and load the wheelchair into the back, then jumped into the back seat behind Luke. By now the afternoon was wearing on toward evening and there was snow in the air. Back at the orphanage, Luke's birthday cake was ready for the evening meal with its eleven candles arranged in a circle.

On the way home, Carl drove by the hospital, which stood about a half mile beyond the orphanage north of town. Every year the hospital displayed a life-size Christmas crèche on the lawn in front of the main entrance. Carl pulled into the hospital parking lot and stopped. He and Gary again helped get Luke out and into his wheelchair, then the three made their way across the lot to the crèche. They stood gazing at it for several minutes in silence. Whatever was on Carl's mind he did not divulge to the two boys. But he was clearly moved by the sight.

Luke's thoughts, too, later that night as Carl gently lifted him into his bed, returned to the sight of the Christmas manger scene. Before Carl left him, he made him to understand that he wanted a pencil, a piece of paper, and a hard board to write on. Carl got them and handed them down to Luke.

A minute later Luke handed him the piece of paper.

Thank you for today, Carl read. *This was my best birthday at the orphanage.*

"You're welcome, my man," he said with a broad smile. "I had fun too. Happy birthday again. Have a good sleep, and I'll see you tomorrow…on Christmas morning!"

Like many children his age Luke had a hard time falling asleep that night. Not because of any gifts Santa might bring, but because he couldn't wait for another Christmas dream. He missed the feeling of being normal — of being able to walk and talk and laugh like everybody else in the world. After a while his eyes grew tired and he drifted off to sleep.

Luke emerged from the now familiar dream-tunnel of light with his feet landing on solid ground with a light thump.

"It's about time," said a familiar voice.

He spun around, treasuring the thrill of feeling his feet beneath him again. There was Vanessa looking at him with a smile on her face.

"You're here again!" Luke exclaimed. "Your dream must have started before mine. How long have you been waiting?"

"Not long," replied Vanessa. "We're in some kind of building. A hospital, I think."

As in every dream, neither Luke nor Vanessa questioned what was happening because in a dream things just happen. The dream pulled them into it of itself. They found themselves walking through a long hallway decorated with red, white, and gold Christmas decorations on walls and strung across the ceiling. The doors of most rooms were open. Luke was surprised to see children in them. At the end of the hall they came to a large room filled with children of all ages, some playing games on the carpeted floor and at tables scattered around the room.

"Why are all these children here?" said Luke. "I thought hospitals were for older people."

The smile faded from Vanessa's lips. Her face was filled with compassion as she gazed about. "Hospitals are for children too," she said. "Children get sick or injured...they even die. They need care too."

A voice interrupted them from behind.

"Welcome to the playroom Christmas party," it said. "There's plenty to eat, and we'll be starting our Christmas Eve play in just a few minutes."

They turned toward the man who had spoken. "Thank you," said Vanessa softly. "We will enjoy that."

Luke stared at the man a moment. He was dressed in a white doctor's smock. His face, especially his eyes, were vaguely familiar. He reminded Luke of the referee at the soccer game in last year's dream. His eyes were filled with pleasure as he gazed about the room and saw the smiles on the faces of the children.

As they continued to walk around the room, Luke could not help staring. He had never seen children like this before. Some wore casts on their legs or arms. One boy had a bandage covering one side of his head. Several were bald. One girl had patches of red, bumpy, scarred skin on her face that stretched down the length of her neck and beneath her hospital gown.

"Don't stare," Vanessa whispered beside him. "You may not think they notice, but they do. They're very self-conscious about their conditions."

"Oh...sorry," said Luke. "I didn't think about that. What's wrong with her face?" he added in a low tone.

"She was in a house fire," replied Vanessa when they had moved to one side of the room. "That's what happens to your skin when you get burned really bad. The pain is horrible. They have to take skin from other parts of your body to cover the burned areas. It's called a skin graft."

Luke was quiet for the next several minutes.

"All right, boys and girls!" said a large woman dressed in blue-green hospital clothes as she stepped to the middle of the room. "It's time for the Christmas play to begin. Let's gather round."

The lights in the room dimmed. The girl with the burn scars on her face stepped to the front and read from a white paper in her hand.

"In those days, Caesar issued a decree that a census should be taken. So Joseph and his wife Mary traveled far, from Nazareth to Bethlehem on a donkey. Mary was pregnant and it was about time for her baby to be born."

One of the girls with no hair now walked forward beside a boy who had needles poking out of his arm attached to tubes leading beneath his robe costume.

"Here come Mary and her husband Joseph," said the girl who was the narrator. "They're on their way to Bethlehem."

The boy and girl playing Joseph and Mary wore long brown robes tied at the waists, and held walking sticks in their hands. The girl had a pillow under her robe to make her stomach look fat. They walked to a small cardboard shack on which was painted the word INN. Some of the older children had helped make it. Joseph knocked on the pretend door. A small boy, also in a robe, wearing a fake beard, ducked low and came out through the door.

A brief silence filled the room as the boy tried to remember what he was supposed to say.

"Uh...I'm the keeper of the inn," he said after a moment. "May I help you with something?"

"My wife is expecting to have a baby tonight," said Joseph. "We need a place to stay."

"We have no room here." The innkeeper boy said, trying to make his voice sound low and gruff. "You'll have to go somewhere else."

"Please, sir," said Joseph, dropping down to his knees. "You must have some place we can stay. I promise, we will cause no trouble. I'm just a poor carpenter from Nazareth."

The innkeeper rubbed his fake whiskers and pretended to be deep in thought. "The only place we have left is out back in the stable with the animals," he said. "If you can stand the smell, you can spend the night there."

Joseph and Mary walked slowly to another part of the room where some cardboard props had been placed to make it look like a barn — fences and gates with some bits of hay on the floor. The boy and girl sat down around a cradle with a baby doll lying inside it.

The girl with the burned face stepped forward again. "Mary gave birth to a baby boy that night," she read from her paper. "She wrapped him in tattered rags and laid him in a manger."

More children dressed in ragged robes now walked to the front, with other children dressed to look like sheep. The narrator continued to read. "There were shepherds in a field nearby keeping watch over their flock, when an angel of the Lord appeared to them and the glory of the Lord shown all around them."

A bright light now beamed down from the ceiling. A tall girl dressed in a white gown with white-painted cardboard angel's wings attached to her back walked toward the shepherds. "Do not be afraid," she said. "I bring you good news of great joy that will be for all people. Today in the town of David, which is Bethlehem, a Savior has been born to you. He is Christ the Lord. This will be a sign to you – you will find a baby wrapped in cloths and lying in a manger."

More children now walked toward the shepherds and angel. They were dressed in dark purple robes and had fake beards taped to their faces and wore crowns on their heads. One of them spoke loudly to the shepherds. "We are three kings from the east. We bear gifts for the new king born tonight. Let us all go to Bethlehem to see this Savior."

As the three kings and shepherds shuffled across the floor toward the stable where Mary and Joseph sat beside the cradle, the girl with the burns continued to read. "When the three kings saw the baby Jesus, they bowed down and worshipped him. They opened their treasure and presented him with gifts of gold, incense, and myrrh."

The three Wise Men took gifts from under their robes and placed them in the cradle beside the baby. "And that is why," the narrator continued, "we celebrate the birth of Jesus on Christmas Eve, and why we give presents to each other, just like the presents the Wise Men gave to baby Jesus."

Those who had acted in the play, Mary and Joseph and the shepherds and Wise Men, the innkeeper and angel, now came together and held hands in a line. In unison they spoke loudly, and said, "We wish you a merry Christmas, with peace and goodwill towards men. The end."

Several parents who had come to share Christmas Eve with their children led the clapping for the performers. Parents and hospital staff and the other children made their way forward to congratulate those dressed in their costumes. As they did, Luke's eyes wandered about the room. He noticed a boy sitting in a wheelchair at the back of the room.

"I'll be back in a minute," he whispered to Vanessa. He rose and walked over to the boy, greeting him with a smile .

"The play was great, wasn't it?" he said in a friendly voice.

"I didn't think it was so great," replied the boy sullenly.

"Are your parents coming to celebrate Christmas Eve with you?" asked Luke.

"I don't have any parents. I'm an orphan."

"Really! Me too."

The boy looked Luke over skeptically. "Who's that girl over there with you?"

"Just a friend. We came together. But you don't see my parents here with me, do you?"

"I guess not. Maybe you are an orphan after all. At least you can walk. It's not as if you're stuck in a wheelchair."

Luke couldn't keep from breaking out in laughter.

"Are you making fun of me?" said the boy.

"No. I'm sorry," said Luke. "I couldn't help it. Let me tell you something," he went on, kneeling beside the boy and gazing earnestly into his face. "This may be hard to believe, but it's the truth. I know a boy who has not only been in a wheelchair all his life, he can't talk either. He's never spoken a word in his life. He's an orphan besides. He lives in an orphanage and all the others think he's stupid because he can't talk. They call him terrible names and make fun of him. How would you like to be him? At least you can talk. I bet you're smart, too, and I bet all the people around here know it, even if you are in a wheelchair."

"So who is this boy you're talking about?"

"It's me."

"You! What do you mean? I saw you walk over here, and you're talking to me just like anyone else."

"I'm telling you the truth. All my classmates think I'm mentally retarded besides being a cripple. And there's nothing I can do about it. But," he went on quickly before the boy could object again, "a special gift comes to me every Christmas Eve. And this is it!"

"What is?"

"You...you're part of my gift for this year."

"Now you're really talking nonsense!" said the boy, laughing for the first time.

"I mean it," said Luke. "Every Christmas Eve I receive a special gift, which is a dream that I can walk and talk and do all the things I can't do in my other life. So you're my gift this Christmas Eve."

"You mean I'm part of your dream?"

"Yep."

"Then if I'm in your dream, how do you know if I'm real?"

"I don't," laughed Luke. "That's a good question. But I think you are real."

"Why?"

"Because I learn things in my dreams that I remember later. Mostly I am learning to be thankful for who I am, even if I am crippled. I am learning something my mother told me before she died — that the person I am becoming on the inside is more important than the person I may look like on the outside. I may never be a great athlete in my other life, but if I can grow on the inside, that will be more important in the end. That's what my dreams are helping me do. I'm learning to be thankful, and to help others when I have the chance. I think meeting you will help me remember. So if I will remember you, how can you not be real?"

"I'm not sure I follow you," said the boy. "But you may be right. I suppose being in a wheelchair isn't the worst thing in the world. Look at Jason over there — he's not only in a wheelchair, he's got no legs. But you never hear him complaining. And poor Sally over there with her burns — she is in pain every day, but she always tries to smile, and every time I see her she says, 'Hi, Brandon,' as nice as if we were best friends. I don't see how she can be so cheerful. I never feel cheerful"

"Is that your name, Brandon?"

The boy nodded.

"I'm Luke. Why don't you and I shake hands and make a deal that being in a wheelchair won't keep us from being thankful ever again?"

"Okay." The two boys shook hands to seal their agreement. "But I'm still not sure how you can be crippled."

"If you could come with me out of my dream into my real life, you would — "

Luke stopped suddenly.

"Uh, oh!" he said.

"What is it?" asked Brandon. His voice began to grow faint.

"I think my dream is about to end. You are starting to fade away."

"But I want to come with you and see you in — "

"I think it is time for us to go," said a voice at Luke's side.

He turned. There stood Vanessa. She had a peculiar look on her face.

"You too?" said Luke.

91

She nodded. "Everything is growing fuzzy and dim. But – "

She continued to glance about with a puzzled expression.

" – but some part of me doesn't want to leave. I want to stay in this dream. I've got the strangest feeling that I know this place, and that I'm supposed to stay."

"We never stay in our dreams," said Luke. "I always wake up in my bed and it's Christmas morning."

"Not me. I don't wake up. I mean, I do wake up – but it's always in another dream with you."

They left the room and walked down the long corridor the way they had come in. Their surroundings continued to grow blurry and run together in strange colors.

Suddenly Vanessa stopped where two corridors came together. She was staring to her right at a sign on the wall above two wide double-doors that read: "Carnegie Wing."

"I do know where we are," she said.

The next instant a nurse came through the two doors holding a small tray of vials and glass bottles. She stopped in her tracks as she saw them. Her eyes widened and she stared intently at Vanessa.

All at once the nurse let out a piercing shriek. The tray fell from her hand. Shattered shards of glass and liquid flew in all directions.

Luke turned again toward Vanessa. Already she was fading into a white mist. The next instant he was swept up into clouds of brightness. Seconds later he was sound asleep in the oblivion of peaceful slumber.

TWENTY

THE KINGS INN

Eaglescliff, Monday, August 18, 1947

Janet spent Monday morning again at the Courthouse, going from office to office, clerk to clerk, and file cabinet to file cabinet, trying every possible line of inquiry she could think of. All the people she spoke to were helpful. But their efforts were unable to turn up any trace of Leslie Holiday, or any clue what her married name might be.

Janet descended the Courthouse steps to the sidewalk. Storm clouds were rolling in, the sky was growing dark with a disheartening color of gray from horizon to horizon. It could not have more perfectly matched her discouragement. More rain was forecast, most of what had fallen over the weekend had long since dried up. The air remained warm despite the clouds. Without a plan what to do next, Janet began to wonder if her mission was already coming to an end. A gnawing in her stomach reminded her that it was well past noon and she was hungry.

Remembering her exchange with the young man at the soda fountain, she set out along Main Street in the direction he had indicated. Passing Rafferty's Drug, she looked up and down the side street for Gary's brightly painted hot rod. But she saw it nowhere. Still thinking about Gary as she continued on, she noticed a sign alongside the street that read, *Wyoming Children's Home ½ Mile, Roosevelt Hospital 1 Mile*. Within two blocks the sign of The Kings Inn came into view.

She walked inside a few minutes later, thinking what a more pleasant atmosphere this was than the café downtown.

A waitress greeted her with a pleasant smile.

"Hi...go ahead and sit anywhere," she said. "I'll be with you in a jiffy."

Janet moved further inside and sat down in a booth as far away from the door as possible. The waitress returned when she was comfortably seated. She wore a blue uniform-dress with a tiny white apron. A nametag read, "Welcome to the Kings Inn, I'm Karen." She set a glass of water and menu down on the table."

"You look a little warm!" she said. "Can I get you some iced tea or lemonade?"

"I think I would like a glass of tea," replied Janet. "I'm from Texas. I'm used to heat, but I've been doing a lot more walking around than normal. Guess I'm a little out of shape."

"Iced tea it is."

The waitress returned a minute later.

"I think I'd like a BLT and a small salad," said Janet, handing her the menu.

"Good choice. Our lunch cook makes a killer BLT. Anything else I can get you?"

"I don't think so," sighed Janet as she dropped a straw into the glass of tea and took a sip. "Not unless you've got a spare miracle I can borrow."

"Sorry. I'm fresh out of miracles," said the young woman with a sympathetic smile. "Wish I did."

She turned to relay Janet's order to the kitchen, then busied herself with other customers.

While she waited for her meal, Janet sipped at her tea and set the manila envelope of information she had been showing around town on the table in front of her. She pulled out the contents and looked them over again one at a time. Her daughter's whole life up to her sixteenth birthday was here — birth certificate, high school records, medical files, and numerous photographs.

"Where are you, Leslie?" she whispered under her breath. *Where did you go?*

Still preoccupied with her thoughts five minutes later, Janet was surprised as she glanced up to see the waitress standing in front of her, holding a plate with her sandwich in one hand and the salad in the other. She was staring down at the photographs on the table. Her face wore a curious expression.

"It's my daughter," said Janet, smiling up at her. "That's why I'm here—I'm trying to find her."

Still thoughtful, the waitress set Janet's lunch across the table. Janet began to gather the papers and replace them in the envelope.

"I haven't seen her in years," Janet went on. "I've been showing these around town, hoping to meet someone who knows her. I've been to the hospital, the police station, the Courthouse, and the post office, though they said they couldn't give out private information. I've gone through every name in the phone book but I didn't find anyone in Eaglescliff with the first name Leslie other than two men who weren't particularly pleased that I had called asking for a *woman* called Leslie."

"Why didn't you look up her last name?"

"I did. I mean I looked up my *own* name— Holiday...Leslie Holiday. There was nothing. And if my daughter is married, I'm afraid I don't know her married name. She left home seventeen years ago."

"You are Mrs. Holiday?"

"Yes—I'm Janet Holiday."

"I'm pleased to meet you, Mrs. Holiday," said the young woman. Her smile as she spoke seemed oddly uneasy. "I'm Karen...Karen Sanders."

"Haven't I heard that name somewhere?"

"You probably saw the sign at the Studebaker dealership. Clint Sanders is my uncle—one of the pillars of the community as they say. A small town, you know. Everyone's related. He's my husband's uncle, actually. I'm only a Sanders by marriage. But once you're a Sanders everyone forgets what you were before.—May I get you another glass of tea?"

"Oh, uh...yes—thank you. That would be nice," replied Janet. "I guess I should eat. It smells delicious."

The young woman called Karen left again. Janet watched her go, thinking that she was probably about Leslie's age. She returned a minute later with more tea.

"I hope you don't mind," said Janet, "may I ask you a question?"

"Of course…sure."

"How old are you?"

"Thirty-six."

Janet nodded thoughtfully. "You are about my daughter's age. Leslie would be thirty-five. I last saw her when she was sixteen. I've been trying to imagine how she would have changed if I saw her walking along the street, whether I would even recognize her. It's not easy. My mind is full of what she looked like then."

"That picture you were looking at a minute ago…"

"It's her school yearbook picture. I thought for a second that you recognized her. But I've had so many disappointments in the last few days…to be honest, I was afraid to ask."

"Could I see it again?"

Janet quickly fumbled for the packet and removed Leslie's graduation photograph. Karen took it and stared at it for a moment or two.

"It's really hard to tell," she said slowly. "It does seem that I might recognize her. But I can't be sure."

"Is she still in Eaglescliff?"

"I doubt it. If she is the girl I'm thinking of, someone I knew briefly years ago, I've not seen her since. Sooner or later everyone in town comes in here. If she was here I'm sure I would have seen her."

"I knew I shouldn't have asked," sighed Janet. "I'm probably on a wild goose chase."

"Could I ask *you* a question, if you don't mind?" said Karen.

"Of course."

"Where are you from, Mrs. Holiday?"

"Dallas," replied Janet.

"You've come a long way."

"In nineteen years, we heard from our daughter only once. I thought it was finally time I did something about it. My husband was killed recently—"

Janet's words tumbled over each other in a rush, as her emotions ricocheted back and forth off the walls of her brain.

"I am very sorry to hear that," said Karen, gently easing onto the padded bench opposite Janet.

"Thank you," said Janet, smiling though blinking hard. "It was very abrupt, and a great shock. Suddenly I realized that I was all alone in the world. I decided to come here and try to find Leslie, though I don't know if she is still here, or even if she *ever* lived here."

"Why Eaglescliff then?"

"I received a Christmas card from Leslie some years ago. There was no return address, but it was postmarked Eaglescliff, Wyoming. No one here seems to ever have heard of her...until you."

Janet looked up and stared into the eyes of her new acquaintance with an expression of fragile hope that went straight to the heart of Karen Sanders.

"I am so sorry for your loss, Mrs. Holiday," she said. "The last thing I want to do is get your hopes up. I don't even know if it's the same girl I knew. Like I said, it was a long time ago. But *if* she is the same girl..."

Her voice trailed away and she did not complete the sentence.

"But she was here...in Eaglescliff?"

"I don't know. I mean...the girl your pictures reminded me of...I knew her somewhere else — no, it wasn't here. And I really can't tell if she's the same person."

"Maybe if I showed you some more pictures," said Janet excitedly. "They might jog your memory."

She dumped the remaining contents of the envelope onto the table and began shoving picture after picture across the table. "That's when she was a cheerleader in the eighth grade," she said. "There she is on her first date her sophomore year in high school...on the track team...and this was taken one summer at the lake."

"She is a very pretty girl," said Karen.

Janet watched closely as Karen's eyes went back and forth among the pictures of her daughter. "*Do* you think you recognize her?" Janet asked hopefully.

"These are all so much younger than when I knew someone that she reminds me of...I just can't be certain," answered Karen. "I'm sorry, Mrs. Holiday. I wish I had something more definite to tell you. but I just don't know."

TWENTY-ONE

THE SEVENTH DREAM—OUT IN THE STREETS

Christmas Eve, 1942

"There's something I need to tell you, Luke," said Carl as he left the cafeteria while Luke wheeled his wheelchair along beside him. "I'm going to be gone most of this afternoon and all day tomorrow and the next day."

Luke glanced up at him. Carl saw the panic in his eyes.

"I know it's your birthday today, and I've never deserted you like this before," Carl went on. "But you're twelve now. Your arms are getting strong and you can mostly get around without me. I made a promise at the church in town that runs the shelter. They're putting on a special meal this afternoon for the poor folks in town and families that are down on their luck. I told them I'd help. I'm also going to spend the next few days with my sister."

Again Luke looked up at Carl. This time in surprise.

"That's right, my man," said Carl, beaming from ear to ear. "I found my sister—just last month. You know I grew up in a home too—Saint Mary's Children's Home in Billings. I never knew I had any family left in the world. A few months ago I got a letter from one of the ladies there. She told me a young woman had found some adoption records after the death of her mother. It turns out that the lady was my own mother, and the woman who called the home was my sister. We met a little while after that and have been getting together as often as we can. Her name's Timmy—that's her nickname. She lives down in Cheyenne. I've been going to tell you, but I just never found the right time. Anyway, I'm driving down tomorrow to spend a couple days with her. And," he went excitedly, "I've just about got enough money saved up for that "32 Model B Roadster I've been dreaming about. I'm going to look when I'm down there and see if I can find one."

Luke nodded and smiled.

"I'm going to give you your birthday and Christmas gift now," said Carl. He pulled a brightly wrapped package out from behind his back where he had kept it hidden.

Carl handed the package to Luke. "Open it," he said.

Eagerly Luke pulled off the bow and ribbon, then tore at the paper. From inside he pulled out a small leather box. He set it on his lap and lifted the hinged lid. Inside were paper and envelopes, several pencils, a sharpener, two pens, and a small leather-bound book.

"It's a writing set," said Carl. "I don't know why I didn't think about you being able to write. I never see you in your classes. But after you wrote me that note last year, it dawned on me that you're probably a good writer. I saw this writer's box in Daly's and I knew it was for you. It's got everything you need, and a blank book there for you to write your own book in."

Already Luke was pulling out a piece of paper and a pencil. He closed the box, set the paper on the lid, then began to write. A minute later he handed the paper to Carl.

Thank you, Carl, Carl read. *This is a great gift. I hope you have a good Christmas – and that you find your car! Have you told Gary?*

"No," laughed Carl.

Luke reached for the paper again. *He will be excited,* he wrote. *Try to take a picture of you and your sister.*

"Why?" asked Carl when he had read it.

Because Christmas is about family. I am happy for you.

Carl nodded. "Thanks," he said. "Is there something I could get for *you* in Cheyenne?"

Luke thought a moment. *I would love to read Robinson Crusoe,* he wrote. *We don't have it in the library here.*

"Consider it done," said Carl.

Luke got himself into bed by himself that night, struggling a little, but happy for Carl. He turned out the lamp on his nightstand thinking about what it would be like to suddenly have a family after so many years. Carl deserved it, he thought. He was one of the best people he knew in the world. He was glad he had found his sister.

The next thing Luke knew he was walking along the street of a large city. He was having another Christmas dream. It was dusk. Night was falling rapidly. A thick fog hung over the city. Ahead he saw a building whose windows were bright from the light inside. As he came closer he saw a sign over the door:

"Shelter — Free Christmas dinner served all afternoon and evening."

He walked toward the building and through the door. Warm air met his face. A dozen aromas assaulted him at once — ham and dressing, sweet potatoes, vegetables and fruits and pumpkin and mince pies. Eight or ten tables were lavishly spread with food, steaming and fresh from the kitchen. But the place was empty.

Something told him he had to help people find this place. Luke instantly forgot his own hunger. He turned and ran back outside. He loved the feel of running. It seemed colder and darker than only a few minutes earlier. He ran through the streets until he saw a raggedly dressed man sitting on a curb holding a tin cup. The man glanced up as Luke came toward him

"Help a man down on his luck, sonny?" he said.

"I'm sorry. I don't have any money," replied Luke. "Are you hungry?"

"Famished, Sonny. Haven't had a square meal in days."

"Then get up and come with me." Luke knelt down and helped the man to his feet. As he led him back along the sidewalk, the man was so weak with hunger he could hardly put one foot in front of the other. "Put your arm around my shoulder, Mister," he said. "I'll help you. There's plenty of food. It's free and it's waiting for you."

Ten minutes later, still walking slowly, Luke saw the bright lights of the shelter ahead. He led the man inside and helped him find a chair. The man sat down, then turned his eyes toward Luke. A light of knowing flashed from them. Suddenly Luke felt that he knew him from somewhere before. Then the man smiled.

"You have done well," he said. His voice was no longer weak and tired. "Now go, find others who need the food of life — the nourishment of love and kindness."

Luke was out the door again. He ran up and down the streets, venturing into dark alleys and lanes, seeking to find more who were hungry but did not know where the food was to be found. All night he roamed the streets, bringing now one, now another, sometimes several at a time, back to the shelter to eat. Gradually the great room and tables filled. But as much as they ate, the food on each table never ran out.

Luke only saw Vanessa once, and then it was from a distance. She was on the same errand, it seemed, for she was helping a struggling elderly woman toward the shelter as Luke hurried through the door and back out into the city. They waved, but no words passed between them. They were too busy spreading the gift of Christmas among the lonely hearts of the downtrodden.

TWENTY-TWO

DIM MEMORIES

Eaglescliff, Tuesday, August 19, 1947

Karen Sanders had not been able to get her customer from Dallas out of her mind. Everything she said to the woman was true—she *hadn't* been sure she recognized the girl in the photographs. But neither had she been able to stop thinking about yesterday's conversation. The more her subconscious replayed Mrs. Holiday's words, the more images from the past came back to her.

Karen had a bad feeling in the pit of her stomach. But she could say nothing unless she was sure, which she hoped she wasn't.

She and her husband had been living over in Wheatland when she became pregnant with their first child. She had shared a room for the five days of her recovery with a young mother a year younger than herself. They had formed a fleeting hospital friendship, though she never even knew the girl's last name. An aura of melancholy hung over her. She spoke vaguely about being estranged from her parents, about wishing her mother was with her. Karen assumed that her husband had abandoned her after learning she was pregnant. She talked about needing to find work. She had mentioned hearing that the Holly Sugar Company was hiring. It had all been in the way of small talk. Karen's recollections were hazy at best.

Something had gone wrong with the other girl's delivery or with the baby, though Karen never knew what. She never learned the reason for the hushed tones of doctor and nurses, nor for the occasional soft crying from the young mother who shared her room. Her newborn was never brought to her. She did not want to ask, but eventually Karen concluded that the poor girl's child must be dead.

Karen was released and went home with a healthy baby, leaving her brief acquaintance in the hospital and learning nothing more about her. She only knew two facts for certain — the girl's name was Leslie…and she was from Dallas.

Perhaps it was a coincidence. The feeling in the pit of Karen's stomach for the last two days, however, said otherwise.

Two years after the birth of their son, her husband was offered a job at his uncle's car dealership. They moved back to his home town of Eaglescliff and had been here ever since. At first it never crossed her mind that perhaps the sad girl she had met had also relocated to Eaglescliff. Karen forgot all about her.

Until the day of the accident.

Everyone in Eaglescliff knew about it. The circumstances were so tragic — Christmas approached…a young girl leaving her grandparent's house…the heroic act of a stranger…the ongoing uncertainty of a grieving family. Karen was busy at the time with her own young family. She hadn't thought much about it, but the coincidence of names struck her. *Could the woman be the same girl she had known briefly in Wheatland?* Once again, however, as the years passed, the circumstances faded into the recesses of Karen's mind…and were forgotten.

Until yesterday, when Janet Holiday walked into The Kings Inn with her own sad story to tell.

As her memories returned into focus out of the dim fog of her recollections, Karen dreaded seeing Janet again. What would she tell her? As she hadn't wanted to raise her hopes, neither did she want to dash them with wild speculations.

Late Tuesday afternoon, seeing Gary's Model B hot rod parked nearby, Janet returned to the Soda Fountain.

"Hello, Mrs. Holiday," said Gary, greeting her with a friendly smile as she walked in. The place was bustling.

"Hi, Gary," said Janet. "You look busier today than you were on Sunday."

Peabody Public Library
Columbia City, IN

"The kids come over from the public high school after school. Can I get you another root beer float?"

"I don't know, what other specialties do you have?"

"I like the orange soda float too—orange and vanilla ice cream seem made for each another."

"That sounds good. I'll try one."

Gary hurried off, seemingly taking care of several orders at once. Janet watched him work, still finding it hard to believe he was an orphan. She had never known an orphan before. Her mind was filled with so many stereotypes. He was good-looking, well-mannered. He didn't *seem* like an orphan…whatever that meant.

He returned a few minutes later with her drink.

"Are you going to watch the parade tonight?" he asked.

"What parade?" asked Janet.

"The annual Fair and Rodeo parade. It's always the week of the fair. It starts at six-thirty. I'll be on the home float."

"What's that?"

"The orphanage float. It's always the first float in the parade."

"Will I be able to see it from the hotel?"

"The parade goes the whole length of Main Street from Holly Sugar all the way to the hospital."

"Then I won't miss it. I'll look for you!"

"Good! Gotta go, Mrs. Holiday."

As she walked back to the hotel a short while later, Janet saw activity all about her. Scores of people were busy putting decorations along the streets The whole town seemed to be involved trying to get everything ready for tonight's parade.

After a late lunch at The Kings Inn, seeing Karen nowhere and having no idea that the waitress was avoiding her, and also after a filling orange float at Rafferty's Soda Fountain, Janet was not hungry for supper. She watched the parade from the sidewalk in front of the hotel, waved to Gary as he passed on the back of a decorated truck bed jammed with thirty or forty shouting boys and girls whom she assumed were from the orphanage Gary called home.

It took half an hour for the parade to pass. Slowly the music from the high school band faded in the distance and the boisterous crowd along Main Street gradually dispersed.

TWENTY-THREE

A Difficult Conversation

Eaglescliff, Wednesday, August 20, 1947

Karen was scheduled to work the breakfast and lunch crowds on Wednesday. Her back was turned when Janet came through the door about eight-thirty, found an empty booth, and sat down. Once she saw her and their eyes met, Karen knew she could not put off the questions she knew were coming.

"Good morning, Mrs. Holiday," she said, greeting Janet with a smile.

"Hello again, Karen," said Janet. "I've come in three or four times hoping to speak with you again. I'm glad to find you at last."

"Here I am!" rejoined Karen, laughing nervously. "Would you like some breakfast?"

"Just toast and coffee, please. Oh...and a glass of orange juice."

"Coming right up," said Karen, turning and hurrying away. She paused at the coffee maker and tried to marshal her thoughts. Finally she picked up the steaming pot in one hand and a cup and saucer in the other, then drew in a deep breath and returned to Janet's table.

"Here you are, Mrs. Holiday," she said. "I'll have your toast and orange juice in a minute."

"Thank you. Karen. Do you mind if I ask you another question, you know...about what we were talking about before?"

"Uh...sure," replied Karen.

"I was watching your eyes when I showed you the pictures of Leslie. I'm sure you recognized her."

"I told you…I thought I *might*."

"Couldn't you at least tell me where you knew her from — or *thought* you did?"

Karen was silent a moment. She glanced around the restaurant. It's wasn't too busy at the moment. BJ could handle it.

"Let me get your toast and orange juice first," said Karen.

Two minutes later she slid into the booth opposite Janet. She stared down at the table. She could feel Janet's eyes staring straight at her. At length she glanced up and tried to smile.

"I hate to say anything in case I'm wrong," she said. "But after you left the other day, as I thought more about it, I remembered that the girl I met was named Leslie."

"You *did* know her then!" said Janet excitedly.

"It *may* have been your daughter, Mrs. Holiday. I never knew her last name. I had the idea that her husband had left her and that she was alone in the world. She mentioned her mother. She said she wished her mother was with her."

Janet's eyes filled with tears. "Where did you meet her?" she asked in a husky voice.

"When I was pregnant," replied Karen. "We met in the maternity ward at the hospital."

A gasp of astonishment escaped Janet's mouth. "The *maternity* ward!" she exclaimed. "My Leslie had a baby!"

Karen nodded. "But…" she went on, "I think there were complications. That's why I've been hesitant to say anything. Leslie was sad. I never saw them bring the baby to her."

"Her name *was* Leslie, then?"

"Yes. But I didn't want to say anything, and I was afraid to ask her. I thought maybe the baby died in childbirth."

"But you didn't know for certain?"

"No. Then I was released. I never saw her again."

"Was it in the hospital here in Eaglescliff?"

"No. We were living in a town called Wheatland. It's west of here. That's all I know to tell you."

Unconsciously Karen's eyes darted away.

"There's more, isn't there?" said Janet.

"Please, Mrs. Holiday, I'd rather not say."

"Karen, please. This is my daughter we're talking about. My only daughter. I haven't seen her in seventeen years. I have to know. Please tell me whatever you haven't told me."

Karen stared at the table. This wasn't going to be easy.

"You have to understand," she began, "I'm not trying to keep anything from you. I honestly don't know if it's the same person. I was busy with my own life. It just crossed my mind, that's all, because of the coincidence of the names. I didn't think of it when you first asked me. But as I began to remember things...I wondered, that's all."

"Wondered what? What coincidence are you talking about? *What* did you remember?"

"There was...Mrs. Holiday, please—you must understand...I don't know for sure, but...there was an accident—a traffic accident—several years ago. It's probably been ten years or more. I had nearly forgotten. But the woman's name who was involved...I think it may have been Leslie."

Janet's hand went to her mouth as her eyes flooded with tears.

Karen went on to tell her the few sketchy details she could remember after so long. She suggested that perhaps Janet investigate the newspaper's old records.

By two o'clock that afternoon, Janet had walked probably four miles around town, north past the orphanage, where she paused for a few moments watching the children on the playground and thinking of Gary before continuing on. She stopped as soon as the hospital came into view. With the uncertainty and terrible possibilities plaguing her brain, she did not want to think of hospitals! She turned back toward town.

When she returned to the restaurant, where she had arranged to meet Karen as soon as she was off work for the day, the initial tumult of emotions had subsided. She had cried several times. She tried to keep telling herself to think positive. At last she was stoically prepared to face whatever news awaited her.

She and Karen left the Kings Inn together and walked the two blocks south on Main Street, and into the office of the region's weekly newspaper, the *Eaglescliff Telegram*.

"Hi, Billy," said Karen to the man busy at the press behind the counter.

"Hi, Karen. I thought I heard that you and the family were off somewhere for summer vacation?"

"The rumors do fly in this town!"

"People keep track of the Sanders."

"We haven't left yet," rejoined Karen. "The children haven't seen their grandparents, my husband's folks, in two years. They're coming with us for our annual get away in the mountains. But I'm here about something else, Billy. Something important. I would like to introduce you to Janet Holiday.—Janet, meet Billy Grimes, Eaglescliff's one man reporter, editorialist, and printer."

"Pleased to meet you, ma'am," said Billy. "You'll excuse me if I don't shake hands. My name couldn't fit the profession more to a tee—I'm afraid my hands are usually full of ink."

Janet nodded and smiled.

"Mrs. Holiday would like to see some of your old papers."

"How old?"

"We're not sure, really. Ten years probably, maybe twelve. We're trying to find out the details of that accident that happened...you remember, I think it was sometime before Christmas."

"Yeah, that was at least ten years. We don't keep papers that long. Don't have the space. We've got every issue back five years is all."

"Isn't everything on microfilm?"

Billy nodded. "Those records are down in the archives in the capital in Cheyenne."

"Could you get them for her?"

"Reckon I could. Take several days."

"That's fine. I assume you have a reader here?"

"Yep. What years do you want, then?"

"Let me think...ten years ago would be thirty-seven. I think maybe thirty-four to thirty-eight." She glanced with a questioning expression toward Janet. Janet nodded in agreement.

"Take you forever to go through that many papers, Mrs. Holiday," said Billy. "We publish fifty editions a year."

"I'll work on them all day, and as long into the night as you'll let me," said Janet. "I have to find out what happened."

"Then I'll make the call and we'll get that microfilm on its way."

TWENTY-FOUR
THE EIGHTH DREAM—A GIRL AND A DOLL

Christmas Eve, 1943

All year the vision of his last Christmas Eve dream remained with Luke. The feeling that helping people out of the cold and dark into the warm, bright shelter, where they could find food and friends never left him. It was a better feeling than being able to walk and talk in his dreams, better than being able to kick a soccer ball fifty yards, better than having a friend like Vanessa. It was the best feeling he had ever had—the satisfaction of being able to help *other* people find happiness. He had been trying to practice doing that at the orphanage too. But it wasn't so easy when there wasn't much he could actually *do*.

All he could do was try to think good thoughts toward them. When they were mean to him, he tried to return their words with a smile—though that was hardest of all. But it helped him remember his mother. He knew what she would say.

"Don't worry about their words, Luke, my little man. They don't know any better. All you have to do is become the best person *you* can be. Remember, you are growing bigger on the *inside* than you are on the outside. I know what you are thinking, Luke. You want to ask how that is possible—how a person grows bigger on the inside. By being good, that's how. Even a smile of kindness grows you a tiny bit. Every time you do a good deed or think kind thoughts or are unselfish toward

110

another person, you grow a little bigger inside. And you will keep growing bigger and bigger on the inside all your life. That is where the *real* you is growing into the person who will one day see God in heaven."

All year he had been using the writing set Carl had given him to write everything he could remember rabout his mother in the blank leather book and everything she had ever told him. He realized that he wanted to become a person his mother would be proud of. And she would have wanted God to be proud of him too.

He was also writing down his dreams. The first dreams he had had were so long ago, some of them were already growing fuzzy in his mind. But as he began to think about them again and write down what had happened in them, gradually the memories returned more vividly.

As Luke lay back in his bed on the Christmas Eve of his thirteenth birthday, he left the blank leather book, which he now called his Angel Dreams, on his nightstand beside him. He left it open to a new blank page in anticipation of being able to fill several new pages tomorrow with the story of the dream he would have tonight.

Suddenly a startling thought came into Luke's brain. What if the *real* him was the him of his dreams! What if his *dreams* were real and his life as a mute cripple bound to a wheelchair was not as real as the dream? What if the inside Luke that was growing bigger was the Luke of the dream!

It was such an amazing idea that it kept him awake another fifteen minutes.

Gradually he began to grow drowsy. "God," he thought sleepily as he reached up and pulled the chain of his lamp to turn out the light, "please give me another wonderful dream tonight. Please give me someone else to help. Let me meet someone else whose Christmas I can help make special."

As sleep overtook him, Luke felt the familiar swirl taking him through the white cloud-tunnel, spinning him happily through the air until his feet hit the ground with a soft thud. His dream-waking was similar to that of last year. Again he found himself in a town with a cold wind knifing through him. Christmas music came from somewhere.

111

Luke began walking. Christmas lights hung from decorated streetlamps lining the sidewalk. The place had an eerily familiar look. Gradually he became aware that someone was walking at his side. He knew it was Vanessa.

"Have you noticed," she said. "There's something strange about this town?"

"It doesn't seem like a dream," said Luke. "It feels too real to be a dream. But I just went to sleep, and you are here, so I know it's a dream."

The rhythmic beat of drums, and the music of trumpets and trombones and a tuba cut crisply through the wintry air. They were playing one carol after another – The First Noel was followed by Angels We Have Heard on High, and then Silent Night. More and more people lined the streets as they went. Now the music of a large band approached in the distance.

"It's a Christmas parade!" exclaimed Vanessa.

They found a place to stand as the parade came closer – led by the high school marching band, followed by floats and horses and groups and clubs in uniforms and a line-up of old cars.

"There's Carl!" Luke shouted. "Look, he's driving his new black convertible! He loves that car!"

"Who's Carl?" asked Vanessa.

"A friend of mine…from where I live. And that boy sitting in the car with him. He's a friend of mine. – Carl! Gary!" he shouted, waving frantically. It was the first time he had spoken either of the two names. But his voice was drowned out by the siren of a red fire engine, lights flashing, signaling an end to the parade.

Luke and Vanessa continued on. The street was lined with booths and tables displaying every imaginable kind of food, as well as crafts and homemade gifts. All the shops on both sides of the street were brightly lit, their windows full of clothes and toys and gifts and cowboy hats. The music of the brass band began again. Carolers strolled along the streets from one end to the other.

"It's a Christmas fair!" said Vanessa.

As they came to the center of town the street was closed off. Booths and tables extended across it from sidewalk to sidewalk. Men and women walked about everywhere, with children scurrying amongst them in a great hubbub of happy activity.

Suddenly Vanessa darted off. Luke followed. When he caught up with her she was standing at a booth talking to an old man with a white beard wearing a white shirt with red suspenders and a faded green Alpine hat. As Luke approached, he heard the man's thickly accented voice. Spread out on the table in front of him, and on several shelves behind, was the most exquisite assortment of handmade dolls Luke or Vanessa had ever seen.

"I am from Switzerland, you see," the man was saying in broken German. "I bring my dolls from old country. One new doll only every year I make."

Vanessa's eyes were wide as she gazed at the dolls wearing the native costumes of dozens of countries.

"I see you like Anika," said the man with a kindly smile as Vanessa gently picked up a doll dressed in a blue and white dirndl of the Austrian alps. "She also one of my favorites."

"Look at her eyes," said Vanessa. "They are so blue, so peaceful. I feel that she is alive, that she is looking straight into my heart. It is almost as if she knows what I am thinking."

Luke watched the face of the Swiss doll maker gazing at Vanessa while she spoke. He would have said the same thing of him. He was looking at Vanessa as if he knew her.

Vanessa handed the doll back to the man. She and Luke slowly continued on their way.

"You really love that doll, don't you?" said Luke

"I have never seen such a peaceful face," replied Vanessa. "I searched all my pockets the moment I reached the man's booth. They were empty. I guess you don't have money when you dream."

They wandered in and out of several shops, then across the street through more booths and tables. Suddenly a brainstorm struck Luke. He knew where he could get some money — he could borrow it from Carl!

"I'm going to go try to find that friend of mine," he said, turning to Vanessa. "I need to see him about something. Wait for me…let's see," he said, glancing about. "I'll be back as soon as I can…let's meet over there where the Salvation Army band is playing."

He dashed off, leaving Vanessa wondering what was so important all of a sudden.

Luke sprinted through the crowd in the direction where the parade had disappeared. Finding Carl among so many people wouldn't be easy. But his '32 Roadster shouldn't be hard to spot!

Luke slowed as he passed the Swiss man's booth again. He stopped and ran panting up to the man.

"I see you are back," said the doll maker.

"I'm on my way to find someone to borrow the money to buy the doll my friend was looking at it. How much will I need?"

The man broke into a good-natured laugh.

"My boy," he said, "you need no money! We don't use money here."

"What do you mean?" asked Luke, confused. "How do people buy things?"

"Christmas is the season for giving, not getting. No one here desires to profit from Christmas."

"Then what are all the stores and shops and booths for?"

"For giving, son. Giving! For spreading the gift of Christmas to those we love, and to those people less fortunate."

"So is everything...free? Can people just take whatever they want?"

"Oh no. Nothing is free. Everything for giving. Nothing for oneself, everything for others. That is their price."

Luke stared back at the man still perplexed.

"Haven't you guessed it yet, my boy? This is town where Lord is king. There is no selfishness here, no greed, no desire to have or possess. The only motive here is to give, to make others happy. No one purchases anything because of personal want, only need...or to give others. So I make dolls to give, another provides clothes, another shoes, another food, another shelter. No one takes from another more than he needs. Thus all have exactly what they need, for we all give and receive in equal proportion. Money is unknown among us. But blessing and happiness and contentment are ours in abundance. All possessions are merely commodities passing through our hands for the benefit of others, not ourselves."

Luke tried to take in what he had heard. He had hardly realized it, but as he spoke the man seemed to lose his accent. Unconsciously Luke's eyes came to rest upon the doll called Anika.

"My dolls are very special dolls," said the man with an even more serious expression. "Their eyes are magical eyes. They look deep inside to help their owner become who they are meant to be."

The man paused, then gazed intently into Luke's eyes.

"I believe," he said, "that your young friend needs my doll. The eyes spoke to her. That always how I know. Anika has something to give your friend which may be as important as life itself."

He reached down, took hold of the doll with the pale porcelain face of white and the penetrating eyes of blue, then slowly handed her to Luke.

"Spread life, my boy," he said. "Take what is given you, and spread life wherever you go."

In a daze, Luke made his way slowly back to where he had left Vanessa. Suddenly all around him, everything looked different. He realized that none of these people had so much as a penny in their pockets. Yet every face was radiant with smiles and laughter. They were happy because Christmas was a season for families, and for giving. None were thinking of themselves, but for how they could make others happy.

Now it was his turn. In the distance he heard the Salvation Army band. There was Vanessa standing listening. Luke put one hand behind his back, holding the doll, and walked up to join her.

"You weren't gone long," she said when she saw him.

"I changed my plans," said Luke.

"Did you find your friend?"

"I didn't have to. I got you a present."

She turned to face him. Her eyes wandered down to the arm stretched behind him.

Luke brought the doll around from behind his back and handed it to her.

Vanessa gasped. Her eyes filled with tears as she gently took it from him. She held it several moments so tenderly that it might have been her own child.

"No one's ever given me such a gift," she said. "Just look at her eyes! They're so full of life. Thank you so much, Luke."

Luke's heart swelled. It was the same feeling he had had in last year's dream. The old doll maker was right – to give gave more happiness than to get.

Luke and Vanessa began walking again. The sounds of the band faded. The whole Christmas fair receded behind them. Soon they were walking in a lonely part of town. Night had descended. Snow had begun to fall. Within minutes it covered the streets and sidewalks and their footsteps crunched as they went. Vanessa's face wore a peaceful smile as she cradled her new doll next to her heart.

A flicker of orange light caught their attention from a side street. Curious, they turned toward it. Halfway down the block, they came to an alley. It appeared deserted, except that at the far end a small fire was burning in a garbage can. Luke led the way into a brisk wind whipping through the alley. As they drew closer, two seated figures became visible among the shadows cast by the light of the fire.

"What do you want?" said a gruff man's voice.

"Nothing," replied Luke. "We just saw the fire, and — "

"Well, it's ours," the man growled. "So you can keep moving on."

They turned to go. A woman's voice stopped them.

"If you're cold," she said, "you can stay and warm yourself. What's the harm, Howard? After all, it's Christmas Eve."

"Thanks," said Luke, stretching his hands toward the fire. "It is awfully cold tonight. I'm sorry — we didn't mean to intrude on your Christmas Eve like this."

"Bah, Christmas Eve!" said the man. "What's Christmas to people like us?"

"Christmas is for everyone," said Vanessa, taking a step or two closer. Behind the fire, the light flickering upon them, she saw an unshaven burly man in a tattered dark coat, and a woman beside him with long dark hair and a kindly face, whose eyes reflected the bouncing light of the fire.

"You're not intruding on anything," said the woman. "To tell you the truth, it's nice to have someone else to talk to. Howard's too much a scrooge for his own good these days. Our car broke down, you see, and we've got no place to go. We've been a little down on our luck and we were on our way to Chicago where Howard hopes to find work. I keep telling him that as long as we've got each other, we'll get by. He's had some odd jobs around here so we can get the car fixed."

"I'm sorry it's a hard time for you, Mister," said Luke. "I would still like to wish you a Merry Christmas. Is there anything I can do for you?"

"You're just a boy. What could you do? Unless you got a job to give me."

"Shush, Howard," said the woman. "This is no time for grumpy talk like that. And Merry Christmas to you too, both of you," said the woman.

"Mommy, I'm cold," said a tiny voice from somewhere in the darkness.

The woman turned toward the voice and emerged a moment later and sat back down. The pale face of a little girl of four poked out from within her coat where she was now comfortable in her mother's lap.

"This is our little Marie," she said. "She'll be warmer now. I keep telling Howard that as long as we've got our family, we've got *the best gift Christmas has to give."*

"She's right, Mister," said Luke. "Family's everything, especially at Christmas. I know because I'm an orphan."

He turned to Vanessa and smiled.

"I never had a chance to tell you, did I?" he said. "It's true – I've got nobody. So the three of you are lucky because you're a family. Your little girl has a more priceless gift than anything you could buy her – even if you bought her this whole town. She's got you, Mister. She's got her daddy."

It was silent. The fire spat and sparked as an occasional snowflake exploded upon it. The man named Howard rubbed the back of his hand across his eyes.

"You're right, young man," he said. "Sometimes a man forgets what's really important. Takes a kid like you to remind me. Sorry I groused at you before."

"Hey, that's okay," said Luke cheerfully. "I know what it's like. Sometimes it's hard for me too remembering all I've got to be thankful for."

"Mommy," interrupted the little girl's innocent voice, "will Santa Claus know where to find us tonight?"

"Honey," said her mother tenderly, "I have the feeling that Santa will know that the best place for your presents is in Chicago. I'm sure they will be waiting for us there."

Another few seconds of silence followed.

"It will be all right if he doesn't leave me anything," said the girl after a moment. "I heard what that man said. I think my best Christmas present is my daddy."

By now Howard was blinking hard. He wiped at his eyes again.

Little Marie now noticed Vanessa for the first time. She gazed up at the girl who seemed so big and old in her young eyes.

"Who are you?" she asked.

"My name's Vanessa," said Vanessa kneeling down in front of Marie's mother.

"I'm Marie. Merry Christmas, Banessa."

"And Merry Christmas to you too, Marie. Do you know what?"

"What?"

"I saw Santa Claus tonight. He asked me if I would bring you a Christmas present."

"He did!" Marie exclaimed in innocent delight.

"Yes, and here it is – just for you."

Vanessa brought the doll from inside her coat and handed it to her. Marie stretched out two tiny hands and clutched it to her.

"Oh, thank you, Banessa. This is almost as good as my other present."

"Her name is Anika," said Vanessa. "She's from Austria."

"Is that far away?"

"Very far away, I think, though I'm not really sure myself."

"Look at her eyes! She looks like she's alive."

Luke now took off his coat. Even as he did, it seemed to enlarge and expand. He handed it to Howard. "Here," he said. "You take it. I'm plenty warm, and I have the feeling I won't be needing it much longer. It will help keep your wife and daughter warm."

Suddenly Luke remembered the Christmas fair, and what the doll maker had told him.

"Wait – what am I thinking!" he said. "Come on, Howard! I know where you can find food for a Christmas meal and everything you need for your family and it won't cost you anything."

But his voice sounded hollow and distant. The mother and father and their little girl became faint and blurry. The fire flickered upward and disappeared into a blizzard of snow. The town became white all around him as everything swirled and faded.

"Vanessa!" he called out.. "Vanessa...good bye...and Merry Christmas!"

But she too had disappeared from his vision, and whiteness engulfed him.

TWENTY-FIVE

THE EAGLESCLIFF TELEGRAM

Eaglescliff, Wednesday August 27, 1947

Janet Holiday sat at the microfilm reader poring through the negatives of the past issues of the *Telegram* that had finally arrived in the morning's mail. It had been a miserably long week with several sleepless nights, alternating between despair and attempts to convince herself that Karen had been right and it *wasn't* the same person. Janet was at the paper at eight-fifteen Wednesday morning. The instant the microfilm arrived with the mail a little after nine, Billy showed her how to load it into the reader.

Karen told her that the accident had occurred around Christmas time. That narrowed the search. Janet began with the December issues of the *Telegram* from 1934, then went on to 1935 and 1936, and finally to 1937. By late in the morning, in the *Telegram's* final issue of 1937, at last she found what she had hoped she would *not* find. With tears in her eyes, she read the tragic story as it had been pieced together from various eyewitness accounts.

The young mother was walking along the sidewalk of Buhne Avenue. All indications suggest she was returning from a shopping errand. Whether she saw the veering headlights of the drunk driver approaching is uncertain.

Suddenly a girl had emerged from a house in front of her and ran toward the street. Shouts imploring her to stop erupted from a station wagon parked opposite her. But the girl was heedless of the warnings and hurried across the sidewalk.

Eyewitnesses say that a small package fell from the young

mother's hands as she sprinted forward trying to save the girl. Frantic screams echoed from both the house and station wagon. Mingled with them was the screech of tires. The reckless car swerved. The next instant the woman and girl, strangers in tragedy, lay senseless on the pavement as the car careened into a telephone pole and smashed to a stop.

A man and woman jumped out of the parked car and rushed forward. Three or four nearby houses emptied of all who had heard the terrible sounds of the crash, yelling out in the night for someone to telephone an ambulance.

It was all Janet Holiday could do to continue on. Her vision was blurry and her eyes full of tears.

"Police are withholding the name of the girl hit by the car," she read with her heart in her throat. "The woman involved has been identified as Leslie Payne—"

With a terrible choking sound, Janet burst into sobs. Billy was already on the phone to The Kings Inn asking Karen if she could break away and hurry over. This was out of his league.

When Karen arrived, Janet was still crying. Billy had done his best under the circumstances, which amounted to setting a box of Kleenex beside her. Karen came forward and sat down in a chair beside her. Janet turned toward her, bursting into tears again. Karen took her in her arms and held her as if they had known one another for years.

"It *was* her," sobbed Janet. "I don't know why, but she must have been using her middle name. It's *my* maiden name! We named her Leslie Payne Holiday."

As she continued trying to comfort her, Karen now read the story on the screen that had sent Janet into a whirlwind of heartbroken anguish.

"Miss Payne," she read, "was employed by the Holly Sugar Corporation, and had apparently moved to Eaglescliff a short time prior to the accident. Both woman and girl were rushed by ambulance to Roosevelt Hospital. Payne, who has no family that could be located, was pronounced dead within minutes of her arrival. The girl remains in critical condition and is under round the clock supervision."

The *Telegram* office was quiet. As soon as Karen had come, Billy went on with his work, though making scarcely a sound.

"We still don't know absolutely if this is your daughter," said Karen after a moment.

"How could it not be!" wailed Janet. "*No family*—the thought of her dying alone breaks my heart!

"Payne isn't an altogether unusual name. This might not be the girl I met in the hospital."

"You thought it was.

"I just had a bad feeling when I heard the name *Leslie*. It could still be a coincidence. We have to—"

Karen hesitated.

"Would you like me to go to Colyer Funeral Home and see if I can learn anything further? With a last name now, and the date of the accident…"

Janet closed her eyes and struggled to draw in two or three halting breaths.

"I'll go with you," she said softly. "I have to know."

Karen helped Janet to her feet. She cast Billy a look as they left the office, silently mouthing the words, *Thank you.*

"Why don't we go over to the restaurant first," suggested Karen. "You could have a glass of water or something. I can't imagine what you must be going through. I am so sorry, Mrs. Holiday."

Janet did her best to smile. "You have been more kind to me than a stranger could possibly expect," she said. "I already feel that I've known you for years. I wish you would call me Janet."

Karen nodded and returned her smile.

"I do feel like a mess" Janet added. "But I don't want to go back to the hotel. I don't want to be alone right now. Could I use your bathroom at the restaurant and wash my face?"

"Of course."

TWENTY-SIX

DREADED CONFIRMATION

Eaglescliff, Wednesday August 27, 1947

When Mr. Colyer glanced up to see Karen Sanders walking into the funeral home, arm in arm with an older woman, obviously distraught, he assumed they had come to discuss arrangements for a recently-departed loved-one. He put on his gentlest and most sympathetic demeanor and went to greet them with soft-spoken words and a smile intended to convey peace and comfort.

"We are hoping you can help us, Mr. Colyer," said Karen. "This is Mrs. Holiday. We believe that you may have handled arrangements for her daughter about ten years ago."

"I see," the funeral director nodded. "But if...that is, you were not aware of your daughter's death?" he asked, turning toward Janet.

She shook her head.

"If we could perhaps see the death certificate," said Karen. "We need to know about the young woman who died in the traffic accident that December — I'm sure you remember...the woman hit by the drunk driver about ten years ago."

"Yes, of course...and the young girl. A tragic case. I will see what I can find in our files. The originals are kept in the Courthouse, you understand. But if we handled the arrangements, I should have a copy. What was the name of the woman."

"Payne," replied Karen. "Leslie Payne."

"And the date, you say?"

"It was ten years ago — December of 1937."

Colyer nodded, then disappeared into his office. Karen helped Janet to a chair, where they sat waiting as Janet quietly wept.

The man returned five minutes later. He held a single sheet in his hand. Karen rose and walked toward him. He handed it to her and she glanced over it.

"I have to ask you a question, Janet," she said.

Janet looked up, blinking hard and trying not to start sobbing again.

"What day was Leslie born?"

"May 17, 1912," Janet replied softly.

The paper fell from Karen's hand. Her eyes now filled too. She walked heartbroken toward Janet. Janet rose. All Karen could do was nod her head, and Janet knew.

The widowed woman, who had now also lost all hope of seeing her daughter again in this life, and her new young friend embraced, held one another, and wept.

Two hours later, as a cool breeze blew down across the prairie from the north, Janet Holiday stood before a simple grave stone in the Eaglescliff Cemetery. Her emotions were numb. She felt as though she was attending a second funeral in three weeks. Beside her stood the young woman who had known her daughter for those few fleeting days. She was young enough to be her daughter. She was the only friend she had in this place other than a teen age orphan at the Soda Fountain.

The two women stood arm in arm, staring down at the stone: *Leslie Payne, b. May 17, 1912, d. December 24, 1936.*

"Why was she using her middle name?" whispered Janet.

Her question was lost in the breeze. She might never know the answer. At last her search had come to an end. She was standing in a lonely cemetery gazing down at the grave of her only child. It was a pain no parent should have to endure. Janet Holiday had to bear it without a husband to share in her grief.

"Would you like to spend the evening at my house?" asked Karen as they walked back to her car ten minutes later. " I know my family would love to have you."

Janet smiled. "That is very kind of you. But now I think I

123

do need to be alone. I suppose I need to think about going home. I've found what I came for. It wasn't what I hoped to find, but at last I know where my daughter is."

Karen looked into Janet's eyes with a tender expression and smiled.

"I am sorry, Janet," she said. "I wish it had turned out differently."

Janet forced a smile. "You've been a good friend through this," she said. "I feel like I've known you longer than a few days. Even though you only knew Leslie briefly, somehow that is a lifeline to her."

"I wish I could have done more, or have made it easier for you," said Karen. "But I am glad I was here to share it with you."

They embraced again. A short while later, with darkness descending around them, Karen let Janet off in front of the hotel, and they parted.

Janet watched her new young friend drive away, then turned toward the building. A late summer cold front was blowing in from the north as it could only do in high mountain regions. The ninety degree temperatures they had experienced all week make the seventy degrees now seem colder than it was. Fresh tears began cascading down her face again the moment she was alone. A light drizzle drifted down, settling silently on the ground. As she stood on the sidewalk looking around Janet noticed the Main Street of the little town was nearly empty. She was alone in a lonely place.

All this was too much to take in at once. She was not sure she could handle it. *God, are you there?* she said silently. *Are you listening? Please help me.*

Her discouragement mounting with every step she took toward the hotel. Once inside Janet slowly climbed the stairs to her room. By the time she entered, she was crying in earnest.

The moment the door closed behind her, she fell on the bed in the dark and burst into sobs of lonely despair.

God…God help me! she cried. *I don't know what to do. I don't know where to turn. I'm all alone. What's the use of going on? Are you even there? I don't know anymore. God…oh, God…show me what to do!*

TWENTY-SEVEN
THE NINTH DREAM—THE SHEPHERD AND HIS SHEEP

Christmas Eve, 1944

Do you know why your name is Luke?

Luke remembered his mother's words every Christmas. It was both a special time of year and a sad time of year. It was the season when he was born, and when Jesus was born. It was also the season when he had lost his mother. But every year as he grew older, he gradually learned to take comfort from his memories, and gain strength as he learned to be a young man of character, as he knew she would want him to be.

It is because you were born on Christmas Eve. Her words were as clear as if she had spoken them yesterday. *You were such a beautiful baby. You were the most perfect Christmas present I could ever imagine. I had just been reading the Christmas story about the baby Jesus written by a man named Luke. So I named you after him, so that your name would always remind me of Bethlehem and the night the star shone bright over the manger and the Christmas story.*

Two men who called themselves Gideons had come to the orphanage last week. They spoke to everyone between the sixth and twelfth grades about their work of placing Bibles in hotels and hospitals. Then they made a presentation to Mr. Pratt of several big boxes of Bibles, telling him they were donating enough Bibles to the home for one to be placed in every room. Then they encouraged all the students to read the Christmas story for themselves.

125

Luke knew most of those in his seventh-through-ninth grade class didn't think he could read at all. Because he couldn't speak, they assumed he was mentally retarded. But he could read better than half the twelfth graders. He spent most of his free time browsing about the orphanage school library. The shelves were wide enough for him to get around between them with his wheelchair. The librarian was always happy to assist him getting down books higher than he could reach. Every week or so he left a stack of books with her for Carl to carry up to his room.

He saved the bright red new Gideons Bible in his room for his birthday. He didn't want to read anything in it until he could read the Christmas story on Christmas Eve. Carl helped him into his bed, though Luke's arms were getting strong enough by now that he could maneuver in and out of his wheelchair on his own. But Carl was always there to make sure he didn't fall.

"Got your new Gideons Bible by your bed, I see," said Carl with a smile as Luke eased back into his bed. "Planning on doing some bedtime reading, are you?"

Luke nodded.

"Well you couldn't do better than the good Book, I always say."

After Carl left him, Luke reached for the Bible on his nightstand. He flipped through the pages to the New Testament until he came to the book written by his own namesake. As he lay with his head on his pillow, thinking of his mother and the first Christmas and how happy he was to be cozy in his bed in his room on Christmas Eve, he began to read.

"And Joseph also went up from Galilee, from the city of Nazareth, to Judea, to the city of David, which is called Bethlehem, because he was of the house and lineage of David, to be enrolled with Mary, his betrothed, who was with child. And while they were there, the time came for her to be delivered. And she gave birth to her first-born son and wrapped him in swaddling cloths, and laid him in a manger, because there was no place for them in the inn.

"And in that region there were shepherds out in the field, keeping watch over their flock by night. And an angel of the

Lord appeared to them, and the glory of the Lord shone around them, and they were filled with fear. And the angel said to them, "Be not afraid; for behold, I bring you good news of a great joy which will come to all the people; for to you is born this day in the city of David a Savior, who is Christ the Lord."

"And suddenly there was with the angel a multitude of the heavenly host praising God and saying, "Glory to God in the highest, and on earth peace among men with whom he is pleased!"

"When the angels went away from them into heaven, the shepherds said to one another, 'Let us go over to Bethlehem and see this thing that has happened, which the Lord has made known to us.' And they went with haste, and found Mary and Joseph, and the babe lying in a manger.

"And when they saw it they made known the saying which had been told them concerning this child; and all who heard it wondered at what the shepherds told them. But Mary kept all these things, pondering them in her heart. And the shepherds returned, glorifying and praising God for all they had heard and seen, as it had been told them."

Luke drifted to sleep. Images of the Christmas story and the sound of his mother's voice filled his thoughts as if she had been reading the story from the Bible to him.

Luke awoke again into the world of his dream. He was walking through desolate, desert country. His feet sank into sand as he went. He saw no people, no trees, no towns, no signs of life. The air was hot and arid. Nothing grew except desert grasses and low scraggly sagebrush. It was a country where it seemed nothing could survive.

He walked for what seemed hours until he was thirstier than he had ever been. As he crested a small dune of sand, a welcome sight came into view. Palm trees and lush green grass appeared in the distance. He thought he could hear the sound of running water.

"It's an oasis!" he cried, running down the slope toward the garden flourishing in the middle of the desert.

He drew closer and felt a change in the air. The atmosphere became moist and filled with the pleasing smell of growing things. He drew it into his lungs with pleasure, as if the air itself could sustain life. The babbling and rushing of water was clear now. In the center of the oasis sat a stone well surrounded by palm and other trees laden with every variety of colorful fruit imaginable. This was more than a mere oasis in the middle of the desert. It was a paradise!

And there was Vanessa! She was sitting on the stones of the circular well talking to a man in a white homespun robe. He held a tall shepherd's staff with a large crook on top. She glanced toward him as he ran toward the well.

"Luke!" she exclaimed with a great smile on her face.

"Vanessa — how did you get here?"

"I walked, from over there," she said.

"I guess we came from different directions. I'm so thirsty!"

"Then come and drink. That's what I did. It made me feel so strong. There's something strange happening inside me — I feel like I'm coming awake, coming back to life or something. I can't explain it. But this water makes you feel things you never felt before. This man has been trying to explain it to me, but it is a little hard to understand."

Luke came closer and peered over the side of the well. He saw that the watery sounds had been coming from inside it. The water was swirling and rushing around to the very top of the stones.

"Wow — it's bubbling up like crazy!" Luke exclaimed. "It's like a geyser or underground river. No wonder I heard it from so far away."

He leaned over and drank and drank until he had had his fill. He stood up again, calm and satisfied and at peace. It seemed that after drinking this water, he would never be thirsty again.

He now glanced toward the man who stood watching him with a curious smile. He seemed to recognize him, but he could not tell where he might have seen him before.

"Is this your well, Mister?" Luke asked.

"The well of life belongs to no one, and it belongs to everyone. Its waters cannot be possessed, they are for drinking. I am merely the shepherd of the oasis. Those are my flocks you see, there on the hillside."

Luke looked to the hills surrounding the oasis and saw that they were dotted with white sheep grazing across the slope of green grass.

"That's a lot of sheep. There must be hundreds."

"Several thousand, actually," replied the shepherd. He gazed intently into Luke's eyes. "Look closely," he said. "Look to the hills. Tell me what you see."

"Your flock of sheep," replied Luke.

"Closer, my boy. Look closer."

Luke squinted and continued to stare into the distance. Slowly a light began to dawn on his face.

"I think I understand you," he said. "I see sheep…but they look like people."

"They are people, Son," said the shepherd. "People are just like sheep. They need a shepherd. But most of them do not know it."

"Can't you tell them?"

"I do tell them," he said, a little sadly. "I am always telling them. But they have forgotten how to listen. Their ears are plugged and their hearts have grown dull. So it is not easy."

"Is there nothing that can be done?"

"I need the help of people like you."

"What can I do."

"People need to know about the water you just drank. And they need you to pray for them."

"How does prayer help?"

"It unplugs their ears so they can hear what I am telling them. There is a woman right now who is in trouble and needs my help."

"What can I do?" asked Luke.

"I want you to pray for her, that she will hear my voice."

With the words, everything around him began to fade into white. The shepherd's voice became his mother's voice praying at his bedside. "Lord, I pray for my little Luke. As he grows help him to know your voice when it speaks to him. Teach him to pray also."

Even as his dream faded, Luke's voice joined his mother's. "God," he prayed, "help the woman who needs the shepherd." And then he knew no more.

TWENTY-EIGHT

BILLY GRIMES

Suddenly in the middle of the night, Janet started awake. Memories from the previous day rushed back into her mind like a waking nightmare. Just when Leslie had been planning to return home, a tragic accident had taken her life. Tears again ran from cheek to pillow as she lay in bed with images of her daughter's lonely end.

Janet wept for another several minutes until the torrent was past. Gradually she began to breathe more easily. She sat up, wiped at her eyes, and turned on the lamp beside the bed. She reached for a tissue and dabbed her eyes. As she did, her eyes fell on the book on the hotel nightstand. She had scarcely taken notice of it before this moment. It was a Gideons Bible.

She drew in another steadying breath, then slowly reached for it. She sat a moment with the book in her lap, then opened it. She flipped absently through its pages, pausing at the red letters at the beginning of the New Testament, the words spoken by Jesus.

Scanning through them, her eyes fell upon a familiar passage. Suddenly the words were filled with new meaning...for her...for this moment. She had heard them a dozen times in church. Now in her heartbreak and loneliness, she felt that they were being spoken directly into her own heart.

Come to me all who labor, and are heavy-laden, and I will give you rest. Take my yoke upon you, and learn from me; for I am gentle and lowly in heart, and you will find rest for your souls. For my yoke is easy, and my burden is light.

Janet lay down and wept again. Slowly and invisibly the words of the Great Shepherd entered her soul.

Jesus, she whispered, *I am so alone. Show me what to do…give me your rest.*

With the prayer came peace.

Janet lay awake for several more minutes. Gradually she realized that her time in Eaglescliff was done. She had found what she had come for—certainty about Leslie. It was not what she had hoped to find. But at least now she *knew*. There was no longer anything to keep her here. It was time to move on to the next chapter of her life.

With the realization, gradually Janet drifted back to sleep.

She woke in the morning feeling clean, empty, pure, purged of emotion. It was neither a good feeling nor a bad feeling. It brought no tears, no smiles. Only resolve. It was time to go home.

After breakfast and after checking the day's Greyhound schedule, she spent the morning gathering her things and packing up. She would spend the afternoon saying good bye to her daughter's final home. It was a day to be alone. In the short time she had been here, she had made a few friends in this town. But she did not want to see anyone. She needed to grieve for these last final hours in solitude.

She took a taxi out to the cemetery and spent one last hour with Leslie. The Rocky Mountain air remained cool, in the seventies, it felt comfortable as she walked back into town. The remainder of the day she walked about, full of memories of Jack and Leslie, drinking in the melancholy of being in the charming little town where Leslie had lived the end of her life. The hours passed slowly but eventually the sun began to sink toward the purple mountains in the west. She returned to the hotel. Her suitcase was packed and waiting in the lobby. She said good bye to the hotel's manager, thanking him for his kindness during her stay, and set out to catch the 5:30 evening bus to Cheyenne.

Halfway there, walking toward her on the sidewalk, she saw the *Telegram's* Billy Grimes. He paused as she approached.

"Mrs. Holiday, isn't it?" he said as they met.

131

"Yes. Hello, Mr. Grimes," replied Janet with a smile.

"Leaving town?"

"I'm on my way to the bus station. There's nothing keeping me here now."

"That's, uh…actually that's what I wanted to talk to you about," said Grimes. "I was on my way to the restaurant to see if Karen or BJ knew where I could find you."

"*Me*…what did you want to see me about?" asked Janet.

"When you and Karen were in yesterday—you know, looking at the microfilm and all…after you left I looked at the article about your daughter."

Grimes paused and glanced down nervously at the sidewalk. It was obvious that he wanted to say nothing that would send Janet into a new round of tears right here on the sidewalk.

"Something didn't seem right about it to me," he went on hesitantly. "I've been trying ever since to jog my memory about what it was. Then just a little while ago it came to me. So I checked our editions for the next few weeks and I was right. That's what I was coming to talk to you about."

"What was it?" asked Janet, with no idea what he was talking about.

"If you'd want to come back to the office with me, Mrs. Holiday, I think it'd be best for you to read it for yourself."

"The bus is due through town in thirty minutes."

"There's time, if we hurry…if you still want to leave after reading the second article. I'll take your case for you."

Billy grabbed the suitcase where Janet had set it on the sidewalk. He turned around and sped off back the way he had come. Janet hurried after him. By the time she caught him, he was already turning the key of the door into the office of the *Eaglescliff Telegram*.

"Come over here, Mrs. Holiday," Billy said. "The microfilm's in the reader just where I left it."

With mounting curiosity, Janet followed him across the floor. "It happened when I was away for the holidays that year," Grimes went on. "I'd forgotten when you were in yesterday, but then I remembered. I had a new man working for me and had to get the issue out. With Christmas Eve and trying to get the paper in before the deadline, he wrote up the story of the accident without having his facts all straight. When I got back and heard about the accident, first thing I did was get the police report. That's why I printed a correction in the January eighth issue. That's what I've got here." He turned on the microfilm reader and pointed to the chair.

Janet looked at him with a questioning expression, then sat down in front of the machine.

"See, there on the upper right," said Billy. "That's the correction from a week after the first story about the accident."

Janet read the brief notice. When she came to the last line, an audible gasp left her mouth.

"It says here that the paper was wrong in reporting that my daughter had no family...that—"

Janet squinted and leaned toward the screen.

"The victim, Leslie Payne," Janet read aloud, *"is survived by a son who was remanded to the care of the Wyoming Children's Home pending investigation of the father's whereabouts."*

Janet turned and looked at Billy with wide eyes. "Do you know anything more about...about this boy, this son?"

"I'm sorry, I don't, Mrs. Holiday. But I thought you ought to know."

"Yes...yes, thank you," said Janet, her brain spinning in a whirlwind.

"You, uh..." said Billy, glancing at the clock on the wall, "the bus you know, uh...it's only fifteen minutes, Mrs. Holiday."

Slowly Janet rose. "Oh...yes, but I...maybe I won't be taking the bus tonight after all."

She walked toward the door in a stupor.

"Your suitcase, Mrs. Holiday," said Billy behind her. "On second thought," he added, "I'll walk you back to the hotel."

He picked up the suitcase, followed Janet back outside, and locked the door. The two made their way along Main Street back to the hotel in silence.

"I guess I'll be needing my room for at least one more night after all," said Janet as she walked up to the hotel manager at the counter."

"Miss the bus, Mrs. Holiday?" he asked.

"No," she answered, "just a change of plans."

Janet heard the hotel door open behind her. She turned and saw the newspaper man on his way back outside.

"Mr. Grimes," she said after him. "Thank you!"

TWENTY-NINE

THE WYOMING CHILDREN'S HOME

Eaglescliff, Thursday August 28, 1947

Alone again in the familiar hotel room that had been her home for more than a week, Janet sat down and tried to think. This threw a bombshell into the middle of everything!

Over and over the words she had just read replayed themselves in her brain.

Leslie Payne is survived by a son who was remanded to the care of the Wyoming Children's Home pending investigation of the father's whereabouts.

Survived by a son…

Survived by a son…

A son! thought Janet. Leslie's baby *hadn't* died in the hospital. Leslie had given birth to a son.

That made her a grandmother!

The thought was so new, so huge, so jolting, it took several minutes for her brain to take it in. She sat in the quiet room trying to absorb it.

From somewhere the words filtered into her brain. *Don't give up, Janet. Don't give up.*

They came as a whisper. She repeated them to herself, then again.

If he was still at the home, her grandson might be less than a mile away at this very moment! Then more words she remembered hearing somewhere returned from out of her memory. *If the mountain won't come to you, you have to go to the mountain.*

She had to go to the orphanage and try to find

him...Leslie's son...her own grandson!

The rest of that evening and night passed as slowly as if the sand in the hourglass was thick black molasses. How much Janet slept, she could not tell. She dozed on and off, but always came awake, startled anew by the electric thought in her brain that she had a grandson.

Gradually the thin light of a gray dawn outside began to show glimmers of light. On it came. Slowly...slowly. At last Janet could stand the waiting not a minute more. The clock beside her bed read six-forty-seven, but she could not lay in bed another second. This was the second morning she had awaken with the knowledge that both her husband and daughter were dead. The pain was more overwhelming than anything she had ever experienced.

Yet in the midst of her grief, perhaps she *wasn't* alone. Up and down and around and back and forth her emotions bounced between heartbreak and hope like the ball of a pinball machine.

She tried to calm herself with a hot bath. She walked into the hotel dining room a little after seven-thirty. Most of the regulars she had come to recognize over the past few days were all in their customary places, some finishing their breakfasts, the later arrivals just wandering in.

She sat down at one of the small single tables she had gradually claimed as her own.

"Good morning, Mrs. Holiday," said the pleasant middle-aged waitress with graying brown hair who was always on hand at the breakfast hour. "Still with us, I see. Would you like some coffee?"

"Yes, please."

She returned shortly and poured out a cup and set it in front of Janet. "And for breakfast?" she said.

"I think just one egg, scrambled, and toast," replied Janet.

Janet had hardly been hungry since Jack's death. All she knew was a constant burning hollow feeling in her stomach. It was not food she was hungry for, it was for family. She ate just to fill the time, for something to do. But she needed something in her stomach, especially after a nearly sleepless night.

By eight-fifteen she had summoned her courage and was

ready. She left the coffee shop and went to the hotel's main desk.

"I need a taxi," she said to the man at the counter. "Do you think I'll find one out on Main Street?"

"Probably not this early. I'll call Jimmy for you, Mrs. Holiday. He'll be here in five minutes or so."

"Thank you. I'll watch over there by the window."

Four minutes later, Janet left the hotel. Cool, brisk sixty degree mountain air snapped her senses yet more fully awake the moment she swung the glass door open. The cabbie pulled up in front and hurried around to open the door for her. Janet scooted in.

"Where to, ma'am?" said the man's voice from the front seat as he glanced back.

"The Children's Home," replied Janet.

The driver whom Janet assumed was called Jimmy pulled away from the curb and sped off north along Main Street. A few minutes later he turned off the highway to the right. They passed open gates beneath a large black iron arch leading onto the orphanage grounds. The driveway was two or three hundred yards long. It led to a circular drive in front of an aging red rectangular brick building several stories high. The cab pulled up in front and stopped.

Jimmy hurried around and opened the door. "Would you like me to wait, ma'am?" he said as Janet got out. "It's a long walk back to town in this cold?"

"No, thank you. Do you have a card or something so I could call you later?"

"No card, ma'am, but wait just a jiffy."

He opened the glove compartment to find a pencil. A moment later he handed Janet a torn scrap of paper with a phone number on it. "You just give me a call when you need to, ma'am, and I'll be right out for you."

Janet paid him, then turned and climbed up the front steps to the main door of the imposing building. She reached the landing, pulled open the large wood door, and stepped inside.

A dozen sensations assaulted her. Janet found herself standing inside a large entry hall with a high ceiling. The vacant, sterile, institutional atmosphere was as unwelcoming as the northern wind blowing across the prairie outside. The combined smells of mildewing plaster, food cooking somewhere, dust, sweaty children, and chalk reminded her of every school where she had taught. The sounds and smells of a school were universal. To her left a wide staircase led to the upper floors. Coming from somewhere in those regions above echoed children's voices.

Getting her bearings, she walked forward. White plastered walls amplified her footsteps as she made her way across the oak floor toward a wall of glass bricks on the far side of the room. A door stood at its center with the single word "Office" painted on its frosted glass. She turned the knob and walked inside.

A silver-haired receptionist a few years older than herself glanced up from behind a desk and eyed her with suspicion. Neither smiling nor by any other sign did she convey a hint of greeting. Janet stopped in front of her.

"May I help you?" she said, still expressionless.

"Uh, yes…I would like to find out about one of the children living here," said Janet.

"What is your business? Why do you want to know?"

The question took Janet off guard. The woman's tone made clear that she was on high alert. Janet hadn't stopped to consider necessary protocol, or what procedures might be required in the highly secretive world of parentless children.

"I think it possible that my grandson may be here," she answered. The word sounded unreal when she actually heard it coming from her own lips — her *grandson*.

The receptionist glanced toward Janet's empty hands. The hint of a smirk came to the edges of her mouth. "Do you have the permission forms with you?" she asked.

"What permission forms?"

"We cannot give out information on any of our children without authority from the state."

"Oh, of course. I should have realized that. Where would I get the forms?"

"You will have to petition the state. You can fill out the forms down at the courthouse."

Janet nodded and left the office, then realized she had sent her ride back into town less than two minutes before. She turned back inside and reluctantly approached the receptionist again.

"I'm sorry," she said, "but would you mind telephoning for a taxi for me. Here's the number."

She handed her the crumpled slip of paper. The woman took it with a sigh, then picked up the phone on her desk and made the call.

Janet left her again and returned to wait in the entryway. As she stood looking out the front window, her eyes were drawn to a large bulletin board just inside the doorway. Casually she wandered toward it. Amid dozens of small pieces of paper tacked to the cork, a few business cards, announcements, and scheduling reminders, the large letters of a familiar notice jumped out at her:

English teacher needed K-12, immediate opening. Interviews conducted by Principal Pratt.

It was the same ad she had seen in the paper her first day in Eaglescliff. Even as she saw the yellow cab pulling up in front of the building fifteen minutes later, a new plan began to take shape in her mind.

The cabbie called Jimmy greeted her as if they were old friends. She asked him to take her to the courthouse. More than six frustrating hours followed during which she discovered the discouraging reality that as much red tape surrounded inquiries into the orphans living at the Wyoming Children's Home as would an investigation into the identity of an adopted child. The records for the two branches of the state's child protection agency were supervised by the same regulations. By three o'clock that afternoon, Janet realized it would probably be easier to bust into Fort Knox than unlock Wyoming's sealed orphanage records. It didn't help that she had no idea of the boy's name, date of birth, or even what last name he might be going by. The puzzle of Leslie's middle name confused her search all the more.

As the Friday afternoon waned Janet left the courthouse and wandered back to the hotel, deep in thought. The new idea that had been revolving in her brain all day was crazier than coming to Wyoming in the first place. But if her husband and daughter had both been taken from her, she wasn't going to give up trying to find her grandson. If he was in this town, she would find him whatever it took!

She wasn't about to let bureaucratic red tape and permission forms and grouchy receptionists stop her!

THIRTY
THE TENTH DREAM—POIGNANT REFLECTIONS

Christmas Eve, 1945

"You're fifteen today, Luke, my man," said Carl. "You're a full-fledged teenager now. Fifteen—that's the big time. And from that growth on your lip and cheeks, I think I need to be showing you how to shave any day now! But today I want to take you somewhere. I haven't taken you before because it's a man-thing not a boy-thing. So grab your coat and we'll head downstairs and get you into the van. You and me are going to take a little ride."

Later that afternoon, the white orphanage van, with Carl at the wheel and Luke in the passenger seat, left Eaglescliff on Route 85 south. Two miles past the Holly Sugar factory, Carl slowed and turned into a narrow one-lane paved road. A few minutes later they passed a sign that read "Eaglescliff Cemetery." Gravestones and memorials surrounded them on all sides. Carl continued another hundred yards, then stopped. He jumped out, unloaded the wheelchair, and was soon pushing Luke over brown frozen grass toward a small, plain stone marker. There he stopped.

"It's your mom's grave," said Carl. "I thought it was time you saw it."

Luke glanced toward Carl with a look of question.

"I know," nodded Carl. "I don't know why, but it's her. I made sure before I brought you here."

The young man and his helper and mentor, the one standing the one sitting, stared down at the simple inscription

141

in silence. Tears filled Luke's eyes and he let them come. He was neither embarrassed nor ashamed. He was indeed, as Carl had said, nearly a man. He was not afraid of a man's emotions.

"You're at a time in life, Luke," said Carl at length, "when the choices you make will determine the kind of man you become. You may not know it, but I've been watching you since the day I first laid eyes on you. You were only seven. You were alone and afraid. I kept watching as you struggled to find your way with your mother gone. I watched when the others made fun of you and called you terrible things. I knew you got angry. You're a boy—who wouldn't get angry the way they treated you. But I watched you learn to control your anger. I watched you learn to return unkindness with the only kindness you knew how to give—a smile. It takes a big heart to do that. Yes, my man, I watched. You probably don't know it, but you inspired me to be more forgiving too."

Carl paused. His eyes were moist by now too. What he was trying to say, in his own way, was that he had come to *love* this young man with whom he had spent more time than any other boy or girl at the home. He loved him like the father neither of them had ever known.

"I know your mother's been watching you too, Luke," Carl went on after a moment, his voice husky. "I know she's proud of you like I am. None of us understand how things work out sometimes—why people are taken from us. It's hard to know what God's up to, or why he does what he does. But I've got to believe that he's watching too, and that he's doing all he can to make life a good thing for us, even though we can't see all the ways he's doing it. Life's confusing for guys like us, Luke. I've been confused about a lot of things in my life. But we've got to try to make good come of it, even if it is harder for us. And we've got to believe...always *believe*, Luke my man."

Again Carl paused. He took in a deep breath, then turned down to Luke.

"I'm not much at making speeches," he said. "But I brought you out here because I wanted to tell you something, and that's this. Your life's ahead of you. Make the most of it. Make good choices. Even if you can't talk, you can look folks straight in the eye, and give them a firm shake of your hand. You've turned into a fine young man, Luke. Sometimes the others aren't nice to you. But you've got more going for you inside than a lot of these kids will ever have. Don't forget it. Don't ever look down on yourself because you can't walk or talk. There's a lot more to life than that. Your mom would want you to be strong. I know you will make her proud, Luke. You will see your mother again. When you do, you will run on strong legs to greet her. I believe that with all my heart.

"So give me a grip of your hand, Luke," he said, reaching out his hand.

Luke took it. Both were weeping freely by now. They shook hands, firmly, strongly, each holding the other's eyes as they did.

"I guess what I want to say more than anything, Luke," said Carl, struggling to get the words out, "is that I love you as if you were my own son."

Luke's heart was full as he lay in bed that night. Carl's words had remained with him all day. With them had come many reminders of similar things his mother had said. For one of the first times in his life, his heart overflowed with more thankfulness than he thought he could contain. He had been blessed with two people who truly *loved* him.

What more in life could anyone wish for than that!

Luke awoke in his Christmas Eve world, which he now considered the most real of the two worlds in which he lived, floating above an endless carpet of green. It was springtime and the whole earth — or heaven…or wherever he was! — was bursting with life. He was floating on the aerie fragrances of grass and blossoms and buds and trees whose perfumes exuded life itself.

As he looked below him, the flowers were alive with the life of heaven, which was just the life of the earth. All around him, the petals of the flowers below him, blown into motion by the fragrant breezes, began to rise off their stalks, flapping as if trying to fill the air with their perfume.

Suddenly Luke was surrounded by a million butterflies, each one a different flower come alive, intricately colored, every one as unique as if it were a live springtime butterfly snowflake of red and blue and green and yellow and purple and orange and black.

Luke laughed with delight. Love was alive in the air! And he was surrounded by it.

Now came toward him from the distance a butterfly as big as himself. But it wasn't a butterfly – it was Vanessa!

"Vanessa!" he cried. "Isn't it wonderful! I feel so light – as if I could fly to the moon!

"I was just thinking the same thing," said Vanessa happily. "I've never been so happy in my life! Do you suppose we're in heaven?"

"Maybe we're angels?" said Luke. "I feel like an angel flying around like this."

"Don't you have to be dead to be an angel?" rejoined Vanessa. "I don't think we're dead...are we?"

"We would have to be dead to be in heaven. If we are, then I like it! This is better than my other life. I'm crippled there, or did I ever tell you?"

"No. Really?"

"I am. Where I live the rest of the year, I can't walk a step."

"I don't think I can either," said Vanessa thoughtfully. "Though actually, now that I think about it, I can't remember. I wonder if that's why we share each other's dreams."

"Wouldn't it be amazing if we could know each other in the other world too?"

"You keep talking about your other life," said Vanessa. "I don't think I wake up in another life. So maybe I am dead and you're not."

"That's too complicated for me!" Luke laughed again. "I would rather believe that we're both just Christmas angels, whatever we are and wherever we live the rest of the time."

"I like the sound of that," said Vanessa. "But I think I must be in heaven, because this is the only world I know. I think in some way God makes it possible for you to come visit me, though I don't know how the two worlds could mix. But God probably knows how to do things like that."

"Well if you are in heaven," said Luke, "will you try to find my mother, and tell her that I am doing fine, that I love her and I know she loves me, and that God is taking very good care of me."

"I'll try. But I don't think I know anyone else here except you...when you come to visit me, that is."

"Then I shall just have to keep coming to visit you until I meet my mom myself."

"But then you would have to be dead."

"Oh, yes. I forgot. But that would be all right, because I really do like it here best!"

THIRTY-ONE

WANTED: ENGLISH TEACHER

Eaglescliff, Tuesday September 2, 1947

Janet spent all weekend debating back and forth with herself about her crazy idea. First she thought it was brilliant, then decided it was stupid, then went back to thinking it good again. As she debated with herself Janet became even more familiar with the wonderful little town, enjoying fifty degree mornings and seventy degree afternoons while strolling through the streets. She smiled despite herself knowing Annie was probably sweating back home in triple digit Texas heat. Eaglescliff celebrated Labor Day Monday with a wonderful picnic and concert in the city park, free to everyone, just a few blocks from her hotel.

When she woke up Tuesday morning Janet still wasn't sure what to do. Did she go home or did she stay? After breakfast, Janet returned to her room and spent some time reading the Gideons Bible. One verse stuck out to her in particular as she read, John 8:32. "Then you will know the truth, and the truth will set you free." The verse spoke to her. She knew exactly what she needed to do, she had known all along but just been afraid. She needed to know the truth. If she didn't stay and find out whether or not she had a grandson she would regret it forever!

"Telephoning for Jimmy's yellow cab at ten minutes after eleven Janet was again seated behind him on her way out of town toward the Wyoming Children's Home. The chill of the morning was gone. The day had begun to warm and Janet rode in the back seat with the window down.

She instructed Jimmy to park at the far end of the lot where she could see the front door. While she waited and watched, the talkative cabbie battered her with friendly questions, filling in his own answers to most of them. By eleven-thirty she knew more about him than she did anyone in Wyoming. He probably knew more about her than anyone else too.

At quarter till noon, Janet's patience paid off. She saw the silver-haired receptionist from her brief interview earlier leave the building, walk to a car in the lot, and drive away. Her hunch that the woman would leave for lunch had been right!

"Thank you, Jimmy," she said, opening the door and stepping out. "I think this time I *will* have you wait, if you don't mind. I have no idea how long I will be. If it looks like I might be a while, I'll come and tell you."

She hurried across the parking lot, up the stairs, and back into the large brick building upon which she had suddenly pinned so many hopes. The aroma of lunch now filled the place. The energetic sounds from above were louder than before. She walked straight across the oak floor and into the office. A much younger woman now sat behind the glass half-wall. She glanced up with a smile.

"Hello, how may I help you?"

"Good morning," said Janet, doing her best to put on a confident air. "I'm here to inquire about the teaching position. I read about it in the paper — English teacher K-12, interviews conducted..."

"Yes, conducted by Principal Pratt," said the young woman, laughing lightly. "We're all familiar with the ad. To tell you the truth, he's frantic to find someone — this is a terrible time of year to be short, with the new school year starting and winter just around the corner, you know. Actually, it's a little awkward — Mrs. Cracker, she just left for lunch...she usually handles all applications."

"I should tell you," said Janet, "I did speak with her late last week."

"Did she give you an application?"

"No. I had asked about a boy who might be living here."

"Did you find what you were looking for?"

"No, she sent me back to the courthouse. I spent the rest

of the day there."

"Any luck?"

Janet shook her head. "To be honest, I don't think Mrs....what did you say her name was?"

"Mrs. Cracker?"

"Mrs. Cracker—I don't think she liked me very much. If she is in charge of hiring, I might as well not even apply for the job."

The young woman laughed. "Join the club. She doesn't like anybody. So you are interested in the position?"

"Yes," replied Janet.

"You're an English teacher."

Janet nodded.

"You don't have an appointment?"

"No, sorry."

"Then, hmm—just a minute."

She picked up the phone on the desk and shoved a wired plug into its connection on the switchboard in front of her. "Hi, Jeanie," she said several seconds later. "It's Mary downstairs. There's a lady here to see Mr. Pratt about the teaching job...yes...I think so, I didn't ask. No, she hasn't spoken with anyone yet—she just saw the ad in the paper...right, okay. I'll tell her."

She hung up the phone and glanced back to Janet.

"Mr. Pratt's office is on the third floor. The stairs are out there where you came in," she added pointing behind Janet. "There's an elevator in back of the building if you prefer. But the stairs are faster. The elevator's a clunky old thing."

"The stairs will be fine."

"You can go on up. His secretary—that's Jeanie who I was talking to—today is the first day of classes for the new school year but she said he has a little free time. With lunch just starting, all the kids will be in the cafeteria."

"Thank you," said Janet with a smile. "I appreciate your help very much. They ought to make *you* the head receptionist."

"Don't even whisper a word like that around here. My husband is one of the teachers and I am on staff for the orphanage. I'm Mary Crosby, by the way. I just fill in here occasionally. But nobody gets in the Cracker's way."

"I'll keep my thoughts to myself!"

Janet reached the third floor landing a couple minutes later. A long wide hall stretched out in front of her, with offices on both sides. She wandered slowly down the corridor, looking at the labels on the doors. At the end of the hall a door stood open. She saw painted in black letters on it, *Mr. Pratt, Principal*. She walked inside.

A large woman behind a desk immediately rose.

"You must be the English teacher Mary just called me about. I'm Jeanie, Mr. Pratt's secretary. Welcome to Wyoming Children's Home."

She reached across her desk with a friendly hand and Janet took it.

"Thank you," said Janet. "My name is Janet Holiday."

"Have a seat over there," she said, motioning to a row of chairs lined against the wall opposite her desk. Janet sat down as the secretary walked to the door of an office behind her. She knocked lightly, then opened the door and disappeared inside. She returned in less than a minute.

"You caught him at a good time," she said with a smile. "Mr. Pratt would like to see you." She motioned Janet toward the open door.

Janet stood and walked toward her.

"This is Janet Holiday," said the woman as Janet entered the office.

"Hello, Miss...or is it *Mrs.* Holiday," said the principal from where he stood behind his desk.

"*Mrs.*," said Janet with a smile.

"I see. I am Charles Pratt, principal of the school here at the Home." He reached across the desk and shook Janet's hand. He indicated a chair as the secretary closed the door behind them. Janet sat down and gave the man a quick study. He was probably about her own age, short and stocky, five foot seven or so, balding, a little paunchy and wearing a brown suit that could have come from a goodwill shop. But she liked his look. He appeared comfortable.

"You've come about the English position I understand?" he said, resuming his seat.

"Yes."

"The job has been open for a month. To tell you the truth,

149

you're the first person to inquire. The opening produced itself quite by surprise and, most teachers already have their positions for the school year already secured. And if you don't mind my asking, why are you applying for a position just as the school year is starting?"

"A major change has come to my life recently," replied Janet.

"Oh?"

"I lost my husband earlier this year."

"I am sorry to hear that. And you are looking for a change?"

"Something like that."

"You have not been teaching, then?"

"Not since Pearl Harbor, no. I resigned my teaching job to focus on being a volunteer. I helped raise war bonds and worked with injured soldiers at the veteran's hospital."

"Thank you for your service, Mrs. Holiday. Our son fought under General Patton in Europe. He made it back — so many didn't you know."

They were both quiet for a moment before Mr. Pratt spoke again. "Do you have a resume? I presume you have the necessary qualifications?"

"I don't have a resume," replied Janet. "To be honest, this is sort of a spur of the moment decision. I saw your notice in the paper and I thought, *Why not?* Maybe I need a change, I said to myself. I didn't really come prepared. But I am qualified."

"What is your experience?"

"I have a degree in Education and a teacher's certificate from Abilene Christian University in Texas," said Janet. "I graduated in 1917. After that I taught in the primary grades for several years, grades three and four mainly, then as an English teacher in grades seven through nine. That was at Lincoln Junior High in Dallas."

"I see," nodded the principal. He was hoping that this lady who had walked in without an appointment might be the solution to his problem. The room was silent a minute.

"As I am sure you can imagine," Pratt went on, "this is an unusual situation here. We are essentially a boarding school, and children come to us from throughout the state. There are unique challenges involved in working with orphans. They're mostly good kids, but they carry hidden pains the rest of us can never know. Sometimes this results in problems, but not often. Communication is always the key. Orphans tend to build up walls of self-protection early in life. It's a defense mechanism against allowing the world to hurt them. Most of the children feel that they're not worthy of parental love, or love of any kind for that matter. Getting beyond that barrier is our constant challenge. It takes a level of compassion and understanding that doesn't come naturally for everyone. The older teenagers are anxious to be out on their own. Yet deep inside they don't know if they are worthy of success or relationships or whatever else they may want. Getting through to them is not an easy job. Do you think this is an environment you would be comfortable working in?"

As Janet listened, she realized, in spite of his frumpy appearance, why she had been drawn to the principal's demeanor. He cared deeply about the children in his school.

"I can't honestly say, Mr. Pratt," she replied. "It would be new for me. I recognize that. But I would like to try."

He took in her candid answer thoughtfully, then nodded slowly.

"I think you would do fine," he said. "I will need references, and a copy of your teaching certificate. Wyoming will have no problem recognizing a certificate from Texas, especially a prestigious school like Abilene Christian. But if everything checks out, it would be my pleasure to offer you the job."

"Thank you!" said Janet enthusiastically. "I will get working on what you need today. I will make some telephone calls immediately."

Pratt rose and again extended his hand. Janet stood and shook it a second time, then made a move in the direction of the door.

"Actually…" said the principal's voice behind her.

Janet paused and turned toward him.

" —You don't strike me as the kind of woman who would try to con me," Mr. Pratt said. 'I'm sure your papers will check out. You will be replacing Mr. Bigby. Until just now I was afraid I was going to have to take over the classes. English was never my strong suit. It would be a great relief to me for you to start as soon as possible, pending receipt of your certificate. Then I could get back to my regular duties. I would love to have you start next Monday, if that fits in with your plans."

"That would be fantastic!" said Janet.

"Let's plan on it, then," he said, leading the way out of his office.

"Jeanie," he said to his secretary, "Mrs. Holiday is going to be our new English teacher. She will start on Monday."

"That's wonderful! Congratulations, Mrs. Holiday," said the secretary, standing and again shaking her hand.

"I want to show her around briefly before lunch is over. Would you gather what paperwork is necessary for her to fill out tomorrow, give her all the keys she will need, employee signatures, and whatever else there is."

"I'll have everything ready."

"Then come with me, Mrs. Holiday," said the principal. "I'll give you the five cent tour."

They left the office and proceeded along the corridor toward the stairs Janet had come up a short while before.

"You will have to excuse the mess here and there," said Pratt as they went. "We have had such an influx of war orphans the last few years that we have been expanding and adding classrooms, as well as trying to modernize our facilities as funding becomes available."

Janet took in what the principal said with interest.

"The living quarters for the resident children are on the fourth and fifth floors," Pratt explained. "Girls on the fourth, boys on the fifth. Most of the children share rooms, except in unusual cases. We do not often have young people with handicaps, but when we do they are more easily managed in rooms by themselves. We have resident nurses on staff for both boys and girls. You'll like them. They are very good to the children. Also a staff psychologist. The third floor here is comprised of the administrative offices for the home and school. A large cafeteria and gymnasium was built as an extension to the first floor many years ago. That's where everyone is now."

They reached the stairway and descended to the second

floor.

"Most of the classrooms are here on the second floor. We usually have between sixty and seventy young people on hand. The younger grades are grouped in four classes — kindergarten and first grade, grades two and three, grades four through six, and finally seven and eight. Then the high school ages are taught by subject as in a traditional high school. You will have one class of ninth and tenth English, another of eleventh and twelfth English, as well as a twice-weekly literature class which is an elective for all the high school grades. Additionally, you will assist in the younger grades with early childhood reading and writing, penmanship, and introductory grammar and reading discussions. Of course all the teachers are well qualified reading and writing instructors, but we like to give as much individual instruction as possible. That's why we have an English teacher on staff to help with the lower grades as well as for the high school ages. All in all, it amounts to about six hours in the classroom a day — as well as the normal shared playground and lunchroom duties and that sort of thing."

They left the stairs and proceeded down a mostly deserted hallway. As they went Janet noted the nameplates and subjects of the doors they passed.

"You mentioned occasional handicapped children. What kinds of handicaps does your staff deal with?" asked Janet.

"As I say, we are not equipped for extreme cases. We have people who are skilled in the usual things — speech therapy, obviously psychological trauma, basic learning problems, that sort of thing. We do have one young man enrolled who is confined to a wheelchair, and is also mute. He has represented a particular challenge. He is pleasant enough, but we do not seem to be helping him a great deal."

"Is he deaf?"

"No, only mute. He seems to learn well with a normal IQ level, but in other respects he remains something of a mystery to us."

"I will look forward to meeting him."

"Unfortunately that won't be possible...at least not right away."

"Why, what happened to him?"

"Nothing, he's fine. Luke and one of our staff members, a wonderful man named Carl Elkin—you'll like him—anyway, Luke and Carl will be in Denver for the next couple of months. Carl arranged for them to participate in an extensive training program that runs through the fall. It's for teens with MS and other major physical handicaps. From what Carl told me it helps kids learn to cope with life in a wheelchair, teaches them life skills and helps them develop a sense of independence. More than anything, I think it's a great way for kids to be around other people their own age with similar handicaps, and to realize they're not alone."

"Sounds like a great opportunity."

"We hope so. In any event, they left for Denver in the orphanage van only a few days ago and won't be back until the first week of December.—Ah, here we are," said Pratt. "This would be your classroom." He stopped in front of a closed door. It read, *Room 234, Mr. Bigby, English.*

The principal turned the knob and led the way inside.

The room smelled musty. The aroma of recently departed youth still lingering in the air. It was warm, the windows all cracked open to let in a breeze to freshen things up. Old steel radiators lining the far wall would obviously be needed in the winter months. Four rows of wooden desks were lined in straight rows facing an oak teacher's desk. An American flag and Wyoming state flag extended on poles from the wall in one corner. The blackboard was filled with notes and scribblings.

"It looks like you've had them diagramming sentences," said Janet.

"Yes," sighed Pratt. "Not very successfully. The thing is a mystery to me, so it's hard to know how to make it make sense to them. I will be very relieved when Monday comes!"

They left the room.

"Do you mind if I ask a question?" said Janet. "Do you have a boy here by the name of Payne?"

"Hmm...no," replied Mr. Pratt. "No one by that name's ever been at the home that I know of, unless it might have been a pre-school-age child who was here briefly. Why?"

"Just curious," said Janet. "There's a boy I'm trying to locate. Perhaps he's not here. What about Holiday?"

"No—no Holiday either."

As they turned back toward the stairs, three boys who appeared eleven or twelve came running along the hall. They slowed slightly as they eyed the woman with their principal. "Slow down, men," he said. "No running in the halls, remember."

The three slowed to a fast walk and hurried on.

"The student lockers are behind us," said Pratt, "at the far end of the hall. "The children don't use them that much since they all live here. If they need something they can go up to their rooms for it. Those boys are probably after something before dashing outside for lunch recess."

Janet turned and watched until they were about halfway down the corridor, then broke into a run again.

"I suppose children are the same everywhere," said Janet laughing. "Always in a hurry."

"Sometimes I wonder why I bother," sighed Pratt. "It just makes them think of me as an old grouch always correcting them. And it does no good anyway. Still, that's a principal's job."

THIRTY-TWO
THE ELEVENTH DREAM—THE GREATEST GIFT

Christmas Eve, 1946

After coming to the orphanage, Luke remembered wishing he could again have a Christmas like he had known with his mother. But then he realized that he at least had a memory of such wonderful times. Most of the children didn't even have that. Some of the others had never known what it was like to hear their mother thank God for the food they had on the table, or the gifts under the tree, or even for a son who couldn't walk or talk. He wished the orphanage could be full of such memories of love that none of them would ever forget!

God, Luke prayed in the quietness of his own mind, *I'd like to ask you to give every boy and girl in this orphanage a gift that only you can give – the gift of knowing they're loved, of knowing they're part of a family, even if they never know their real fathers and mothers. Maybe some are like Carl and might have brothers or sisters or aunts and uncles or cousins out there that they don't know about. But you know where they are. So maybe you could help them find their relatives so they would know what it feels like to have a family. I knew what it was like to have a mother. Some of them don't. I wish you could do that for them. I don't know how you manage to keep track of everyone. That's one of the things that's hard to understand. But however you do these things, if you do have a little time left over, and it's not too much to ask, I'd like to have a family Christmas again too some day.*

Luke reached up and turned out his light. Soon he was sound asleep.

When Luke came awake in his dream it felt more real than before. He had no sensation of air or clouds or flying or being in an unreal place. He was still in the orphanage. But he was a grown man and in charge. He walked around telling people what to do, greeting the boys and girls, refereeing games at recess. No one recognized him as the wheelchair-bound boy who couldn't walk or talk.

Homemade holiday decorations were everywhere with cutouts of Christmas trees, silver stars and golden tinsel on the walls, not to mention strings of blinking Christmas lights.

A flatbed truck drove up to the building. Luke went out the front door to meet it. The back of the truck was full of everything needed for the most perfect of Holiday feasts, turkeys and hams were steaming hot and ready for the table. There were also large bowls full of stuffing and mashed potatoes and brown gravy in yet another large bowl. Three workers got out, picked it all up, as only they could in a dream, and carried it inside. Under Luke's supervision all the food and even some magnificent deserts of pumpkin pies and chocolate cake were placed on a large table.

"Now for the loved ones," he said. "The families will come. I must just believe."

He stood patiently waiting. Before long a bus came along Route 85, slowed, then turned into the orphanage entryway. It passed through the iron gate, turned in the circular drive and stopped in front of him. The bus driver got out. Luke went down the steps to meet him. The man's eyes sparkled with laughter and looked familiar.

"Is this the Wyoming Children's home?" he asked.

"It is."

"I have some people who would like to spend Christmas with your children."

"Fine, good!" said Luke. "I will show them the way to the feast."

Luke looked behind him to see all the children of the orphanage standing behind him. A woman stepped out of the bus and looked around for a moment. A young girl squealed with delight and ran forward to hug her. "Mama! Oh Mama!" she cried in ecstasy. "Thank you for coming to my Christmas!"

Next an older man walked off. A boy from Luke's class hurried forward to greet him. "Grandfather, welcome to the orphanage. It is so good to see you again!"

The wonderful reunions continued. Every new visitor to step off the bus was joyfully greeted by one of the young orphans rushing forward to love and be loved.

He had believed, thought Luke. And the love of Christmas had come.

When the reunion bus was at last empty, Luke walked back inside the building. The table spread with the upcoming feast was gorgeous to behold. Even more food seemed to have appeared. Steam rose from dozens of platters and bowls and serving dishes as the happy children and their loved ones scurried to find their places. When everyone was at last in place, every person around the table gave brief thanks for their own personal blessings on this special day. It was the best Christmas ever at the Wyoming Children's Home.

Suddenly the man-Luke who had supervised the day's activities disappeared. Luke was himself again at sixteen. He walked across the floor, out the door, down the steps, along the drive, through the gate, and to the highway beyond. He was not surprised to see Vanessa at the intersection waiting for him.

"What took you so long?" she said merrily. "I've been waiting for you for what seems like years."

"I was busy with a feast and bringing family members back together again. It's Christmas, you know?"

"How could I forget that? That's always when you come to meet me.."

They turned and walked into town. Few words passed between them.

They made their way along one street, now another, through the center of town, then onto side streets that led past nice houses and a few apartment buildings. They moved as with one will. Neither was leading, but somehow both felt compelled to go in the same direction.

"There is something familiar about this street," said Vanessa at length. "It seems I have been here before."

"I know. Me too," said Luke. "But I don't recognize it from any of our dreams. That's the only time we're together."

"It has something to do with you," added Vanessa. "When I saw this street, I thought of you. But not you as you are now, but maybe how you were a long time ago."

They continued on in silence.

"Do you remember what you used to do for Christmas when you were with your family?" asked Vanessa.

"It was only my mother and me. She always made it fun, even

158

though we didn't have much money. But I remember how thankful my mother was for everything we did have. She always thanked God for me most of all. I suppose hearing her pray that prayer is one of the most special memories of my life. What did you do?"

"Every Christmas Eve we visited my grandparents and had a wonderful dinner. After that we went home for cider and dessert and then sat around the tree and sang carols. But all that seems like a very long time ago. I have no more Christmas memories after that, except with you."

"It sounds like you had a nice family."

Vanessa did not reply. A tear stole down her cheek.

They found themselves walking back out of town on the same road as before. They had been walking for hours and night had fallen. It was a cold, clear night and the heavens were alive above them. Luke thought he had never seen so many stars. They filled the sky like millions of sparkling jewels.

He and Vanessa slowed as the lights of the large brick building of the orphanage, set back from the road on the right, came into view.

"This is where I was waiting for you," said Vanessa.

"I think I am supposed to go back inside," said Luke.

"I need to keep going," said Vanessa pointing. "Just over the hill there ahead, that's where I think I am supposed to go."

She turned to Luke. Her face wore a sad expression like he had never seen.

"What is it?" asked Luke.

"I don't know," replied Vanessa. "I have a strange feeling that I'm not going to see you again. I think this is my last dream."

"Don't say that. We will meet again next Christmas, like we always do!"

"I don't think so, not like this. This is the last dream."

She smiled. "You're so much bigger and older than when I first met you. Your voice is getting deep like a man's. You're a big handsome sixteen year old boy."

Luke laughed. "What about you! You're sixteen too, and beautiful. Sixteen year old girls look like they're seventeen. Sixteen year old boys look like we're thirteen."

Now it was Vanessa's turn to laugh. "That's really funny. But maybe you're right."

The two grew serious again, then embraced. When they stepped back, they gazed earnestly at one another.

"I will never forget you," said Luke.

"I won't forget you either. I know it sounds peculiar, but I have the feeling that somehow you saved my life. Good bye, Luke."

Vanessa smiled again, then continued her way along the road. Luke turned into the drive, and walked slowly through the iron gate ahead of him. As he approached, the large brick building gradually faded into nothingness, and slowly his dream came to an end.

Something strange and amazing happened at the orphanage the next morning. The children all woke up with the memory of having a wonderful dream the night before. In their dream each remembered enjoying an amazing Christmas feast with a favorite family member. Many of those family members had passed away years before. Others had simply disappeared from the children's lives. But for one special night, thanks to one young man's heartfelt prayer before falling asleep, each of the children in the orphanage had a chance to share in the magic of a special Christmas dream — a dream they would cherish for the rest of their lives.

THIRTY-THREE

DECISION

Friday, September 5, 1947

For the rest of the week Janet's emotions swung from the heights of excitement to abject terror. *What had she done!* she asked herself a hundred times.

The idea of walking into an 11th and 12th grade English class, never having taught high school juniors and seniors in her life, struck her heart with so much fear that she nearly decided to call Mr. Pratt, apologize profusely, and tell him she had changed her mind. Just as quickly her thoughts returned to Jack's death and the circumstances that had led her here, followed by the horrifying wave of realizing anew that her daughter was also dead. Suddenly she found herself plunged all over again into despair. And so it went — from heartbreak to hope and back again.

Janet's fear of intimidation by the older students was given a temporary respite during a brief teacher's meeting on Friday. There she met the rest of the staff and Mr. Pratt handed her the schedule for the following week. Her first class on Monday morning would be with the youngest children in the kindergarten and first grade class. She would introduce herself and read a few stories and talk about words and language. For the first week, he said, he expected nothing more than that she become comfortable. She could simply read aloud in all the classes if she chose. She did not need to work up more specific lesson planning, he assured her, until she found her teaching legs again, and was able to assess the needs of each class and its students. She would want to go

161

through Mr. Bigby's files, he added, to familiarize herself with what he had been doing. Thankfully, and to her great relief, Janet saw that she would not encounter the juniors and seniors until the last hour of the day, from 2:30 to 3:30.

After arranging with the hotel manager to stay on at a reduced weekly rate until she decided what to do, Janet finally called Annie. She had not spoken to her friend since arriving in Eaglescliff.

"You did *what*!" Annie nearly shouted into the phone.

"I told you, I took a job."

"What kind of job?"

"Teaching. I know, I know…it's crazy!" laughed Janet. "I've been telling myself the same thing. But I did it."

"But why? Did you find Leslie?"

Annie's question jarred Janet back to reality.

"Oh, Annie…" she began, then broke into sobs. The sound of her friend's voice speaking her daughter's name unleashed the torrent all over again. In a halting voice Janet told her of the events of the last several days, along with the astonishing news that she had a grandson who may still be living in Eaglescliff.

"I am so sorry, Janet," said Annie. "I can't imagine what you must be going through."

"Thank you, Annie. It's hard, but I'm trying to deal with it."

"And you don't know the boy's name or anything?"

"Nothing," replied Janet, beginning to breathe more easily once again. "That's the odd thing. Leslie was going by her middle name—Leslie Payne. I don't know why. But there is no student at the orphanage by the name of Payne."

"What about Holiday?"

"No, not that either. I may be on a wild goose chase. But the orphanage runs its own school. My hope is that by being there…I don't know, that somehow I will be able to find him."

"*If* he's even there."

"Right—a big if."

"No word about Leslie's husband?"

"Not a thing. The girl who was with her in the hospital thinks he may have abandoned her."

They continued to chat for several minutes.

162

"Well, don't worry about a thing here," said Annie. "I've got the key to your house and will continue to pick up your mail. Now that I know where you are and have the hotel number, I can call you if there's anything you should know about. Oh—I just thought of something! You'll need some new clothes!"

"You're right. How exciting! I'll go out tomorrow."

"Does the place have any decent stores?"

"A small town department store. It's not exactly Macys or Gimbels, but I'm sure they'll have everything I might need. If I stay longer, I'll have you send me a box of clothes from my closet."

"When do you start?"

"Monday. A full day. I'll be spending the weekend frantically trying to get prepared, going over the records of what's been happening in each class."

"Are you nervous?"

"You bet I'm nervous. I haven't been in a classroom in six years!"

"You'll do great."

"I'm glad for your confidence," rejoined Janet, trying to laugh through her lingering tears. "But it's me that has to walk into that classroom, not you! Added to having to sharpen up my teaching skills, I will be looking at every boy wondering if he is the one."

When Janet got off the phone with Annie, it suddenly dawned on her how little she knew about Leslie's son. She knew neither his first name nor his last name...she did not know his exact age. Why hadn't she thought to ask Karen *when* she and Leslie were in the hospital together? How could she have overlooked such an important detail?

She hadn't seen Karen since applying for the job. She wanted to tell her all about it anyway. She would go over to the restaurant right now and see what more she could learn.

She walked into the Kings Inn, glanced around quickly, but saw no sign of Karen. The other regular waitress saw her come through the door and walked up to her.

"Hi, I'm BJ," she said. "Aren't you Mrs. Holiday?"

"Yes I am. I came to see Karen. Is she here?"

"She wanted to see you too. She went over to the hotel

trying to find you, but you weren't there."

"Well I'm here now," smiled Janet, "and I really need to talk to her."

"I'm afraid that won't be possible for a while, Mrs. Holiday. Her mother just fell ill and is not doing well. Karen caught the bus to Denver this morning and will take the train from there back east."

"Where does her mother live?" Janet asked.

"West Virginia, her daddy was a coal miner. I think they are pretty isolated there—that's why she was trying to find you."

THIRTY-FOUR

THE NEW ENGLISH TEACHER

Monday, September 8, 1947

Janet's initial self-doubts about being able to connect with the orphans at the Wyoming Children's Home was swept away within five minutes of walking into her first class. The sight of ten pair of innocent kindergarten and first grade eyes staring up at her went straight to her heart.

Those lonely, parentless children!

If only she could adopt them all! She had lost a daughter. But these poor boys and girls had never felt a mother's tender caress. They didn't know the feeling of being tucked into bed and prayed with and kissed goodnight by their own mother. They were all looking at her as if hoping *she* might be such a mother to them.

By the time of her 9th and 10th grade English class just before lunch, Janet had already learned to look into their eyes and see the hopes and fears of each one. How could they intimidate her? She *loved* them.

She spent the day, as the principal had suggested, getting to know the students, and allowing them to know her. She did not, however, divulge her personal reasons for being in Eaglescliff. Yet it could not be helped that her enthusiasm throughout the first day's round of classes was energized by the obvious thought as she gazed intently into the eyes of each young boy — Could *this* be Leslie's son?

With the weight of such a question constantly on her mind, it was a wonder she was able to keep her concentration at all.

165

As the 11th and 12th graders filed out of her last class at 3:30 that afternoon, when the day's thousand smiles were at last behind her and she was finally alone, she realized that she was completely exhausted. She sat down at Mr. Bigby's desk—her desk now—and laid her head down on the desk. Mr. Pratt found her unmoved five minutes later when he stopped by to see how her first day had gone.

Half an hour later, after asking Mrs. Cracker to make the call for her, it was all she could do to keep from falling asleep waiting for Jimmy's cab. She was glad she wasn't driving! The weather had changed suddenly again and another early mountain cold front had blown in bringing a cool rain with its gusty winds.

Janet had not, as she and Annie had talked about, gone shopping on Saturday. She thought she ought to wait until she had at least had a day under her belt. There was no sense buying a new wardrobe if she decided to quit after Monday!

Riding into town in Jimmy's cab with her first day behind her, she thought that if she could brave the wind and rain she would spend what was left of the afternoon at Daly's Department Store. Otherwise she would probably fall asleep in her room! By the time she deposited her things at the hotel and was back outside, it was nearly 4:30. Daly's was open till 6:00. The day was gloomy under heavy gray clouds. By closing time, she walked out of Daly's carrying two new blouses, a sweater, a skirt, and one dress, a light jacket and a heavy winter coat. Perhaps she would visit Olson's Shoe Store in the next block after school tomorrow.

Still carrying her purchases, and seeing the brightly painted hot rod parked on the street, she paused for a brief stop at Rafferty Drug.

"Hi, Mrs. Holiday!" a familiar voice greeted her as she walked in.

"Hi again, Gary."

"That was sure a surprise when I saw you in class today! I didn't know you were a teacher."

"I was a little surprised myself," said Janet with a smile, taking an empty seat.

"Can I get you something?"

"No thanks," replied Janet taking an empty seat. "I just

166

stopped in to say hi. I'm going back to the hotel to drop these things off, then have some dinner."

"What do you mean you were surprised?" asked Gary.

"Only that I hadn't expected to be applying for a teaching job when I arrived in town. But I enjoyed myself today, nervousness and all. I was especially glad to see you in class. It made it nice seeing a friendly face in the crowd. I've never taught upper high school classes before—but don't tell anyone!"

"I promise!" laughed Gary.

Janet lifted herself wearily off the red stool. "I'll see you tomorrow, Gary."

All through dinner at the hotel dining room, and through the evening in her room, Janet's mind replayed images from the day just past. Her initial uneasiness had evaporated in compassion. She had brought home all her class lists. As she scanned them in the quietness of her room, face after face rose in her mind's eye—now a first grader, now a junior, now a girl from her 7th and 8th glass. It would be some time before she knew every name and face. But even a single day was enough to sting her heart with deeper emotions than she had felt when occupying any previous classroom.

She had lugged back to her room six or eight books from the orphanage library. She'd brought along only a couple books from home to read. If she was going to teach high school literature, she needed to brush up on her classics—*Moby Dick, Jane Eyre, Silas Marner, Sir Gibbie*, and the rest. She needed to come up with some good reading ideas for her 7th and 8th grade class too.

But as she sat in her room, she couldn't concentrate on the book in her hand. She kept returning to the pages of her class lists. Was it possible that one of these very names, someone she had actually met today, could be her grandson?

If only she had thought to ask Karen more specific questions. Now she was out of reach, at some remote family homestead in West Virginia. *When* were she and Leslie together in the hospital in Wheatland?

Leslie had left home seventeen years ago. So her son could be no older than sixteen. The accident had been in 1937—that was ten years ago. So Leslie's son had to be at least eleven.

That narrowed the possibilities to somewhere between the 5th and 11th grades.

She scanned the names of the students in her classes again.

Where are you, young man? she thought to herself. *And who are you?*

Thirty-Five

AFRAID OF THE TRUTH

Thursday, September 11, 1947

The final days of Janet's first week as the new English teacher for the Wyoming Children's Home were full of enthusiasm and hopefulness. Having so many young lives to give herself to helped immeasurably in dulling the ache of loss in her own heart. She quickly learned her students' names. The young ones especially, desperate for attention and affection, were wide-eyed and eager every new day, pressing close, telling her the little stories of their lives, crowding about to scramble into her lap when she sat on the floor to read. By week's end she had every boy and girl in the six younger grades enchanted by Thornton Burgess's world of the Mother West Wind stories, and the antics of Old Grannie Fox, Jimmy Skunk, Uncle Billy Possum, Chatterer the Red Squirrel, Buster Bear, and Reddy Fox.

Even in the older classes, no longer was she concerned whether she could still teach the minds of these children, but rather whether she could somehow reach their hearts. The older children were more closed off emotionally than the 1st and 2nd graders. But though they were reluctant to show it, their need of love was no less. All their hearts—young and old alike—were crying out for love more than anything. Every one was missing that deepest part of self-knowing—knowing where they came from, and the mother and father that gave them life.

She could not give that to them. She could, however, give them love from her own mother's heart. What she had lost, they had never known—the bond between a mother and her child. In a way, she was like an orphan now too—she had no family either. That loss helped her identify with every one. She was still a mother. Love still beat in her heart. Therefore, she would love them as if they were her own.

It did not take long for Janet's goals to change. No longer was her quest merely to find her grandson, if he was there. Now she hoped to be able to convey in some way to every child, to every boy and girl, even the older ones, the reality that they each had some special gift to offer the world. Perhaps, she thought, it was a truth she needed to take hold of for herself as well.

The other teachers and staff members were warm and friendly and embracing, with the exception of Mrs. Cracker, from whom she had not yet succeeded in drawing a smile. She looked forward to her morning taxi drive every day at 7:30, to the staff meetings, to the exchanges in the teachers' room during the day's breaks, even to her lunch room and recess supervision duties when she had the chance to mix with the older students who were not in her Lit class.

Janet was so busy with her new job and the new children who quickly found their way into her heart, she delayed the start of a concerted search for her grandson. She told herself she would get serious about it as soon as Karen returned from helping her mother. For the first week or two, she needed to get her teaching legs back, and put her time and energy into her new students. They were so much in need of her love. Her teaching provided an excuse to put the search for her grandson on hold until she got used to the idea. Everything had happened so fast!

However, with a few minutes of free time at the end of the day she could not help looking through a few of the files and records of her students. In truth Janet could not help being afraid of what she might find. *Not* knowing the truth was a blessing of sorts. As it was, if she could keep putting off the search, then she could keep the hope of finding her grandson alive and well.

She didn't consciously admit it to herself, but she was afraid that when she did finally get all the answers, that her heart would be broken again. Janet therefore put her time and energy into serving her new students. Not that she could ignore the burning question that was always at the back of her mind. She could never predict when an expression or glance from one of the children might unexpectedly draw her attention. But just as quickly the glimmers of potential recognition would fade, and another of the children suddenly drew her into new speculations.

It would be easier, she thought, if the child she was looking for were a girl. Perceiving the hint of a mother's features in a young boy was not so easy. She might, of course, ask which of the children knew their mother's names. But such a question would be cruel. She would have to prosecute her search by other means. And there remained the very real possibility that Leslie's son wasn't here at all.

The days and weeks sped quickly by.

September turned to October and then suddenly November had arrived. Janet accepted an invitation to join Mr. Pratt and his wife for a lovely Thanksgiving dinner. Classes resumed the following Monday, December first, and Janet was delighted to be back with her students. They had become her new family.

THIRTY-SIX

A GIFT AND ITS PRICE

Wednesday, December 10, 1947

Luke knew something was troubling Carl.

It had begun when they were away in Denver. Several times, after receiving mail, Carl had been quiet for the rest of the day. He'd also left Luke on his own at the program two or three times throughout the fall. Not for long, just a day. All Carl said was that he had some personal things to deal with.

He had not been his usual cheerful self ever since they returned to the orphanage last weekend. He seemed distracted, even worried. Once when he left, Luke wheeled his way to the library floor window overlooking the parking lot. There he watched Carl walk across the lot to his prized '32 Model B three window coupe, then he did a peculiar thing. Carl paused, laid a hand on the car's hood, patted it two or three times, stood another moment, then got in and drove away.

Luke waited by the window reading. An hour and a half later he saw a taxi cab come through the orphanage gates. He was surprised to see Carl get out, then walk slowly up the steps and inside.

For years Carl had done everything possible to make Luke's life in this place more pleasant. He had researched about the program in Denver for nearly a year. He had jumped through all the hoops of applying for the grant and doing all the paperwork that made it possible.

All for him.

Now it was his turn, Luke thought. What could he do for Carl? Christmas was approaching, his favorite time of the

172

year. He hated the thought of Carl being downcast during the Christmas season.

At the first opportunity the next afternoon when they could talk after classes were over, making sure he had paper and pencil, Luke handed Carl the note he had written out.

"What's this?" said Carl.

Luke simply nodded, his expression serious, and gestured to the paper.

I can tell something's wrong, Carl, Carl read. *You've been a great friend. You're always there for me. I may not be able to talk, but I am a good listener.*

Carl smiled a little sadly. "It's that obvious, is it?"

Luke nodded.

"Nothing gets by you, does it?"

Luke took the paper from him and wrote again briefly.

Not much.

The straightforward simplicity of the words struck Carl as humorous. "All right, Luke, my man," he chuckled. "If anyone deserves to know, you do. Let's go up to the lounge and have a chat. I'll tell you about it."

But again Luke took the paper.

Where's your car? Carl read.

"You noticed? What were you doing, watching me?" he asked with a wry smile.

Luke nodded.

"Well, my man, that's part of my trouble — though not the main part. Let's head on upstairs."

Carl led to one corner of the expansive room that served as a game room, living room, relaxation room. The newest addition was a small television set. Luke turned his wheelchair toward Carl and waited.

"It's my sister Timmy," Carl began, easing into a chair. "I told you about her, how she found out about me and how we finally met."

Luke nodded.

"It's been great," Carl went on. "For the first time in my life I've got a family. But," he went on, glancing away momentarily, "she hasn't been feeling too good for a while. She went to a few doctors but they didn't have much to say. Finally she went to a specialist in Cheyenne who did some

173

blood tests and other kinds of tests — women tests, you know. They found out that she's got breast cancer. That was a year ago. They've been doing all kinds of things — medicines and hooking her up to machines. Most of it I don't understand. The chances for a woman like that — they aren't too good, you know. Cancer's a nasty disease. I've been going to the city to be with her as much as I can. I was getting news of her condition when we were in Denver. That's why I had to leave you a few times. I don't have much to give, but I can give her a brother's love. Timmy's a fighter and she's been doing good, and the doctors think she's improving. They're now giving her better than a fifty-fifty shot of conquering it. But that medicine and treatment and the doctors, it takes a lot of money. Beating a disease like cancer's an expensive thing. If you don't have the money you're likely to die. And I'm not about to lose my sister so soon after finding her. So we've been putting all the money we had into her treatment. But the money's finally gone, and she's not done fighting yet. We had to do something. So all the time we were gone I was scheming about what to do, and yesterday I did it. I sold my car to Mr. Sanders in town. I explained what I needed the money for and he gave me a good price — probably better than I deserved, but he wanted to help. So I've got the money to keep Timmy's medicines and treatments going, hopefully long enough for her to win the battle. I'd trade a car for Timmy's life any day. So that's about it, Luke. It's just been a hard time for Timmy and me."

Carl let out a long sigh. Luke wrote a brief note and handed it to Carl.

I'm sorry about Timmy and about your car. Thank you for telling me. I will pray for you both.

Carl smiled and nodded. "Thanks, man. I appreciate it."

Carl rose and left him. Luke read for a while in the book he had with him. But he couldn't concentrate. His thoughts were too full of Carl's story. Carl's compassion for his sister, and his sacrifice for her, was what Christmas was all about, thought Luke. It was too bad he had to lose his car. But what greater gift could one person give another than life?

Since the day he had arrived here, Carl had been helping him. What could *he* now do to make Carl's Christmas a little bit more special?

Luke picked up his book and tried to read again. But it was no use. He was filled with the idea of getting Carl a special gift. Yet he couldn't just walk into town like the others. The only time he went to town was with Carl.

But it was only half a mile. His arms were strong. He pushed himself around inside the orphanage all day long probably much further than that. The next minute he was on his way out of the lounge and making for his room. It was just a minute or two after four. He could easily make it into town and back before dinner at six. If he snuck out the back door, no one would even know he'd been gone.

He wheeled quickly in and out of his room, found the five dollar bill Carl had given him for Christmas the year before where he kept it in his writing box, then left the room.

Not many of the other boys were around. Most were in the lounge or at the gymnasium playing basketball, or in the library. They paid no attention to him anyway. He passed two or three in the hallway, but no one even glanced in his direction. A minute later he was in the service elevator at the back of the building pressing the G for the Ground Floor. The elevator creaked into motion, and finally jerked to a stop a minute later at the end of its slow descent. Luke wheeled himself through the sliding doors.

Knowing none of the orphanage staff would allow him to leave the grounds on his own, he glanced back and forth along the corridor to make sure no one was watching, then quickly made for the outside door.

The building sat on a slight incline such that its rear door was at ground level. A shocking blast of wintry air greeted Luke as he guided his wheelchair through the doors and onto the sidewalk. He hadn't realized how cold it was, nor had he thought to get his coat. It was too late now. He had come this far — he wasn't going back to his room now.

The late afternoon's sun reflecting off the snow nearly blinded him. His eyes adjusted as he steered down a slight ramp and onto the long sidewalk that led alongside the brick wall to the front of the building. As he passed the front corner a freezing gust of wind stung his face. It was colder out here than he thought at first. Soon he was passing the parking lot, his wheels crunching over patches of ice and snow that had escaped the shovel.

Luke moved quickly, though his hands were already freezing as they gripped the wheels, a little more snow sticking to them with every revolution. He was in plain view now...he hoped no one was watching from the windows behind him.

Passing through the black iron gates, he arrived at the intersection to the highway and turned left. For the next quarter mile there was no sidewalk. But traffic was light. Only two cars sped by and he managed to keep his wheelchair moving along the gravel alongside the road. Reaching the first buildings of the business district, he maneuvered onto the sidewalk. He was shivering, and his hands were going numb, but it wasn't much farther now.

Four minutes later, his body numb and colder than he had ever been in his life, Luke stopped in front of two large glass doors. It did not take long before a man coming out saw him waiting and held one of the doors open. Luke's teeth were chattering, but he tried to smile as he wheeled himself into Daly's Department Store.

He steered his way to one side and sat, his body shaking, hoping to warm up. When his hands began to thaw, they burned like they were on fire. After five minutes, he drew in a breath, wheeled around, and began moving through the crowded store. He knew exactly what he was looking for. It was in the Toy Department on the second floor. The elevator here was smoother than the one at the orphanage, though the elevator operator seemed determined to talk, and all Luke could do was smile. With relief, he wheeled himself out a minute later and toward the display he had once visited with Carl and Gary.

There they were, just as he remembered them!

He stared up at the boxes on the shelves — replicas of every classic car from the Ford Model T up to the '46 DeSoto Custom Club Convertible.

"Are you finding everything all right, young man?" said a voice behind him.

Luke turned and smiled, then pointed to the boxes above him on the shelf.

"Looking for one car in particular?" asked the lady.

Luke nodded. He held up the fingers of his two hands, showing three on his right hand, and two fingers on his left.

"A '32 ?"

Luke nodded.

"All right," said the sales lady, scanning the boxes. "Let me see, we have Fords, Chevys, Studebakers, Packards..."

She glanced down at Luke and saw him nodding.

"One of those?"

Again he nodded.

"A Ford —"

Luke nodded vigorously.

"Ah, right — a 1932 Ford. So...it looks like we have the Pickup, the Sedan...what's this other one — yes, a black three window Model B Coupe."

Her back was turned as she scanned the shelf. Luke reached out and touched the back of her arm. She turned. He smiled and nodded, pointing to the box whose label she had just read.

"That's the one you want — the '32 Ford Coupe in black."

Luke nodded.

She took down the box and carried it to the glass countertop, then walked around behind it to the cash register. "It looks like this will be...let me see...with tax it comes to six dollars and forty-two cents."

Luke's heart sank. Disappointed he pulled out the five dollar bill from his pocket, smiled sadly, then turned around to go.

"Wait, young man," said the clerk behind him after a moment. "You just happen to have come during today's Christmas sale. I believe that would make the price of this car...let me see...five dollars exactly."

Luke turned again. His face beamed with gratitude. He knew she had dropped the price just for him. He placed the five dollar bill on the counter.

"Would you like me to gift wrap that for you, dear?" the woman asked.

Luke nodded.

She turned to another counter behind her and pulled out a length of blue and white wrapping paper. The box containing

177

the little car soon became a beautifully wrapped package. A minute later she placed the box, complete with bow, in a bag and handed it over the counter down to Luke where he sat in his chair.

"There you go," she said.

With two or three gestures, Luke made her to understand that he wanted something to write on and a pencil or pen. She found a scrap of paper. Luke took it, wrote briefly, and handed it back to her.

Thank you so much, she read. *This is going to make a man I know very happy. Merry Christmas to you!*

"And to you, young man," she said, returning Luke's smile.

Keeping the bag secure in his lap, Luke wheeled himself back to the elevator. By quarter till five, he was leaving Daly's double doors and was on his way back to the orphanage. He would be in plenty of time for dinner!

He had not exactly forgotten how cold it was outside. Whether the temperature had dropped since he'd left the home he didn't know, but one thing he did know, the wind was now blowing straight into his face.

As he began his return journey, he tried to take his mind off the cold by thinking about giving Carl a gift he knew he would appreciate. He tried to smile at the thought. But the wind in his face had frozen his facial muscles and he could not move his lips.

He reached the end of the sidewalk and maneuvered onto the gravel shoulder alongside the road. He moved slower and slower. The wind seemed beating him back. Snow began to fall. Darkness was descending.

He was shaking in every inch of his body. Even his paralyzed legs were shivering. His hands had become two blocks of ice. Snow caked up on the wheels of his chair. But he had no choice but to keep grabbing them and force himself forward. If his momentum stopped, he would never get moving again.

I'm almost there, said to himself. *I'm close. Keep going, Luke...not much farther now.*

Ahead he saw the sign for the orphanage drive. A hundred yards more...seventy-five...fifty.

Keep going, Luke, you're almost there!

He reached the drive and began to turn toward it. In the distance, through the snow drifting down all around him, he saw the lights of the home.

Behind him a large delivery truck came rumbling along the highway. Luke was too close to the road. The truck's front tire bounced in a pothole. An icy sheet of slush flew straight toward Luke's back and shoulder. The impact jolted him sideways and he lost his balance.

Luke toppled to his side and flew out of the wheelchair. The cold wet shock forced the air from his lungs and he lay several seconds unable to breathe.

When he came to his senses, realizing what had happened, Luke struggled with hands and arms to pull himself around and back to his overturned wheelchair. But his hands were frozen. They had become as powerless as his legs.

Come on, Luke, he said to himself. *You can do this…got to get back to your room…it's warm there…warm up…just a little further…nice and warm…*

His face and head were wet with slush. His arms were useless. His head drooped.

Just a little rest…regain your strength, Luke…just a few seconds…get your strength back…

Slowly sleepiness enveloped him. The cold disappeared. A feeling of sublime warmth took over his entire body. All was white…snowy white…and warmth…delicious warmth.

Luke closed his eyes…and slept.

THIRTY-SEVEN

JANET'S IDEA

December 12, 1947

During the second week of December, arriving back on Main Street after a tiring but exhilarating day, the increasing bustle of shoppers suddenly reminded Janet that Christmas was approaching rapidly. She had been so caught up in the changes to her own life, she had hardly given Christmas a thought. Her mind had been completely focused on trying to get to know her fellow teachers and the students, as well as trying to organize her teaching curriculum for the different age groups. Here it was already December 12th. She needed to do some shopping! She had to get Annie something especially nice after all she had done. And Manny's wife. And a few other people back home. She had to get those things in the mail.

The reminder that she would be spending this Christmas alone plunged her into a new round of melancholy. Christmas reminders of her true family, the family now lost, brought reality back all too painfully. What would she even do for Christmas? The dilemma had not until this moment crossed her mind. She could not stay *here*—Christmas alone in a hotel! The very idea was unthinkable. But another long Greyhound ride back to Dallas was not an appealing prospect...nor another day and a half back to Wyoming after Christmas. What did she have to go home for anyway—an empty house with pictures of Jack and Leslie above the fireplace...that wasn't much better than a solitary hotel room. Annie would invite her to her house, of course, and would include her in their family's celebrations. But was that what she wanted?

What did the orphanage do for Christmas?

Gradually an even larger question rose on the horizon of her thoughts: If she returned to Dallas for Christmas, would she even want to come back to Eaglescliff? She loved the children, but one way or another, she knew she had to face reality and find out whether her grandson was at the orphanage or not. If this indeed turned out to be a wild goose chase, what *would* she do?

Too many questions! She couldn't resolve them all right now.

Janet changed clothes, put on a comfortable pair of slacks and her warmest turtleneck over several inner layers, slipped into a pair of tennis shoes, grabbed her coat, and left the hotel. For the next hour she wandered through Daly's and most of the town's other shops. But the perfect gift for Annie eluded her.

Unable to completely shake the doldrums over what she would do for Christmas, she finally gave up and walked the two blocks from the business district to The Kings Inn. As she went, a new thought occurred to her: *What about the orphans?* What do *they* do for Christmas? They have no family...who gives the children at the orphanage gifts?

With much on her mind, Janet walked into the restaurant. BJ greeted her like the friends they had become in Karen's absence.

"Hello, Janet," she said.

Janet had not asked about Karen for quite some time but knew the time to face reality had come. "Have you heard from Karen? How is her mother doing? Will she be coming home soon?"

BJ smiled, "Her husband was in for lunch. Apparently Karen's mother came home from the hospital last week and is doing better. Their family is going out there for Christmas and Karen will come back with them after the holidays—How's the teaching going?" BJ asked.

"I am enjoying it very much," sighed Janet wearily, pulling off her coat as she sat down in her usual booth. "I had forgotten how tiring teaching is. Smiling, talking, having to be aware and up all day, and the endless energy of children—it wears you out! And now I'm thinking about how to make Christmas special for them."

"How are you going to do that?" asked BJ.

"I don't know," nodded Janet. "I'm sure the orphanage gives them all the perfunctory gift—the orange, the chocolate bar, the new pencil, or whatever. But how do you really personalize Christmas for those poor kids? Why shouldn't they know the joy of opening gifts containing toys and books and games and balls and dolls and new clothes, not hand-me-downs? Most of them have probably never experienced that."

She glanced quickly over the menu. "French dip sounds good," she said. "With a baked potato instead of fries."

BJ, scribbled the order on her pad. "Be back in a bit," she said, then walked off toward the kitchen.

Janet glanced out the window, shivered momentarily as she shook off the remaining chill from outside. The brief conversation with BJ set the wheels of her mind in motion.

The following afternoon she went to the office just as lunch was beginning.

"Hello, Janet," said Jeanie. "From what I hear, it seems to be going well for you."

"I think so," replied Janet with a smile. "I'm feeling more comfortable. I'd like to talk to Mr. Pratt."

"Sure—go on in."

Janet knocked lightly, then opened the door to the principal's office.

"Janet, come in...my favorite English teacher!" said Pratt warmly, motioning her to a chair.

"Your only English teacher," laughed Janet.

"Yes, but one who relieved *me* of those duties!" rejoined Pratt. "I don't know how long I would have survived."

"I wanted to ask you about something else," said Janet once she was seated, "—something that has nothing to do with the classroom."

"Of course. What's on your mind?"

"What do you usually do for the children for Christmas?" Janet asked. "I mean in the way of gifts."

"Whatever we can," replied Pratt. "Unfortunately, that isn't a great deal. Our budget is limited. We have a tree and a Christmas Eve party and of course a turkey dinner on

Christmas."

"Do the children receive gifts?"

"A few little things—whatever we can afford. Occasionally there are donations from the community. But they are so few we can't give them to individual children. We just put them in with our other supplies for the children to use."

It was silent a moment. Janet had been planning how to ask what she wanted to say next. She did not want to come across as a newcomer charging in with a rash of new ideas. Everyone else had invested far more in these children than she had. She was the low man on the totem pole and she knew it.

"What would you think," she began tentatively, "—and I know perhaps you have tried it and it hasn't worked...but I was wondering if we could conduct a gift drive in town. I would like to find a way for every boy and girl to have a personal gift or two to open on Christmas."

Mr. Pratt sat back, his chair creaking, and took in her question with obvious interest.

"Actually...no, we haven't done that," he said after a moment. "There's been no one to take on such a project. I don't think we've ever thought of it on quite the scale you're talking about."

"I would take it on," said Janet, "if it was something you wanted to try. I'm not trying to barge in and—"

"No, no—quite all right. I appreciate your willingness to help, and that you want to do something for our boys and girls. In fact, I think it is a wonderful idea. Tell you what—I'll call a staff meeting this afternoon. You can present your suggestion. We'll see what the others think. We will get everyone's input, then go from there."

Thirty-Eight

Close Call

Luke emerged hazily from a blissful sleep of warmth to be greeted by an annoying beeping noise. A mask was clamped over his nose and mouth. People were standing about talking in low tones.

"...body temperature too low...hypothermia...got to get it up..."

"...pulse strong, Doctor."

"...if you can get him to respond."

"...chart says he's mentally retarded..."

"...do what you can...got to try to save him regardless..."

He was shaking...still cold...so cold... then again Luke slowly slid into the dark cocoon of unconsciousness.

How much time passed before Luke blurrily woke again to lights, tubes, voices, and strange sensations, he had no idea—an hour, a week, a year, ten years. It felt like another lifetime ago when he had been out in the snow. Had he missed his birthday and maybe another holiday dream?

His eyes darted about for some sign of what day it was.

"Hey, look who's back!" said a voice.

Luke tried to turn toward it.

"Can you hear me, Luke...can you hear me?"

Luke strained to turn his head as Carl came around the side of the bed, a great smile on his face.

"Hey, my man—you gave us quite a scare!" laughed Carl.

In spite of being covered by heavy wool blankets, Luke

realized he was still cold. His brief reunion with Carl was peremptorily halted a moment later by the importune approach of the nurse on duty.

"You're lucky someone found you when they did, young man," scolded an aging woman whose white hair stuck out in all directions from under her nurse's cap. "What were you thinking traipsing about in a snowstorm with no coat?"

"Take it easy on him, nurse," said Carl. "He's been through a lot. He doesn't need you reading him the riot act."

Muttering something about interfering do-gooders, the nurse apparently thought better of tangling further with Carl and left the room.

Carl now came to the side of the bed and placed a hand on Luke's arm. "I've been here for three days, Luke buddy," he said. "I wondered if you were ever going to wake up! Some of these nurses have been asking me when I was going home to take a bath!"

Three days! thought Luke. He'd been out for three days?

"Now that you're awake, I suppose I could break away for a change of clothes. But I'm afraid you're going to be here a while. They're talking about keeping you a week. But guess what! I've got your present right here."

Carl walked across the room and returned a few seconds later carrying the blue and white wrapped gift with the bow on top. He set it on the bed beside Luke.

"The paramedics told me they found it next to you in the bushes beside the drive. It was a good thing someone coming along the road saw your wheelchair and stopped to investigate. You'd only been lying there fifteen or twenty minutes they think. Otherwise, you'd have been a goner, man. What were you doing out there anyway? Somebody give you this Christmas present?"

Luke smiled feebly. He reached out one hand, took hold of the box, then extended it toward his closest friend.

"What?" said Carl.

Luke gestured toward the box, and pushed it closer toward Carl.

"You don't mean….this isn't for *me*?"

Luke nodded with a smile.

"You didn't…I mean—did you wheel yourself all the way

185

to town for this?"

Again Luke nodded.

"You snuck out of the orphanage and nearly got yourself killed, to buy *me* a gift."

A third time Luke nodded.

"You rascal!" laughed Carl. "I don't know what to say, man. Should I save it for Christmas, or do you want me to open it now?"

Luke nodded vigorously.

"Now?"

Luke continued to nod.

"All right. Wow, this is really something. I never expected this!"

Trying to be gentle, but with the vigor of a man, Carl tore at the wrapping paper. He too had grown up as an orphan. To open a gift, *any* gift, was as big a thrill as it is to any child on Christmas morning. Slowly he pulled the paper away and lifted the box lid to see the six inch replica of his own perfect little dream car—his '32 Ford three door Coupe.

Carl shook his head in disbelief then wiped at his eyes with the back of his hand.

"This is about the nicest thing anyone's ever done for me, Luke," he said in a husky voice. "You *are* always paying attention to everyone, even me. This is the best gift I could imagine. Thank you."

The next several days for Luke were a blur of sleep, blood tests, needles and tubes, hospital food, and visits from Carl. He never came without his '32 Ford Coupe replica.

Luke felt perfectly fine two days before they let Carl take him back to the orphanage. But at last the day came when he was pronounced fit enough to be discharged.

"You're outta here, kid," said the white-haired nurse. She tried to keep up a gruff front but in fact had grown more fond of Luke than she would admit. "Looks like you're finally thawed out. "And I don't want to see you back here in the Carnegie wing again anytime soon."

THIRTY-NINE

THE GIFT DRIVE

Tuesday, December 16, 1947

A few days after their first discussion about the gift drive, Janet was intercepted in the hall by Mr. Pratt.

"Janet," he called behind her. She paused as he hurried toward her. "After the enthusiastic response from the other teachers, over the weekend I spoke with the members of our governing Board. They are also excited about your idea of a gift drive. So it's on. Whatever you would like the rest of us to do…"

"That's wonderful, Mr. Pratt!" exclaimed Janet.

"Do you really think there's time? Christmas is only a week away."

"We'll never know if we don't try."

"Then I'll leave the planning of it in your hands."

"I am so happy—thank you," said Janet. "I won't let you down."

They chatted a few more minutes, with the result that Janet was late for Mrs. Warpole's second and third grade class. The youngsters were eagerly waiting for the next installment of the antics of Buster Bear before breaking into smaller groups for more individual reading and writing lessons with the two teachers.

"Good morning, Mrs. Holiday," said several of the children in sing-song unison as she walked in.

"Good morning, children. Good morning, Mrs. Warpole," said Janet. "I'm sorry I'm late."

A six year old girl raised her hand and spoke at the same

time. "That's okay, Mithez Holiday," she said. "We bin good."

"I'm sure you have, Carla. I appreciate that. I'm sure you'll get an extra star today for being so grown up."

"Are you going to read some more about Buster Bear?" asked James, the boy sitting behind Carla.

"I sure am, James. But first you all need to pay attention to Mrs. Warpole. It's not quite reading time yet."

Janet took her place at the back of the class while she waited for Mrs. Warpole to finish the drawing project the children were busy with. She surveyed the class on this day with even greater eyes of compassion. Carla's parents had both been killed in a car accident when she was two. Six year old James was not actually an orphan. He had been found alone at home after a neighbor, hearing him crying, called the sheriff. His parents had left for a weekend in Las Vegas. Authorities had subsequently found stashes of heroin in the garage behind the house. Both parents were now serving time in state prison. Every one of the children could have told his or her own story of pain and loneliness, and the effects could be seen in their eyes. Even so, in the faces of the younger ones could also be seen the innocent hope that life could still be a good thing.

"All right, children," she said thirty minutes later, setting aside *The Adventures of Buster Bear* for the day, "before we break into our reading and writing groups, I have a special and exciting project to tell you about."

The whole class broke into chatter, clamoring close around her where they sat on the floor, full of questions and enthusiasm.

"What is it...what is it, Mrs. Holiday!" they cried with childlike exuberance.

"I'm sure you all know what holiday comes in just eight days," said Janet.

"Christmas!" they yelled together.

"And who comes to visit on Christmas?"

A tiny dark-haired girl raised her hand. "My Aunt Molly and Uncle Bunky come visit me on Christmas."

"And you are very lucky, June," said Janet. "But who comes to visit everyone in the whole world on Christmas?"

"Santa Claus," said Jimmy.

"Yes, Santa Claus!" added Janet, expecting more enthusiasm from the children.

"Mithez Holiday" said Carla, raising her hand.

"Yes, Carla."

"Santa Claus doesn't come here. He doesn't know we're here because we don't have mommies and daddies."

The simple words broke Janet's heart. A lump rose in her throat. She struggled to continue on.

"Well we are going to make sure that Santa knows you're here and knows your names," she said. "Not only that, we're going to make sure that he knows just what special gift to bring each one of you."

"How, Mithez Holiday?"

"We're all going to write him a letter."

"I don't know how to wite, Missus Howiday," said a little boy at the back of the circle.

"Don't worry. Mrs. Warpole and I will help you. That's what we will do in our writing groups tomorrow and for the next few days. We'll write letters to Santa Claus!"

"How will he get the letters?" asked a first grader by the name of Jerry. It was the first time he had spoken to her directly since Janet's arrival.

"Don't worry, Jerry. Mr. Pratt and Mrs. Warpole and I will be sure he reads every letter."

Now at last the room erupted into a excited clamor of chatter and questions and a frenzy of requests.

"I want a doll!"

"I want a truck!"

"I want a toy gun""

"I want a football!"

"Not so fast!" laughed Janet. "We're not going to just write Santa to tell him what we want *ourselves*. Each of you are going to write a secret letter to Santa about one of your classmates."

"A *secret* letter?" said Carla.

"Yes, Carla. You are all going to have to try to find out what would be a special gift for someone *else* in the class, not yourself. Then you will write to Santa and ask him to bring that gift to them."

"You mean we're not going to ask him for presents for

ourselves?" said James.

"That's right. You're going to ask him to bring gifts to others."

Whether the significance of Janet's plan was capable of getting through to children so young was doubtful. But the lesson of giving rather than getting would hopefully take root in their hearts to be remembered in later years.

"Here is what you are going to do," Janet went on. "Carla, you will have to discover what would be a special gift for June or James or Jerry or Mary or Willy. Then you will write a secret letter to Santa. You won't show your letter to anyone else. You will ask Santa to bring them that special gift. James, you will do the same—and so will the rest of you. You have to find out what would be most special to someone else, then tell Santa about it. But you have to keep your letters secret. You will begin today, at lunch and recess and after school, asking the others about their favorite things. And remember, *everyone* in class must be included. So you might even want to write to Santa about more than one of your classmates. Then tomorrow in our writing groups Mrs. Warpole and I will help you begin writing your letters."

As she turned the class back over to Mrs. Warpole, the children were abuzz with excitement. And so it was also in the fourth, fifth, and sixth grade class in the next hour when Janet presented it with the same plan. As the day continued into the upper grades, she modified her presentation, shifting away from "letters to Santa Claus" to "Christmas requests," while still asking every student to turn in a brief letter telling what would make Christmas special to one or more of his or her classmates. Enthusiasm ran high even through the 7th and 8th grade classes. Janet could see their imaginations fired with the idea that even in an orphanage, this Christmas might be more fun than any they could remember.

Once she began presenting her idea to the high school students, however, the cynicism of a few of the more outspoken ones nearly put a damper on it. Janet could hardly blame them. But she was determined not to let *her* enthusiasm be squelched.

"Come on, Mrs. Holiday," complained one of the more irascible twelfth-graders who was chomping at the bit to graduate and get away from the orphanage for good. "Who are we trying to fool? Christmas means nothing here. We have no families. There is no Santa Claus. Christmas isn't a holiday for kids like us with no families."

"I'm sorry you feel that way, Reuben," replied Janet. "But I hope you will give this a chance. Maybe you have no reason to think Christmas is special. But I hope you will find it in your heart to perhaps try to make it special for someone else."

Reuben's only reply was to roll his eyes.

FORTY

A BOY IN A WHEELCHAIR

Wednesday-Thursday, December 17-18, 1947

After school that afternoon, Janet told BJ about her idea, asking if she could put up a notice on the window about the orphanage gift drive.

"It's a fantastic idea, Janet," said the waitress. "Of course we'll put up a notice."

"Not all the children were so enthusiastic," sighed Janet. "A few were cynical about the whole thing. I received nothing but blank sheets of paper from some of the 11th and 12th grade boys, and a few joke-requests."

"Like what?" asked BJ.

"Oh…things like, *What Reuben needs for Christmas is a haircut.* And, *Dear Santa, Stuart has been a bad boy, he shouldn't get anything for Christmas. From your friend, Marco.* Or, *Marco could use some new deodorant.*"

"Well the joke will be on them when they receive something nice," said BJ. "They'll see that they can't spoil the spirit of Christmas."

"I hope so. But the younger ones—you should have seen them. Their enthusiasm is so contagious—the whole orphanage is excited. Their letters were so touching. I cried when I read them asking for Santa to bring gifts to the others in their classes."

"What an ingenious idea. How did you think of it?"

"I don't know," replied Janet. "As soon as I thought of the children writing letters to Santa, the idea popped into my head—How can we turn this away from getting just what *we* want into discovering what would make Christmas special for others."

"I think it's great. I'm sure it will be the best Christmas those children have ever had."

"*If* we can get the gifts."

"You will," nodded BJ. "I know the whole community will pitch in. Once you have a notice in our window, everyone will ask about it. We'll have to get moving quickly — Christmas is next week! I'll talk it up and word will get around. Take one to Harv at the Café too. He'll put it in his window. Word will get around. My husband works at the bank and is a member of the Rotary Club. He'll be able to get business leaders involved. And Holly Sugar — he knows the plant manager. If you have something for me to give him for their bulletin board, I'm sure they'll contribute. They're good about things like that. Word will get around."

"I don't know how to thank you, BJ. You ought to be in charge of this thing!"

"It was your idea."

"I just wish Karen was here. She'd be so excited to see how well you're doing. She was worried about you after...well, you know."

Janet nodded. "What do you think," she asked, " — should we compile a list of the kinds of gifts we're looking for? But I wouldn't want the older children to see a wish-list posted on store windows when they're in town and figure it's a charity drive."

"I see what you mean," nodded BJ. "I'll talk to Ken, that's my husband. Maybe you ought to make a list to be circulated only among business leaders, and perhaps church pastors."

Janet nodded thoughtfully. "I appreciate that," she said. "I'll talk to Mr. Pratt and the staff again to see what they feel is the best way to handle it."

Janet left the Kings Inn forty minutes later exhilarated. She hadn't been this excited about Christmas since Leslie was a girl.

She was walking down the corridor late the following morning on the way to her room. She saw the crippled young man from her English class rolling toward her from the opposite direction in his wheelchair. He reached the classroom a second or two ahead of her. He reached for the knob from his chair and opened the door, then with some difficulty inched backward and held the door open for her.

"Why thank you!" said Janet, pausing and smiling down at him. "You are such a gentleman...Luke, isn't it?"

The boy nodded and returned her smile.

"Don't bother wasting your time talking to Luke, Mrs. Holiday," said Marco as he walked by on his way to 12th grade History. "His elevator doesn't go all the way to the top floor, if you get me. Never said a word in his life."

"Knock it off, Marco," said Gary, coming up behind them. "Hi, Mrs. Holiday. And forget what he said — Luke's okay, he just can't talk. But he's just as smart as any of the rest of us. Here...I'll hold the door. — Luke, you and Mrs. Holiday go on in."

"Thank you, Gary," said Janet. "I knew about your trip to Denver from Carl, Luke," she added as she walked into the room. Luke steered his wheelchair in after her, with Gary following. "But then after only a couple days in class, you disappeared again. I hear you had an accident and were in the hospital. I am glad to see you are okay."

Luke nodded and smiled again.

"I would love to hear about your time in Denver and get to know you better," said Janet. "Hopefully we will have time to visit later."

Janet walked to the front of the classroom as the students bustled the way to their seats. Two or three more arrivals walked in and sat down.

"Before we begin today," said Janet, "since he was in the hospital last week, I think we should tell Luke about our Christmas gift letters. — Luke," she said, looking to the back of the room where Luke sat in his wheelchair at a table which every classroom had for him instead of a regular desk, "all the students have written gift requests for Christmas, telling what they believe would make Christmas especially meaningful for one or more of their fellow students. The others have all turned theirs in already, but if you would like to —"

"Don't bother with him, Mrs. Holiday," interrupted a 10th grader named Rusty, a known troublemaker. "He's in his own world. He can't talk or read or write or do anything. How's he going to know anything about the rest of us? Lights on but nobody's home, know what I mean."

A few muttered comments and snickers circulated amongst the older boys.

"Mr. Collins, please keep your comments to yourself." Janet glanced quickly down at her class list. There was only one Luke on it. "—Mr. Kirch," she went on, "I'm sorry to have to ask, but since I only met you for the first time last week...can you write?"

Luke nodded as she went on.

"Very good," Janet continued. "Then if you would like to write out your suggestions for Christmas gifts for one or two of your fellow students, I will include it with the others."

"Yeah, Luke," said Rusty. "Tell her I want a '32 duce coupe. And while we're at it, why don't you get yourself a new wheelchair!"

"That will do, Rusty," said Janet sternly. "What kind of talk is that at Christmas?"

"What does he care? He can't understand what we're saying anyway. He's just a r—"

"Rusty! Stop it! Another comment like that out of you and I'll send you to Mr. Pratt."

"Yeah, and what's that old bag of wind going to do to me?"

As the class settled down, Janet proceeded with the day's discussion of the book they were reading. She glanced every so often toward Luke in his wheelchair at the back of the room. Despite what Rusty had said, and though he had missed all but three days in the entire school year thus far, the boy called Luke seemed completely engaged in the discussion. The look in his eyes, she thought, was an expression of knowing, concentration, and thoughtfulness. It was anything but vacant. As his eyes darted about the room following the discussion, then rested upon her whenever she was speaking. She recognized it as the expression of intelligence and insight.

FORTY-ONE

A SURPRISING LIST

Friday, December 19, 1947

After the expression she had noted in his eyes, Janet was not exactly surprised with what greeted her at 11:15 the following morning when she returned to her classroom for 11ᵗʰ and 12ᵗʰ grade English. On her desk, written in a strong legible hand, was a two-page list of Christmas suggestions from the mute boy named Luke Kirch. Luke was at his place at the back of the room, reading a book waiting for class to begin.

After scanning them briefly, still holding the papers, Janet walked back toward him. Luke heard her step and glanced up.

"Thank you for this, Luke," she said. "I must say, this is a very enterprising list. I will look forward to reading it in more detail. I appreciate very much the time and effort you put into it."

Luke smiled and nodded.

"What's that you're reading?" said Janet, glancing down at the hard cover book laying open on the table in front of him. He took it and handed it up to her. Her eyebrows went up as she saw the title.

"*David Copperfield*," she said in surprise. "This is some very advanced reading."

Luke shrugged and smiled again.

"If you're reading this—most of my 12ᵗʰ graders couldn't that's for sure!—you're probably not feeling very challenged by our discussion of *Robinson Crusoe*."

Luke reached for a blank sheet of paper. Quickly he wrote

down a message and handed it to Janet.

No — I love Robinson Crusoe, Janet read. *I've read it three times. I am enjoying the discussion very much.*

"Good," smiled Janet. "I wish you could participate."

Again Luke scribbled a hasty message.

I am…just silently.

Janet chuckled. "I'm glad. Still, I would like to know what you're thinking. Perhaps we shall write papers on the book when we're through."

As the students filed into the classroom, a few of their eyes were drawn with curiosity to the apparently one-sided conversation taking place in the corner of the room between wheelchair boy and their middle aged English teacher. Mrs. Holiday was talking to him like he was a normal person!

That evening, alone in her hotel room, eyes blurry with tears, Janet could hardly believe what she was reading. In her hands she held the two pages the handicapped, wheelchair-bound 11th grader Luke Kirch had handed her shortly before lunch that morning. After three months at the orphanage, here was a boy who, in the few days she had known him, had already added new interest to her upper grades English class. She certainly had not yet met any others who were reading the classics of English Literature in their spare time!

Once more Janet read what Luke had written.

Mrs. Holiday,

I assume this will remain just between me and you. I would not want the others to know what I have observed about them. They would not be able to see that I care about them. But I watch and listen. I hear what they say. I see the looks in their eyes. They pay no attention to me. But I want them to be happy, and have good memories of Christmas.

You probably know Marco. He is in the 12th grade. He is afraid of leaving the orphanage when he graduates. He doesn't know what he will do. He takes out his insecurity on younger children. If I could give him any Christmas gift in the world, it would be something that gives him confidence in himself so that he will know that he can be a success in life. Robinson Crusoe helped me learn that a person can overcome any obstacle in life — whether it's being marooned on an island, or being marooned in a wheelchair.

Stuart is in the 11th grade. He makes fun of others and calls them names. But it's only because he is lonely inside. He is the school's best soccer player. He lives for soccer and I know he would like nothing better than his own soccer ball.

Sally is in 10th grade. She is actually a pretty girl, but she has pimples and is very self-conscious. I'm sure she would love a make-up kit. But she shouldn't be the only one to receive one or it might embarrass her. Probably many of the high school girls would also like one.

Little Ralph, who is a first grader, was abused I think and first came to the orphanage almost in rags. I'm sure he would like a cool new shirt and pair of shoes.

Reuben is also getting ready to graduate. He is unbelievably artistic. He has so much talent. It would be great for him to have some art supplies to pursue his talent after he graduates.

Jennifer is in 7th grade and is a great reader. She is always in the library. She loves grown up fairy tales. The library has some books by a man named George MacDonald that she is fond of. If there were others by him she could receive, she would love them.

Steven is in the 9th grade. He struggles with school. He needs some books that are easy to read but that do not look like juvenile books — mysteries and adventures perhaps that would spark his interest and make him know that he can be a good reader.

Rusty, a 10th grader thinks he has to be tough. He is always egging the other boys on trying to pick fights. A pair of boxing gloves would be something he would like and he could work out his aggression without actually fighting the other boys. Maybe one of the men like Carl could give him boxing lessons, and at the same time Rusty would find out that he is not as tough as he thinks he is. I'm pretty sure Carl would give him more than he could handle.

Tom is in 5th grade. He is new to the orphanage this year. I remember what it is like to be new. It is very hard. Tom is a good basketball player, but sometimes the boys in his class don't choose him for their teams just to be mean. If he had a basketball of his own, I think it would make this hard time easier for him.

Angela, a sweet soft-spoken 11th grade girl, is very imaginative and likes to write stories. But she is too shy to share them. Most of her teachers have no idea what a good writer she is. I know she would really like a writing set similar to the one Carl gave me as a gift several Christmases ago...

And so it went. Luke had thoughtful and insightful suggestions for thirty or more boys and girls at the orphanage, from every single class—from clothes and books, to sporting equipment and toys and dolls. His list, along with those she had already received, would be all she needed for the gift drive.

Sadly, however, not a single boy or girl in the school mentioned Luke in their gift recommendations. His keen awareness of their needs and aspirations and silent hurts was certainly not reciprocated. They had no eyes to see beyond the wheelchair, and what lay within him deeper than the silence of his tongue. Yet he was almost like an invisible angel, watching and listening in his silence, doing everything he could for the good of those around him.

"Your suggestions have been very helpful to me, Luke," said Janet after class. "But what about you? What would *you* like for Christmas?"

Luke thought a moment, then reached for a piece of paper.

I don't need any presents, Mrs. Holiday, Janet read. *God gives me my very own special gift every Christmas Eve, a wonderful dream where I get to be normal. I look forward to it all the time. But if there is one thing I do wish for, it is someday to be to be part of a family again.*

Normal, young Mr. Kirch? Janet thought with a smile. *You are so far beyond normal already as to be the envy of any teacher or parent!*

Forty-Two

Mysterious Encounter

Monday, December 22, 1947

Janet hardly dared hope that the gift drive would actually produce every gift the children had listed. But as Christmas approached, the entire business community of Eaglescliff, men's groups, women's groups, and all the town's churches, became caught up in it. In less than a week requests were pouring in to her mailbox at the orphanage and to BJ at The Kings Inn for lists of what was wanted. Businesses were not merely posting flyers in their storefronts, they were donating toys and clothes and books. BJ had enlisted what amounted to an army of mothers making pick-ups from merchants and various drop-off locations. There, Janet and Carl and others of the staff pitched in to match gifts with the Christmas lists the boys and girls had filled out. The most difficult part was keeping it from the children.

With Christmas holidays starting after the previous Friday's school day, most of the teachers were glad for the two week break. Several left town. They were wholeheartedly supportive of Janet's efforts, but not to the extent that they wanted to spend every waking minute on it. They had families of their own to make Christmas plans for. Thus it was that most of the matching and wrapping of gifts fell to Janet and Carl and a few others. But Janet had never felt so much purpose in her life. Watching her brain child take wings was so exciting that she was anticipating Christmas almost with the joy as if she were a child herself.

A few days before Christmas, Janet walked into The Kings

Inn shortly after one o'clock for a brief lunch. BJ came over and sat down to chat a few minutes with Janet.

"It will all be over soon!" said BJ. "This week's been a madhouse."

"I can't thank you enough for all you've done," said Janet.

"I wouldn't have missed it for the world. I only wish Karen could be part of it."

Mention of Karen reminded Janet that she was anxious to see Karen for another reason, for the reason that had brought her to Eaglescliff in the first place—to find out exactly when Leslie's baby had been born in Wheatland, and thus how old her grandson would be.

"When will she be back?" asked Janet.

"Her family left for West Virginia over the weekend to join her. Her husband told me they will come back just after New Year's. So, do you have everything organized at the home?"

"There's still a lot to do. Carl and the older boys put up a big Christmas tree a few days ago. The children are having fun decorating it. But we're frantically trying to keep them away from the room where we're storing and wrapping and labeling the gifts."

"I'll make one more swing through the stores today and tomorrow," said BJ. "I'll have the last of the gifts at the home by tomorrow afternoon."

"I need to stop by a couple of churches this afternoon that have been collecting gifts," said Janet. "It will definitely be a busy next twenty-four hours!"

Two hours later, feeling a great sense of relief, Janet walked out of the last church on her pick up list. Boxes of toys and clothes and puzzles and books and candy and fruit were stuffed into every corner of the used car she had been renting for the past month from the Studebaker dealer. She was still nervous about driving on snow and ice. But she could not have done everything she needed to do this past week relying solely on Jimmy's taxi. Slowly she pulled out of the church parking lot and made her way on slushy streets back to the orphanage.

She parked near a side door and hurried into the building to find Carl and Mr. Crosby and his wife to help her sneak the last of the unwrapped gifts into the storeroom. Jeanie, busily wrapping at one of the long tables, saw her walk in.

"Janet, a message came for you."

"A message — who from?"

"A Pastor Emmanuel from All Saints Church. He has some gifts for you."

"I don't know the name. Did he call or bring the message himself?"

"I don't know actually," replied Jeanie. "I just found a note on my desk. No one knows who delivered it."

"Well I will follow up on it as soon as we get my car unloaded."

Thirty minutes later, Janet was on her way back into town. She had attended All Saints a couple times since arriving in Eaglescliff. She did not remember the name Emmanuel. She turned off Main Street, drove another half block, and pulled in next to the curb alongside the building. The church was long and narrow, its lower walls of yellow stone, with beautiful blue stained glass windows accenting the stone construction above. As she climbed out of the car, the tones of what sounded like a children's choir wafted from inside out into the chilly afternoon. The pleasant smell of smoke from neighborhood fireplaces drifted through the air. The sight of the church, combined with the angelic sounds of children's voices singing *O Little Town of Bethlehem,* filled her with peace.

Her breath hung on the air as she approached the building and pulled open one of two huge dark oak doors. A sense of mystery stole over her as she walked into the dimly lit narthex. The singing, of which she had caught but a foretaste outside, met her as a wave of the purest music she had ever heard. Its crystalline beauty took her breath away. She paused a moment at the simplicity and complexity of the harmonies reverberating from inside.

She walked into the sanctuary. It was both familiar, yet strangely new. Hundreds of candles were scattered about, accompanied by dimly lit lanterns hanging on chains from the high, vaulted wood ceiling. Even as her eyes adjusted to the thin light, the stained glass windows above seemed to glow with a strange luminescence. Where their light came from she could not imagine, for the day was advanced and it was nearly dark outside.

Janet stood as one enchanted by a strange spell. The choir of young angels began *O Holy Night,* her favorite Christmas carol. Tears spilled down her cheeks as she listened. They were tears of a thousand emotions and longings and hopes all in one—joy and sorrow, loneliness and yet with it a strange new sense of purpose. She was alone. Yet as she stood listening she felt somehow embraced in love.

Faces and names and images filled not just her mind but her heart—Karen and BJ and Mr. Pratt and Jeanie and Carl and Mr. Crosby and his wife and Mrs. Warpole and even the Cracker…the faces of every boy and girl in the orphanage…faces of those she had grown to love. Then rose in her mind's eye the faces of her beloved Jack and Leslie. Instead of sadness, a wonderful joy filled her heart, the joy of knowing they were together.

Then another face rose in her mind…a face without features. The face of Leslie's son.

She had no time to contemplate what all these sensations meant. In the midst of her reverie, a man's voice spoke.

"Hello, Janet," it said. "I am glad to meet you at last."

It was a voice of peace, as pure in tone as the sounds of the angel voices of the children behind him. Their song reached its crescendo at that very moment—*The night…when Christ was born.*

Janet glanced up. A man approached. Somehow the church was no longer dark. The beams of light slanting down from the stained glass windows, if anything, grew brighter. Shafts of whiteness rested upon the man's shoulders and head, almost as if the light from the windows was following his step.

"I am John Emmanuel," he went on. "This is quite a project you have set in motion in this town. I'm sure it will make many people happy, including those who receive the gifts you have made possible."

"I hope so," replied Janet. "I don't think I know you, yet you seem to know me. Do you preach here?"

"No. I am not especially fond of preaching. But I am always here. I am most often in the background. I am one who prefers to watch."

203

Peabody Public Library
Columbia City, IN

"Who are the children?" Janet asked, glancing to the front of the sanctuary where three rows of boys and girls stood in purple and white robes. "I've been to church here a time or two. There has been no mention of a children's choir. They sing like angels."

Pastor Emmanuel smiled. "Yes, they do indeed!" he said, a hint of humor in his tone. "They are some of my younger charges. They are practicing for the big show tomorrow night. They only sing once a year, you see."

"I've never heard anything so divine."

Unexpectedly, Janet began to cry. The next moment, she found herself taking a tissue from Pastor Emmanuel's hand. He was staring straight into her.

"I don't know what's wrong with me," she said, half laughing as she dabbed at her nose and eyes. "I think the music must be getting to me. I've had a pretty emotional year. This will be my first Christmas alone."

"I understand," he nodded. "Yes, I know something of your history, and the two losses you have suffered."

"Word does get around in a small town I suppose."

Again he smiled a knowing smile. "Do not let your heart be troubled, Janet. You will not be alone."

Janet nodded and tried to smile.

"You are facing one of the great challenges in life down here," the mysterious Pastor Emmanuel went on. "Circumstances often seem unfair, painful, and wrong. Yet it is possible even for the most trying of circumstances to strengthen us and bring comfort. Suffering molds us into people of strength that we could not become otherwise. It is all part of the great plan. But you must believe, and not lose heart."

"That is very hard to do," said Janet.

"If it were not hard, it would not be capable of molding us into men and women of character. It is the *testing* of your faith that produces strength. You are growing stronger than you have any idea."

Janet tried to smile again. "I guess I'll have to take your word for it," she said. "I certainly don't feel strong. I feel weaker than I ever have in my life."

Pastor Emmanuel took in her words as if they were

exactly what he had hoped to hear. His eyes glistened as he nodded with a smile but did not reply.

Janet glanced at her watch. "But...did I understand correctly that you have some gifts for the children at the home?'"

"We do. It has given us great joy to select them and wrap them. They are out in the narthex."

He turned and led the way toward the front of the church. A great stack of wrapped presents sat near the door. Janet had not seen them when she had come in.

"You will see that they are already labeled."

"Do you know all the children at the orphanage?" asked Janet.

"I do. Let me give you a hand carrying them to your car."

The two made three trips back and forth from the front door to the sidewalk. Janet's car was nearly full again!

She thanked Pastor Emmanuel once more. As she turned to go, he spoke.

"With all your efforts to bring joy to others, Janet," he said, "what gift would be most special for *you* this Christmas?"

Surprised by his question, Janet answered hastily. "I don't know, there's nothing I need," she said. "Christmas is for children."

"We are all God's children, Janet," said Pastor Emmanuel. "What does the child in you want this Christmas?"

This time his probing eyes caused her to reflect more deeply.

"I came here looking for my daughter," she answered after a moment. "Now that I know I will never find her, I can only hope to find my grandson. That is the only thing I really want."

Pastor Emmanuel nodded. His expression seemed to say that he had already known the answer. He smiled again, turned, and walked back toward the church. Janet stared after him. He climbed the steps, opened the door, and turned one final time and lifted a hand toward her. As he disappeared inside, as the door closed behind him, a flash of brilliant whiteness shone from within.

Then the door closed, and the light was gone.

Janet was left standing on the sidewalk in the gathering darkness. A mysterious peace rested about her and within her. Then came the haunting refrain from the young angel choir echoing one final time from behind the stone walls of the church, *O night divine…O night…when Christ was born.*

FORTY-THREE

MYSTERIOUS GIFTS

Janet arrived back at the orphanage and found the others wrapping the last of the gifts.

"I don't know how to break this to you," she said as she walked in, "but I have another whole carload of presents!"

A few good natured groans sounded, as Carl and Bert and Mr. Pratt dropped what they were doing to help her unload.

"But this is the strange thing," Janet added. "They're already all wrapped. And labeled."

A few minutes later, with the gifts from the church all stacked on one of the tables, the five gathered around looking at the brightly colored packages and labels. The boxes were of all sizes and shapes, and labeled for children in the home ranging in age from three to eighteen.

"This is amazing," said Jeanie. "How could the people at the church have known what to give them. Look—here's one to Reuben. Nobody in that church could know him! He would never set foot inside a church. And he's from the western part of the state. I don't think he knows a soul in Eaglescliff."

Janet thought of Reuben's comment in her class on the day she had announced the gift drive. *Christmas means nothing here. We have no families. There is no Santa Claus.*

Maybe you're wrong about that, Reuben! she thought to herself.

"And look," Jeanie continued, "here's one addressed to Lyle and Lydia Kingsbury."

"Who are they?" asked Bert Crosby.

"Seven year old twins," replied Mr. Pratt. "They only arrived at the home yesterday—from Casper."

"How could anyone know they are here?" said Janet,

shaking her head.

"Did you know they were coming, Charles?" asked Bert's wife Mary.

The principal shook his head. "I only found out two days ago. It's a sad case. When they arrived they were dressed in old torn clothes several sizes too big. They smelled as if they hadn't taken a bath in weeks. Neither of them said a word. They just huddled together. Their poor fearful eyes—they didn't know what they were doing here."

"There was something very mysterious about that Pastor Emmanuel when he was giving me the gifts," said Janet.

"Pastor Emmanuel—who's that?" asked Mr. Pratt.

"I had a message from him to pick these up at All Saints Church."

"Never heard of him. I thought I knew all the ministers in town."

"And look," said Carl, holding up a small green box wrapped in shiny green paper with a bright red ribbon on top. "This one is labeled for Janet Holiday. How do you rate, Janet! You're the only staff member with your name on one."

"It must be a mistake!" laughed Janet, looking the box over.

"No mistake—there's your name!"

"You're the one whose mistaken, Carl," now said Bert. "Janet's not the only one. Here's a little package with *your* name on it!"

"You've got to be kidding!" laughed Carl. Bert handed him the tiny box which was only three inches square. Curiosity getting the better of him, Carl gave it a shake.

"Sounds like there's something inside all right!" laughed Bert. "Do you collect marbles, Carl!"

"Can't be a marble. It doesn't roll around."

"It looks like you and I will just have to wait to find out about our mysterious gifts, Carl. And I don't know about the rest of you," said Janet, "but I'm bushed. I'm ready to call it a day. Once the gifts are under the tree, I think we'll be just about ready for Christmas!" Janet turned for the door.

"You'll be here for the Christmas Eve party?" asked Jeanie.

"Oh yes—I wouldn't miss it. Don't worry—I'll be here!"

FORTY-FOUR
THE TWELFTH DREAM—
THE DAY BEFORE CHRISTMAS

Wednesday, December 24, 1947

Luke enjoyed Christmas Eve dinner, but as always on this most special night of the year, he was mostly anticipating what lay ahead. It was the one night of the year when the *real* Luke came alive again.

This was also his seventeenth birthday. Although a lot of students and several teachers still considered him an imbecile, over the years he had gradually made enough friends that he was a favorite in the hearts of many. His smile and sweet spirit had at last reaped their rewards, as had the recognition of his intelligence for those who would admit it. Far from thinking him retarded, there were not a few, especially among the younger children whom he was always eager to help with their homework, who regarded him as a genius. This view had gradually come to be shared by a few others. Indeed, his silence created an aura of mystery that, for so long an object of abuse among his fellows, had gradually now become a sense of wonder.

Part of Christmas Eve celebration at the orphanage, as in the past, was the addition of Luke's birthday cake, circled now with seventeen candles, following supper. Not all the teachers at the school attended every orphanage function, especially during Christmas when many were busy with their own families. But Luke made a special effort to invite Mrs. Holiday to the Christmas Eve dinner. In the short time since he had been back from the hospital, he had grown fonder of her than all his other teachers. He felt a special affinity towards her that he couldn't explain. He knew she *understood*. She never talked down to him. She had challenged him in his reading and writing in just a few days beyond what the others in the class were capable of. Recognizing his abilities, she had delighted him by giving him *extra* work to do over the Christmas break. More than anyone other than Carl, he wanted to share his special day with Mrs. Holiday.

The spirit at the orphanage was different this Christmas. Excitement was in the air. The younger children especially were abuzz with anticipation. Rumors had been spreading for several days that the Christmas tree they had decorated would be found Christmas morning with more presents beneath it than any of them had ever seen in their lives. How the rumor began, no one knew. One of the intrepid fifth graders claimed to have seen Mr. Pratt, Carl, and Mr. Crosby carrying brightly colored packages to the Christmas present room, which had been locked once the decorating was complete. It was enough to set the place on fire with speculation. Nor could the smiles and suspicious answers of, "You'll just have to wait until Christmas morning," from the staff to the questions of the eager youngsters dispel their feverish curiosity. Indeed, the expression on the smiling faces of the adults said clearly enough that they knew more than they were telling.

Luke was swept up in the frenzy of anticipation along with everyone else. He thus remained longer than usual into the evening for the Christmas Eve party. A few of the younger children followed him about and clustered around his wheelchair, chattering away and asking him a hundred questions at once about what he thought they would find in the locked Christmas present room. They all knew that he had never spoken a word in his life. But they had learned to watch his face, his eyes, his lips, and observe every glance and gesture for what he might be saying by other means than sound.

"It seems that you have quite a fan club, Mr. Kirch!" said Janet as she approached with a glass of eggnog in her hand.

"Mrs. Holiday…Mrs. Holiday…please tell us if there are presents!" clamored a half dozen voices at once as the little band of youngsters scurried toward her.

"Luke won't tell us!" said Carla.

Janet laughed. "How could he tell you, Carla?"

"He writes us notes, Mrs. Holiday," said James.

"I see what you mean. But even if Luke knew more than you, do you think he would tell?"

"He would tell *me*," insisted Carla.

Luke now joined Janet in laughter. Their eyes met briefly. A chill swept through Janet. But she had no time to think what it meant. Little James was tugging at her elbow.

"But you know, don't you, Mrs. Holiday?" he said. "Won't you *please* tell us?"

"I can't, James. I promised Santa that I would say nothing."

"You promised *Santa*!" he said with wide eyes. Hearing the word, the other children clustered closer.

Unobtrusively, Luke backed his wheelchair away, turned, and slowly made his way unobserved for the door. Once out of the cafeteria where the annual party was held, he made for the service elevator. He was usually in bed almost by now on Christmas Eve. It had been an enjoyable evening. Being around the younger children was exhilarating. But they would be going up to their rooms soon themselves.

Luke emerged three minutes later into the fifth floor corridor, now empty and silent, and wheeled himself down the hall to his room. Carl usually accompanied him to his bed on Christmas Eve. It had been their tradition for years, even after Luke was able to get around on his own. But he had seen Carl enjoying himself downstairs. The staff as well as the children seemed buoyed and energized and excited by this Christmas season. He was well able to get himself to the bathroom and ready for bed.

Half an hour later Luke pulled his blankets up over his shoulders, lay back contentedly, and opened his copy of *Sir Gibbie* from the library. He would read until the delicious warmth of sleep took him over.

When Luke awoke, he was surprised to find himself standing beside his own bed at the orphanage. He was gazing down at a seventeen year old boy sound asleep in his bed. He was looking at himself!

He stood staring for several long seconds, then tried his legs. He danced a brief jig to make sure his feet were working again. His body felt strong and healthy and full of life.

Then what was he doing here!

The next thing he did was look around for Vanessa. He turned and left the room, his own room, and wandered up and down the empty corridor. Vanessa was nowhere to be seen. The hallway was deserted just as he had seen it only a short while earlier.

Luke continued in the opposite direction from the way he usually went. Soon he was walking down the main stairway. He had never walked down these stairs before. On the fourth floor he heard the sounds of the younger children being put to bed, still full of questions about Christmas and Santa Claus and presents and the Christmas tree room.

Down he continued to the ground floor. Everything looked familiar yet different. Slowly he made his way toward the rear of the orphanage, and to the cafeteria where the party was still in progress. The room was full of talk and laughter. The record player was playing Christmas recordings.

Luke walked into the room. No one saw him. There was Carl talking to Mrs. Holiday. He moved toward them.

"Hi, Carl," said Luke. "Hi, Mrs. Holiday."

"...haven't seen Luke anywhere, have you?" Carl had just asked.

"Hey, Carl!" laughed Luke. "I'm right here!"

"No," replied Janet. "He and I were talking with some of the younger children, then I turned around and he had disappeared."

"He always goes to bed early on Christmas Eve," said Carl.

Luke stood listening. This was like none of his dreams before. He had the peculiar sensation that Carl and Mrs. Holiday really were talking about him. They were in his dream, but they could not see him in their world.

"Why is that?" he heard Janet ask.

"Every year he has what he calls an angel dream," replied Carl.

"He is writing a paper for my class about that. I've only read the first few pages. I thought it was only a story."

"Oh, no. It's real enough," said Carl. "Luke says it's the most real night of the year for him. By the way – what's with the two gifts for you and me that were in that batch from the church you visited? Why us?"

"I've been wondering that too."

"You haven't secretly opened yours yet?"

"No," laughed Janet. "It's still in the locked room with the others. What about you?"

"I took mine with me, but I haven't opened it yet. There's something strange about it. I'm saving it for just the right time."

Luke saw Carl look intently into Mrs. Holiday's face.

"I understand it has been a difficult year for you," he said. "I heard that you lost your husband. I am very sorry."

"Thank you," nodded Janet.

"I'm still unsure how you came to be in Eaglescliff. I heard you were from Dallas. Do you have family here?"

"I thought my daughter was here. But I recently learned that she was killed several years ago."

"I'm sorry—I didn't know that. What a difficult Christmas this must be for you. It makes all your efforts to make it special for the children all the more wonderful. I'm sure God will greatly bless your work."

Janet smiled. "I almost feel that the loss of my husband and daughter makes me an orphan in a way too. Maybe that's why I've grown to love these boys and girls so much. But actually," she added, lowering her voice as if speaking in confidence for Carl's ears only, "I had an ulterior motive in taking this job."

"What was that?" asked Carl.

"My daughter had a son. There is a chance he is here. If so, he is my own grandson."

"Your grandson!"

Janet nodded.

"Do you know who he is?" asked Carl eagerly.

"No. I don't even know how old he is or when he was born. Every day when I look into the eyes of the boys, I silently wonder if one of them is my Leslie's—"

Their conversation was interrupted by the arrival of one of the very young men Janet had been thinking of.

"Hi, Mrs. Holiday…hey, Carl—Merry Christmas!" said Gary.

"Hello, Gary," said Janet, probing his eyes and the features of his face far more than Gary realized. "Merry Christmas to you too."

"Sorry to hear you had to sell your Coupe, Carl," said Gary. "It was such a hot ride."

The voices of the three began to blur together. Luke's eyes strayed from them as he looked for the one person he was most anxious to see.

Why wasn't Vanessa here? He continued to look around the

213

room. The older students and teachers and staff were chatting and drinking Christmas eggnog. But where was Vanessa!

Suddenly Vanessa's words returned to him from last year, the last time they had been together. She had grown quiet, almost sad, and then had spoken the words he did not want to remember:

"I have a strange feeling that I'm not going to see you again. I think this is my last dream."

"We will meet again!" he had insisted.

"I don't think so, not like this. This is the last dream. I know it sounds peculiar, but I have the feeling that somehow you saved my life."

Around him the cafeteria and the Christmas party and Carl and Mrs. Holiday, and Mr. Pratt across the room talking to Rusty and Mr. Crosby, all began to fade and blur. Their voices grew faint.

Suddenly across the room, at the far end of the cafeteria, he saw a man standing looking at him – staring straight into his eyes.

It was the Shepherd from the oasis! But he was dressed like any man might be dressed today – in a suit like a teacher or perhaps a minister.

The man smiled and lifted one hand, and beckoned Luke toward him. He started speaking softly, almost in a whisper, and Luke heard what he was saying.

"Never be ashamed of who you are, Luke," he said. "Every obstacle you have faced in your life, every challenge you have overcome, has molded you into a young man I am proud of – a child I am happy to call my own. And now, Luke, it is time. Come with me. This is the last dream."

As Luke walked toward the man with the smiling eyes, he began to fade from view, then disappeared completely. Luke's heart grew suddenly warm within him. He didn't know how, but he could feel the man living inside his heart and his mind. His eyes seemed to open a little more to those around him.

Luke left the cafeteria and returned up the stairs of the orphanage, to the second, the third, the fourth, and finally to the fifth floor where his own room was located. The deserted corridor reminded him of another corridor he had seen. It reminded him of Vanessa...another dream, long ago.

"I know this place," she had said.

As he remembered her words, unconsciously Luke turned to look at the sign they had seen on the wall. But this was not the same dream. He was in the fifth floor corridor of the orphanage. An image rose before him of the nurse saying good bye to him when he left the hospital two weeks ago after his accident. But he could not remember her final words.

Luke continued along the hallway, then opened the door of his room.

He paused and looked back. All was empty and quiet. An eerie feeling came over him, as if he were saying good bye to this place.

He had once hated this hallway, this building, this orphanage, this room that he called his home. Now the thought of leaving it filled him with fond memories. Wherever he was bound, he would miss it.

This was where he had learned to be a man.

Suddenly a voice sounded in his mind, "Come find me, Luke...come find me at the Carnegie Wing." He spun around and looked down the hall in one direction, then the other.

"Vanessa...Vanessa!" he tried to cry out. But no words would come.

He knew it had been her voice! He would recognize it anywhere. "Come find me, Luke...come find me at the Carnegie Wing." She repeated.

What was she saying? What did it mean?

Slowly Luke walked into the room. The door closed behind him. He lay down in the bed...fell asleep...and knew no more.

FORTY-FIVE

CHRISTMAS EVE

After leaving the Christmas Eve party, exhausted from the long day, Janet let herself into the locked Christmas present room. She found the small green package with her name on it where she had placed it with the rest. She took it with her and left the orphanage. Tomorrow was for the children not her. This was her first Christmas without Jack. She would open her one gift—and from a stranger no less!—alone. Carl told her he had removed his gift too. Why the two of them had been singled out remained a mystery.

As she left the orphanage and drove into town in her rented car, the streets were mostly quiet. She could not help being reminded of the Christmas Eve ten years before when her daughter had also been out and a drunk driver had taken her life. She cried most of the way back to the hotel. Christmas was supposed to be a happy time, a family time. Holiday lights and empty streets would always remind her of the last night of Leslie's life.

But she had to move on. Life did not stand still. She had begun to find a new sense of purpose by investing in young lives who, like her, had no families with whom to share Christmas. She was happy about what they had accomplished. But Christmas would always bring melancholy memories. She knew she would cry again.

The temperature was well below freezing. They were predicting a white Christmas, though when the snow would actually arrive was anyone's guess.

A message was waiting for her at the hotel desk from Annie. She went to the pay phone and returned the call.

"Hi, Annie—it's Janet. Merry Christmas," she said when she heard the familiar voice of her best friend on the line.

"Janet—you're out late on Christmas Eve!"

"Big Christmas Eve party at the orphanage."

"How's the gift drive going?"

"It's been unbelievable, Annie. There are more gifts than I dreamed possible."

"Every one of the children will have one?"

"Probably two. They are so excited! They all helped decorate the tree earlier this week, then we locked the room tonight and put the presents under it. Presents nearly fill the room. I doubt if the younger children will sleep they are so excited. They don't actually know what's going on, but they suspect, and rumors about a huge pile of gifts are running through the orphanage. It's really been fun."

"You sound excited too."

"I am. Giving these poor kids a Christmas is one of the best things I've ever done."

"You seem happy, Janet. I am so glad."

"It's a mixed blessing. How can I not think of Leslie? She died during the holidays. I'm missing Jack more than ever now too. But to see the faces of these children can't help but bring love to your heart. So in that way, yes, I suppose I am happy."

"I got the gift you sent—thank you."

"You didn't open it already!"

"No, I'm just thanking you in advance. Yours is on the way. I sent it to the hotel. Sorry, but I was a little late."

"Don't worry about it," said Janet. "I have another gift to open tomorrow."

"Who from?"

"Actually, someone I'd never met before yesterday—a pastor in town...an interesting encounter. A long story. I'll tell you about it later."

"We all really miss you and love you. Merry Christmas, Janet."

"And to you, Annie, and your family. Tell them all I love them and miss them. You probably don't know this, but your family really taught me a lot when I was so bitter over Jack's death."

"Really? You'll have to tell me all about it someday. Call again when you can. I want to hear how your Christmas goes."

"I will."

Janet wearily climbed the stairs to her room. After a bath, she lay down in bed. As she reached for the light on the nightstand beside her, she glanced across the room. There sat the wrapped present on the table where she had put it. An overwhelming wave of curiosity swept through her.

No, she thought. She would save it for the morning. She turned off the light and lay in darkness, unable to stop thinking about the gift that was awaiting her. She was just as bad as the little children.

Visions of the mysterious pastor with the smiling eyes filled her mind as sleep overtook her.

As she lay in bed, she had to admit, she couldn't wait for Christmas morning to come! It *was* almost like being a child again.

FORTY-SIX

EARLY CHRISTMAS MORNING

Suddenly Luke awoke. Something had startled him out of his sleep, as if a voice had called him.

Memories of his recent dream filtered back into his consciousness. Had he *dreamed* the conversation between Carl and Mrs. Holiday? Or was it real?

Their voices gradually came back to him, now echoing into his brain with the reality of true waking.

…recently lost your husband, Carl had said. *I am very sorry…heard you were from Dallas…*

Like an electric current, his mother's words to him the night she died shot into Luke's brain. *"I've got a surprise for you Luke. We are going to turn over a new leaf this coming year. I sent your grandma and grandpa in Dallas a letter letting them know we will be coming to see them. I've been saving up for months. In a couple of weeks we will have enough to buy bus tickets to go see them. Does that sound fun?"*

Dallas. He had forgotten. His mother had come from Dallas!

Now Mrs. Holiday's words returned to him with vivid, stunning clarity.

…thought my daughter was here…she was killed several years ago…silently wonder if one of them is my Leslie's…

Leslie, thought Luke. It was his mother's name!

Then came words that made Luke's eyes shoot open in the darkness.

My daughter had a son…a chance he is here…he would be my own grandson.

Almost at exactly the same moment, a flash of white light

219

from the window awakened Janet in her hotel room. She glanced around in the dark. Where had the light come from? She fumbled for the chain of the lamp beside her and looked at her watch. It was six-seventeen.

Christmas morning in a lonely hotel room in Eaglescliff, Wyoming.

More sleep was useless. She was wide awake. It was almost as if a voice had spoken out of the light.

She turned over in the bed. Her eyes fell on the green box. It seemed to beckon her.

At length Janet rose. She walked across the room and pulled aside the drapes. A flurry of falling white met her eyes, reflecting off the lights of the town. Two inches of snow lay on the ground.

A white Christmas! Janet thought with a smile.

She turned back into the room, then picked up the gift whose mystery had haunted her sleep all night. She sat down on the edge of the bed with the package on her lap.

She trembled with anticipation, as if something momentous awaited her beneath the bright green paper and red bow.

She removed the bow and set it aside. Gently she tore away the green paper to find a plain brown box void of any hint of what might be inside. She lifted the lid. A small blue envelope lay inside. Janet took it out and pulled from it a beautiful card with an artist's simple rendition of the nativity.

She opened the card. Inside she read a single sentence handwritten in red ink:

The son was born on Christmas Eve.

Janet stared at the brief message, then read it over again…and a third time.

Confused, all she could think was that there was some mistake. She closed the card and stared at the image of the manger on front. Jesus was not born on Christmas Eve…but on Christmas day.

Again she opened the card. *The son was born on Christmas Eve.*

What did it mean?

The rush of events from the previous weeks, culminating in the last two days, played through her mind in a jumble of images, visions, and sounds. The gifts…the music…the excitement of the boys and girls…the strange encounter at the church, and the pastor's haunting question, *What does the child in you want this Christmas?*

What could it all mean? Some mystery was here. But her brain could not lay hold of it.

Disappointed that the gift she had anticipated all night had proved a letdown, Janet lay down in bed again and pulled the thick quilt up around her shoulders. She realized she was very cold. Maybe she could get another hour of sleep before driving to the orphanage for the morning's festivities.

She reached for the light and turned it out.

Janet lay only another minute or two. All at once her eyes shot open and her body jerked upright with sudden new energy.

What if—

Was it possible!

What if the note in the card was not a general reminder of the meaning of Christmas, but a personal message to *her*!

Could the note be a reference to *Leslie's* son!

How could anyone know her grandson's birthday? She had confided her secret to no one but Carl. She had said nothing to him until *after* she was given this gift. And if her grandson had indeed been born on Christmas Eve, what was she to do—go to Cheyenne and ask to look through the state birth files for every baby born on December 24 for the last eighteen years?

All at once, the solution to her perplexity hit her like a bucket of ice water in the face. The orphanage files contained birth dates!

The next instant she was flying about the room for her clothes.

FORTY-SEVEN

THE BIRTHDAY FILES

Janet flew down the stairs at ten minutes before seven. The hotel was nearly empty, though the dining room was open for its handful of guests and the smell of fresh coffee filled the lobby. But she had no time for coffee or breakfast now. The adrenalin surging through her system was more powerful than ten pots of strong coffee!

Startled anew as she dashed outside by the fresh snowfall, Janet slowed. The snow on the sidewalk crunched pleasurably beneath her feet. It was Christmas! she thought. A wonderful white, spectacular Christmas. And she finally had the clue she had been praying for that might help her locate Leslie's son!

The parking lot was dark, empty, and cold. She climbed into her rented car and turned it on, heedless of the cold, hardly thinking that she had never driven in three inches of fresh snow in her life. She waited until the defroster and windshield wipers enabled her to see, then pulled the car into gear and crept from the parking lot onto Main Street. She continued north at ten miles per hour. She was too keyed up to be nervous. She had heard Jack talk enough times about driving in the snow in the Rockies to know what to do — go slow, don't hit the brakes, and turn gradually.

Leaving town, she did her best to follow in the tracks of the few cars that had already come and gone on Route 85 this Christmas morning. There was the turn into the orphanage just ahead. With extreme caution she gently eased the steering wheel to the right. Slowly she made her way onto the virgin snow covering the drive.

Just as she passed the black iron gates, suddenly a gasp escaped Janet's mouth.

Christmas Eve...birthday!

Images of yesterday evening's dinner at the home filled her mind...the birthday cake...the singing of Happy Birthday to the boy who had turned seventeen on Christmas Eve.

Could it be Luke!

Yesterday's birthday celebration proved nothing of itself. Hundreds of babies were born every year on Christmas Eve. She had to *know*!

Trembling with anticipation, Janet eased into the parking lot, turned off the car, then hurried across the new snow as quickly as she dared. Her warm breath floated like steam from her mouth. The snow had stopped. Overhead, a clearing in the clouds revealed the morning sky blinking with stars. Janet imagined that it could have been a night like this so many years before when a bright star above beckoned three Wise Men to the manger that held the newborn King. Lights were already on in the top floors of the huge brick building. The children were coming awake on Christmas morning. But she had a more pressing personal errand she needed to take care of before she saw anyone.

She unlocked the front door, closed it carefully behind her, and hurried across the hardwood floor to the administrative offices. Thankfully the Cracker would not be on duty on Christmas morning.

Once inside the main office, it did not take long to find the file she was looking for. Tears flowing like a river from her eyes, she read the brief but elusive biography she had been praying for:

Luke Jack Kirch, born December 24, 1930. Mother, Leslie Payne, deceased. Father, unknown. Admitted December, 1936.

Janet stared at the blurry words, reading them over and over through her tears.

Jack. Leslie had given her son her father's name. In spite of their estrangement, she had loved them to the end.

Images of the boy Luke Kirch were suddenly tinged with reminders of Leslie.

Luke's face filled Janet's mind. She saw what she should have noticed all along—the corners of his mouth, the cheekbones, his thin lips, the full reddish-brown eyebrows. The slightly pug nose reminded her of Jack, though his hair was a darker shade of brown. And the deep green eyes! The very face of her daughter had been staring at her out of Luke's eyes all this time!

Janet sat for several minutes, smiling and weeping and in her mind's eye studying every feature of Luke's face.

Then she pulled the mysterious card from her purse, opened it again, and added two more sentences of her own. She would pass on the gift she had received to the one her heart had longed for, whom she had come to this orphanage to find.

FORTY-EIGHT

CHRISTMAS MORNING

Janet stole down the corridor of the fifth floor on tip toe.

She heard movement in some of the rooms. Most of the boys were just coming awake. She had never been in the fifth floor boys' dormitory before. If any of the juniors or seniors came out now on their way to the bathrooms and showers, they would be in for a shock. It was a risk she was willing to take.

She paused in front of the door labeled *5-J – Luke Kirch.*

This was it—the moment she had been waiting for. She was trembling inside, like a girl anticipating her first date. Whether he was awake yet, she didn't know. But she could not wait a minute longer.

Janet drew in a deep breath, then knocked lightly and turned the knob and opened the door a crack. Light shone from inside. She opened the door wider and poked her head in.

"Luke?" she said.

He was awake, writing at his desk. The moment their eyes met, a radiant expression of happiness exploded over his face. With tears flooding her eyes, Janet rushed forward. She stooped down and stretched her arms around him, weeping for joy.

Suddenly realizing what she had done, Janet pulled back in embarrassment. Luke wiped his eyes, turned to the desk, picked up a sheet of paper, and handed it to her.

"I knew it was you," she read. "I've been awake for several hours. Once I realized the truth I saw how much you look like my mother, Leslie. You are my Grandma!"

At the sight of the word, Janet burst into sobs. Again grandmother and grandson embraced. This time they held one another for several long seconds. As she again pulled back, Janet kissed Leslie's seventeen year old son on the cheek.

"Merry Christmas to you, Luke, my very own grandson!" said Janet, smiling and wiping her eyes. "I have a present for you," she added, sitting down on the edge of his bed. "The first part may require some explanation. But I think the second part you will understand easily enough."

Telling Luke the story about coming to the orphanage in hopes of finding her daughter's son, then receiving the gift, not knowing at first what it meant, and finally figuring it out, filled Janet with joy to replace all the heartache and confusion from the previous days. There was nothing to call it, she said, but a Christmas miracle.

She handed him the envelope. Luke read the top line inside the card, written in dark red ink.

The son was born on Christmas Eve.

"The rest is from me to you," said Janet.

An I.O.U. for all the love one grandmother can give to her grandson. I have missed you all your life.

Almost the next moment, they heard the door to Luke's room open.

"Hey, big guy, Merry Christmas. Time to rise and — "

Carl stopped in mid-sentence when he saw Janet sitting on the edge of Luke's bed.

"Janet…uh, Mrs. Holiday," he said. "What are you doing here? Is everything…I mean, is something wrong?"

Janet stood from the bed.

"Good morning, Carl," she said. "Sorry to surprise you like this. And no, nothing's wrong. I know it's not exactly protocol for women teachers to barge into their students' bedrooms. But I have just been getting acquainted with my grandson."

"Grandson!" repeated Carl. He glanced toward Luke, whose face was beaming. Luke nodded vigorously as if to say, "She's right!"

Janet quickly gave Carl the short version of what had happened since their conversation of the previous evening.

Even as she was speaking, the loudspeaker in the hallway

came to life with Christmas music.

"What time is it?" said Janet, glancing down at her watch. "Oops—seven-thirty! Everyone will be rushing downstairs and clamoring to get into the Christmas tree room before long. I'd better leave the two of you to get ready!"

"Wait…Janet," said Carl. "I've got another question—did you open your gift from that church?"

"Yes—and what an amazing gift it was. It led me here to Luke. What about yours?"

"I opened it, but I don't know what to make of it."

"What was it?"

"This," replied Carl, digging into his pocket and holding out his hand.

"A key? What's it for?"

"I have no idea."

"There was no note or anything?"

Carl shook his head.

"I don't know what to say, Carl," said Janet. "It looks like a bright new car key. But I'm going to have to let you figure it out or I'll be late when they open the door to the Christmas tree and all the gifts underneath!"

She hugged Luke and again kissed him on the cheek, Carl still shaking his head in disbelief at the sudden turn of events.

"All I've got to say," said Carl after Janet had left the two men alone, "is that you don't see that around here very often! Christmas morning and you find your grandmother! Wow— you've got family, Luke! That's the best Christmas gift of all. Let's get you dressed and downstairs! I can tell that this is going to be a great Christmas!"

FORTY-NINE

GRANDMOTHER AND GRANDSON

A few yells and shrieks from those clad in robes or towels accompanied Janet's dash along the corridor out of the boys' dormitory. Within minutes word was spreading throughout the fourth and fifth floors, full of laughter, question, and shock, that their English teacher had crashed the boys' living quarters.

Janet bounded down the stairs and into the cafeteria, smiling from ear to ear. Many of the older children were not downstairs yet. But most of the younger children were already busy with breakfast, chattering and clamoring excitedly. The staff on hand had its hands full keeping the place from erupting into a zoo. Never had the orphanage known a Christmas like this!

"Janet...Merry Christmas—you are positively radiant!" said Jeanie where she stood at the coffee maker. "You must have slept well."

"Actually...no, I didn't get much sleep!" said Janet, giggling as she poured herself a cup of coffee.

"Something's going on!" laughed Jeanie. "What's your secret? Why are you glowing?"

They found seats far enough away from the din that they could hear one another. Mary Crosby joined them as they sat down. Both women stared at Janet expectantly.

"Do you remember that first day I came in and saw you, Mary?" Janet began. "You were filling in at the office during lunch?"

"Of course," replied Mary.

"I told you I had been asking about a boy who might be

here at the orphanage."

"I had forgotten that. Now that you mention it, I do remember."

"I had reason to believe that my grandson might be here."

"Really — your grandson!" exclaimed Jeanie.

"And just this morning, I came in early and searched in those files Mrs. Cracker guards so jealously. I finally discovered the information I've been looking for."

"And!" said both women at once.

"He's here. I found him!"

Before Janet could say anything further, suddenly a clamor arose beside them. Janet turned to see a half dozen youngsters at her side, tugging on her arm and pressing close and all asking questions at once. They knew that the new teacher Mrs. Holiday had been in charge of the gift lists. Once the children realized she was in the cafeteria, first one, then another, then three more, and finally a stampede of eager young boys and girls jumped out of their seats and ran toward her.

"Mrs. Holiday...Mrs. Holiday!" they all cried at once. "Can we see the Christmas tree yet? Can we go in, please, Mrs. Holiday? When can we go in? It's Christmas, Mrs. Holiday... can we go into the tree room!"

Janet laughed as she turned toward all the smiling eager faces. Beyond them, still seated eating their breakfasts, most of the original skeptics were obviously watching. She saw Reuben and Rusty, both trying to keep from smiling but obviously eager to know what she would say. They were excited too!

"Soon!" said Janet, not able to keep from laughing with delight. "Very soon. You must all keep being patient. We will open the room to the Christmas tree and presents as soon as everyone has had breakfast. Then we will all go in together!"

The children all yelled and clapped and scurried back to their places to finish the rest of their oatmeal, fruit, toast, and milk.

Two young children Janet did not recognize remained huddled together beside her. Their fresh little faces stared up into hers as if she were their mother. They seemed bewildered by all the commotion.

"The Kingsbury twins," whispered Mary beside her.

"Are you Lydia and Lyle?" said Janet, smiling and bending down toward them.

They nodded.

"And are you ready for Christmas?"

The girl nodded, but the boy spoke up.

"Santa won't bring us anything," he said. "We just got here. He doesn't know where we are."

"I don't know about that, Lyle," said Janet. "I think there might be a surprise waiting for you in the Christmas tree room too."

She saw a smile of hopefulness come into seven year old Lydia's eyes.

"So why don't the two of you go finish your breakfast. Then in a little while we will go into the Christmas tree room together."

Mary rose from where she sat beside Janet and took the two under her wing back to their places.

When they were alone, Jeanie looked across at Janet. "I'm still waiting," she said. "I want to hear the rest of the story! You said your grandson is here?"

Out of the corner of her eye, Janet saw the door of the cafeteria open. Luke, with Carl behind him, wheeled his way through it.

"I think this will answer your question!" said Janet. She jumped up and hurried over to them. She took hold of the wheelchair and guided it to the table where Jeanie sat, then she reached down from behind, put her arms around Luke's neck and shoulders and kissed him on the cheek. Mr. Pratt and others of the staff who were watching, not knowing whether to be outraged or merely curious, began inching closer.

"Jeanie, Mr. Pratt..." said Janet, glancing about, "and all of you, I would like to introduce you to my grandson, Luke Kirch."

A momentary silence descended, though across the room the cacophony of children's voices continued. Glances of astonishment went back and forth, but the smiles on Carl's and Luke's faces told them all they needed to know.

Gary, who was sitting at a table with the older boys, had

heard Janet's words. He jumped from his seat and ran toward them.

"Did I hear you, Mrs. Holiday—Luke is your grandson!"

All Janet could do in reply was laugh with delight.

"Wow—that's great! I knew there was something special about you from the day you ordered your first root beer float. Congratulations, Luke!" he said, reaching out and shaking Luke's hand.

Gary's obvious enthusiasm broke the ice. Within seconds, all the staff and most of the older boys and girls were clustered around excitedly—full of more questions than the youngsters had been about the Christmas tree!

FIFTY

THE CHRISTMAS TREE

Half an hour later, led by Janet pushing Luke in his wheelchair, Carl and Mr. Pratt at her side, followed by a tumultuous, energetic, clamoring throng of youngsters and boys and girls of all ages mixed together and all talking at once, the entire population of the Wyoming Children's Home and its staff approached the long-awaited door of the multi-purpose room. It would henceforth be known as The Christmas Tree Room.

Mr. Pratt stepped forward and inserted his key. Janet turned around and waited for the clamor to die down.

"Are we ready?" she said loudly.

"Yes!" cried more than fifty voices in unison.

Mr. Pratt opened the door. The throng poured in. To Janet's surprise, the children did not wildly storm the room. A hush descended as they walked in almost reverently, staring in awe at the tree and panorama of gifts. Never had any of them seen such a sight in their lives. Slowly the quiet turned into a hush of whispers, then excited giggles. Before long the noise built to a subdued roar of jubilation.

They had all been instructed on the procedure that would be followed to keep the scene from turning into a pandemonious madhouse. So eager they could not contain themselves, everyone took places around the tree. They were moving and squirming like insects and all chattering at once. The two Kingsbury twins were the only ones maintaining any hint of calm. They walked in huddled close to Mary Crosby, holding her two hands, and stared up with wide eyes at the huge tree. Gradually silence descended over the room like a bird settling its wings.

"I have asked Mrs. Crosby to hand out the first gifts," said Janet when everyone was in place.

Mary walked to the tree, stooped down, and picked up two shiny green packages. To the surprise of the recipients most of all, she handed them to Lydia and Lyle Kingsbury. In disbelief, the two newest members of the orphanage family stared at them with eyes as big as saucers.

"Go ahead," said Mary. "They are for you."

Seconds later, the paper lay shredded beside them and they were shrieking with delight at the doll and toy fire engine in their hands.

"And now," continued Janet, we will let you give one another the gifts you suggested. — Carla, here is a gift for you to give to James."

Janet handed a package to Carla. With a huge smile, she walked to her fellow first-grader. "Here, James," she said. "Merry Chrithmus."

As James took the gift and opened it, Janet saw joy on Carla's face, if anything, perhaps greater than that of James. It was the joy of giving pleasure to another.

"June..." she went on, "here is a gift for you to give to Jennifer."

"And I believe Mr. Pratt has a gift for you, Reuben," said Janet.

Reuben was obviously taken aback by being singled out to receive one of the first gifts. But the smile on the principal's face said that the letter he held out as Reuben approached was something very special he had to give this young man who had given him more than his share of trouble through the years."

"Luke," now said Janet, "don't you have a gift for Tom?"

Janet lifted a square box of approximately one foot dimensions in all three directions, and laid it in Luke's lap. Luke glanced at her with a smile. He stuffed the leather journal that never left his side down next to one leg. Balancing the box on his knees, he wheeled to the other side of the room to find the fifth grader. He held out the gift to him.

Tom grabbed it excitedly and wasted no time tearing into the package.

"A basketball!" Tom exclaimed. "Thanks, Luke!"

By now the room had exploded into a frenzy of excitement. Gradually all the children and older boys and girls were handing gifts to their fellow orphans. Before they were done, they had all begun to anticipate being handed a gift to *give* even more than opening their own. A few of the exchanges were awkward, such as Stuart being handed the gift meant for Luke, whom he had always looked down on. But the giving accomplished its work, and opened many hearts in both directions.

An hour later, when the last gift was handed from Rusty to Gary, and Gary had unwrapped a book entitled, *A Pictorial History of Classic Cars*, everyone noticed that there remained just as many packages under the tree unopened as had been opened.

"Who are all those presents for, Mrs. Holiday?" asked first grader Angela.

"They are for you! There is one more gift for everyone. You may all go and search for the package with your name on it and open it."

Janet's words were followed by such a scramble and rush that she feared the tree might topple over. But in the tumult of searching the gifts, most of the children seemed more eager to shout when they had found someone else's present than to locate their own. Some tore away the paper instantly. Others waited, more eager to see others open their gifts than to open their own.

As she watched, amid the tumult, a quiet calm descended upon Janet. Whether the voice was audible, or whether it was a voice speaking only in her mind, she would never know. That she heard *something* was certain.

They have learned the joy of giving, and the meaning of Christmas because of you, said the Voice. Startled, Janet glanced around the room, as if expecting to see a familiar figure standing at her side. *You have done well, Janet. You asked once if it was enough to be baptized or go to church. No, it's not. My children have to seek me and hear what I have to say. By giving of yourself, you have also received your family back — perhaps not as you had hoped, but as it was ordained.*

Janet's eyes fell upon an eleventh grade girl named Shelly,

who was in her English class along with Luke. She was at that moment opening a box wrapped in the green paper and red bow that distinguished the gifts that had come from All Saints. The girl froze for a moment, then slowly lifted a lavender scarf from the box. With it was a note.

It is a letter from her mother, whispered the Voice in Janet's ear. *The dying woman wrote it before she passed away two years ago. She shared her memories of many of the happy times they had enjoyed together as mother and daughter. She knew she was dying, and wrote to Shelly to remind her that she would always be with her. There was so much confusion after her death, the letter and the scarf have only just now come to her.*

For a moment, Janet imagined that she could faintly make out the figure of a beautiful woman standing over Shelly, smiling with the loving eyes of a mother as tears came to Shelly's eyes. Slowly the girl lifted her mother's scarf and placed it against her cheek and smelled it, then pulled it around her neck and read again the words written in her mother's own hand.

As the image faded from Janet's view, her eyes drifted to dear little six year old Carla, who had already become one of her favorites. She was just opening her tiny green package.

The one thing Carla wants more than anything in the world is a picture of her mother and father, said the mysterious Voice.

Carla now pulled a necklace from the box inside the wrapping paper. Her tiny fingers struggled to open the gold locket hanging from the chain. A squeal of pleasure erupted.

Carla jumped to her feet and ran to Janet, nearly tumbling headlong into her lap.

"Mithez Holiday...Mithez Holiday, look—ith's a tiny picture of my mommy and daddy!"

"May I have everyone's attention please!" called out Mr. Pratt. "Just for a moment—then you can get back to your gifts. I have an announcement to make. You all know about Reuben's artistic gifts. A few months ago I received a letter telling me that some of his drawings made their way to a prestigious art college in Denver, and asking for copies of the record of his work here. I said nothing to Reuben, but sent back the information. Just days ago I received the letter that I gave Reuben a few minutes ago. He has been accepted to attend, with a full scholarship, next year."

Cheers and applause broke out through the room. Reuben beamed with boyish pleasure, then did the last thing anyone would have expected, turned toward Mr. Pratt and gave him a great bear hug.

"Thanks, Mr. Pratt," he said. "After all the trouble I've given you, for you to do this for me—I will never forget it! I'm going to make you proud!"

"I know you will, Reuben. Just promise me that when you become a famous artist, you'll give me one of your paintings to hang in the orphanage."

Reuben laughed. "I promise, Mr. Pratt!"

Janet looked up at Luke where his wheelchair sat beside her. They exchanged smiles. Luke was as happy for Reuben's Christmas gift as he was his own.

The magic of Christmas had infected the whole orphanage, thought Janet. Christmas was not about the size of the gift, but the love that came with it.

Fifty-One

The Carnegie Wing

All this time, Luke had hardly noticed what Carl was carrying in his hand. Now he saw that he was holding the car replica he had bought for him. Carl came over and sat down beside Janet.

"I figured I didn't need much else this Christmas," he said. "I got my Christmas present a couple weeks ago. I don't know if I ever showed you this—Luke bought it for me. It's a replica of a car I used to own—a '32 Ford Coupe. It's not everyone who has a friend who risks his life just to buy you a Christmas present. That's why Luke wound up in the hospital just after you came—he went to town to get this for me."

With the mention of his stay in the hospital. Luke was reminded of his dream of a year ago, and Vanessa's words when she pointed along the road as they parted.

I have a strange feeling that I'm not going to see you again. I think this is my last dream.

He had argued with her. But she had been right. She *hadn't* been in his dream last night. But he had heard her voice. What had she said! The memory was hazy. But it was something important.

Come find me…come find me.

But where? She had said more.

Come find me, Luke…come find me at the Carnegie Wing.

Why did the words sound so familiar?

Suddenly he remembered what sat half a mile north of the orphanage. He grabbed for the journal he always had with him and the tablet inside it. He scribbled a hasty note and handed it to Carl.

What is the Carnegie Wing? Carl read.

Carl looked at Luke with a questioning expression.

"It's at the hospital," Carl answered after a moment. "It's where they keep terminal patients. They were out of rooms so that's where they stuck you three weeks ago. Man, when I walked in and found out that's where you were, I was really worried. The only people who go in the Carnegie Wing are those who are dying."

Luke grabbed the tablet and wrote even more feverishly than before.

I've got to get there, Carl. I've got to go to the hospital NOW. Please, can you take me. It can't wait!

Bewildered, Carl glanced toward Janet. He handed her the tablet with Luke's hastily written message. Now it was Janet's turn to wonder what Luke was talking about.

"Luke...?" she said, "is something wrong? Are you not feeling well?"

Again Luke grabbed hurriedly for the tablet and wrote below the earlier messages, then handed the tablet back to Janet.

No, it's not me. It's someone else. I think she may be in danger. I have to find her. I think she's at the hospital.

With obvious urgency in his expression, he handed the tablet back to Janet.

Luke was staring intently at her and Carl, as if to say, *I know this all may seem weird and out of the blue, but you have to believe in me.* Gazing deep into his eyes, they could almost read his mind. *Please believe me!* his eyes pleaded.

"We've got to go, Janet," said Carl. "Whatever this is about, Luke has proved himself to me thus far. I don't know what is going on, but I believe him."

"That's good enough for me," said Janet.

"Luke has never asked for a selfish thing in all the years I've known him," Carl added. "If he says he has to get to the hospital, then you can be sure he's got a good reason. We can take the orphanage van."

Bidding hasty farewells to the staff and children, and with apologies for their unceremonious departure in the midst of the Christmas celebration, Luke and Janet made for the back door of the orphanage. Carl sprinted out the front, dashed across the parking lot, and was soon driving around to the back of the building, skidding about in the snow, to pick up Janet and Luke. In five minutes, they were on their way.

Driving across the fresh Christmas fall of snow at what he considered a safe speed, which was three times faster than Janet had inched her way to the orphanage earlier, Carl maneuvered the van past the entry gates, and onto Route 85. Enough traffic had traveled the highway by now that the snow had mostly turned to slush. Gently Carl accelerated to 40 m.p.h. In another minute or two the hospital building came into view. He pulled in, drove straight toward the main entrance and slid to a stop.

Carl jumped out and retrieved Luke's wheelchair from the back of the van. The instant he was seated, Luke grabbed at the wheels and tore off toward the doors with Janet and Carl hurrying after him. Carl raced ahead, grabbed the door and flung it open. Luke flew through, then slowed, looking about to get his bearings. But Carl knew the way well enough. He had spent nearly a week here waiting for Luke to recover. He took hold of the handles at the back of the wheelchair, and, paying no heed to the questions of the nurse at the registration counter, wheeled Luke to the right and down the length of the corridor. Janet had to run to keep up with them

The three paused at the elevator. The ride to the third floor seemed to take forever. The instant the doors opened, Carl sped out, turned left, paused as they entered through the familiar double glass doors labeled "Carnegie Wing," then stopped at the nurses' counter. Janet and Carl were breathing hard.

The nurse on duty glanced at them skeptically as they approached. "May I help you?" she said. Her tone did not convey optimism.

"We're looking for someone," said Janet.

"What's the name?" asked the nurse flatly.

Already Luke was busy again with his tablet. He handed it to Janet, who held it across the counter to the nurse.

"Vanessa?" she said as she stared at it.

Luke nodded.

"What's her last name?"

Luke shook his head and shrugged his shoulders.

"Without a last name, there's not much I can do?"

"Please," said Janet. "It is very important. Couldn't you look through and see if there is anyone in this wing called Vanessa?"

The nurse sighed, then picked up a clipboard, scanned it for a second or two, then glanced toward them again.

"There's no Vanessa," she said.

Carl now spoke up for the first time. "Aren't most of your patients in this wing older?" he asked.

"Mostly, I suppose," replied the nurse. "We had a young boy of seventeen here earlier this month from hypothermia."

Luke grabbed his tablet and wrote again.

That was me, the nurse read. *Do you have any girls here near my age?*

"Now that you mention it," she replied, "we do. Several of us commented at the time how unusual it was to have two teenagers in the wing at the same time."

"What is the girl's name?" asked Janet.

"Nissy…Nissy Johnson. She is seventeen."

"*Nissy…Vanessa*—that could be it!—Luke?" said Janet, glanced down at her side.

Luke nodded his head violently.

"What room is this Nissy Johnson in?" asked Janet.

"I can't give out that information," replied the nurse. "You are obviously not family if you didn't know who she was. Besides, it's Christmas morning. Her family is with her now, like they are every Christmas. The poor girl's been in a coma for ten years. She doesn't even know her family is in the room. She certainly isn't going to care about a visit from three strangers. I can't let you barge in like this."

Luke hastily wrote another note, this one longer and handed it up to the nurse.

Would you please tell the family that a friend of Vanessa's is here? she read. *Ask them if I could see her. My name is Luke Kirch. Please.*

She thought a minute. "I don't suppose there's any harm in asking," she said. "Wait here."

She walked down the corridor away from them, then disappeared around a corner. When she reappeared a few minutes later, a man and women were with her. They approached, looking back and forth from Carl to Luke to Janet with obvious confusion.

"I'm Eric Johnson," said the man. "This is my wife Fran. We understand you've come to see our Nissy. You obviously know something about her since you know her name. No one around here has called her Vanessa in years. But I don't recognize any of you. She is in a coma, so I am uncertain how you could know her? Why do you want to see our Vanessa?"

"I'm afraid we don't have a very satisfactory answer," said Janet with an apologetic smile. "My name is Janet Holiday. I am a teacher at the orphanage. This is Carl Elkin, a nurse at the home—"

Carl stepped forward and shook Mr. Johnson's hand.

"—and this young man is my grandson, Luke Kirch," Janet added.

Luke stretched out his hand, smiled, and shook hands with both Mr. and Mrs. Johnson.

"I am so sorry for intruding into your family Christmas like this," Janet went on. "We really do not want to bother you—"

A hand on Janet's arm stopped her. She glanced down at Luke. He took his pencil and tablet again. They all waited. After a minute, he handed the tablet up to the two Johnsons.

I'm sorry too for barging in on your Christmas, they read. *I can't talk, so please bear with me as I write. I hope you can believe me when I tell you that Vanessa and I are friends. I can't explain it all now, but I promise I will when there is more time. Right now I have I see her. Please…please. I really need to see her.*

The husband and wife looked at one another, not sure what to make of the strange request.

"What harm can it do, Eric?" said Mrs. Johnson. Before her husband could answer, she turned toward Janet and tears flooded her eyes. "It's been ten years," she said. "Exactly ten years last night since the accident…ten years without a sign of life other than the hint of a smile and a tear from one eye—and then only on Christmas Eve. The doctors tell us that it is rare for coma patients to do that. It's why we think she can hear us. It is as if once a year she is remembering. She was only seven at the time. Now she is seventeen and—"

She glanced down and began to cry. Janet stepped

241

forward and took her in her arms. "I am so sorry," she said. "I know a little of what you must be feeling. I lost my daughter too. She also died ten years go, though I only just found out. I have shed many tears this last month. What kind of accident was your daughter in?"

"A traffic accident," replied Mrs. Johnson, sniffing and wiping at her eyes as the two women pulled away. "We'd gone out looking at the lights in town," she went on. "We do it every Christmas Eve. Then we stopped by to visit my parents. We were on our way home. The rest of us were in the car on the other side of the street but Nissy had gone back to give Grandma and Grandpa another kiss. Then she came out and ran into the street, when a drunk driver came along the street—"

As she listened, suddenly Janet's face went pale.

"What street was it?" she asked in a faltering voice. "What street did your parents live on?"

"Buhne Avenue...why?"

Janet gasped. "And it was exactly ten years ago last night...Christmas Eve of 1937?"

"Yes, that's right."

"And a woman darted into the street and pushed her out of the path of the car?"

"Yes. The poor woman was killed saving our Nissy's life. How could you possible know?"

Janet's eyes flooded. "That was my daughter," she said in a barely audible voice. "My daughter died on Buhne Avenue on Christmas Eve ten years ago."

Mrs. Johnson broke into fresh sobs. The two mothers fell into one another's arms and wept.

"I don't know what to say?" said Mrs. Johnson. "I'm so sorry. Your daughter died saving our little girl's life. What was her name?"

"Leslie," answered Janet, stepping back again.

"That's right, I remember...Leslie Payne. I have wanted to meet someone from her family all these years to tell them what a hero she was. Now here you are—from out of nowhere on Christmas morning asking about our Nissy. I admit, I'm still confused by it all, and how you knew Nissy was here."

"I didn't. Luke did."

242

Janet turned to Luke, who had been listening incredulously to the exchange between the two mothers.

"But how did he know?" asked Mrs. Johnson.

Luke pulled the leather journal from his side. He flipped through it to the first page of what he called *The Angel Dreams*, which Janet had only seen the beginnings of before Christmas vacation. He showed it to Mrs. Johnson, and pointed to the page."

"Luke is Leslie's son," Janet added. "He was taken to the orphanage after the accident. It has taken me all this time to find him."

Mrs. Johnson turned toward Luke and gazed down at him with eyes of tender love. She stooped forward and embraced him warmly. "Your mother was a hero, Luke," she said. "She gave her life for our little girl. That can't be said of very many people. I'm sorry for your loss. But you can be very proud of her."

Luke nodded and smiled and wiped at his eyes. He took his pencil and wrote a brief message, and handed it to Mrs. Johnson.

When you have read this, she read, *you will know why I said that we were friends. But this is the first time Vanessa and I will have met in real life.*

He handed Vanessa's mother his journal. He was remembering his first Christmas Eve dreams, whose stories he had written down, and was trying to take in the incredible reality that his mother's and Vanessa's fate had been so intertwined.

Mr. Johnson stepped forward and shook Luke's hand again, this time with deep feeling. He then embraced Janet as if they had known one another for years.

"Why don't we go down to her room," he said to Luke, "and you can see your friend."

What the nurse thought of the proceedings, it would have been difficult to determine. But she no longer voiced an objection.

FIFTY-TWO

NISSY JOHNSON

The familiar sights and sounds of monitors and machinery and blipping green screens met them as they followed Mr. and Mrs. Johnson into the room. Three children were sitting quietly around the room, two twin boys reading books, a younger girl playing with a doll. Christmas music played softly from a radio on a bedside table. A small Christmas tree dressed in white lights lit a corner of the pale yellow room. Evidence of open presents was strewn about the floor.

But Luke had eyes only for the still thin form in the bed wired to a monitor that gave off a slow but constant beep. An IV bottle hung from a stand at the end of the bed. Its tube was attached to a lifeless white arm.

Luke recognized Vanessa instantly. She was thinner than she had been in his dreams, her face gaunt and pale, her eyes closed. But she was exactly the same Vanessa he had said good bye to a year ago on the road outside the orphanage.

"It may be silly, I don't know," said Mrs. Johnson, as if apologizing for the mess as if the room were her own home, "but ever since the accident it's been part of our family tradition to come here and open some of our gifts with Nissy on Christmas."

"It's not silly at all," smiled Janet. "I think it's lovely."

Suddenly Janet gasped. Her eyes were riveted on a framed photograph sitting on the shelf of an open cabinet that had been brought in for the family to keep a few personal belongings on.

"What's that...how do you...I mean, why is that photograph here!" she stammered.

"We found it at the scene of the accident," replied Mrs. Johnson. "It was wrapped in Christmas paper, and—"

She stopped abruptly, took two or three quick steps toward the cabinet, then picked up the picture and stared at it intently. She spun around to face Janet.

"It's *you*!" she exclaimed. "And…the boy in the wheelchair," she added, turning toward Luke, "that's Luke, isn't it?"

But Luke was paying no attention. His eyes remained glued to the bed and the girl lying upon it.

Mrs. Johnson handed the frame to Janet. Both women gazed at the two oval photographs, framed together as one, fresh tears pouring from Janet's eyes.

"It's my husband and me," she said quietly. "Look at us! We were so young. I remember the day—it was 1927. Leslie was fifteen. I had no idea Leslie had this picture of us. And then this other one of her and Luke."

"The price tag is still on the frame," said Mrs. Johnson. "We assumed that's why she was out that night. She must have had the photographs framed as a gift. Maybe it was for you."

Janet smiled sadly at the thought. "Or for Luke," she said softly. It's a nice thought either way."

"My mother found the package on her lawn the next day. I guess the police hadn't seen it when they picked up your daughter's purse after the accident. We asked the neighbors if anyone knew anything about it. No one did. When the newspaper said the woman had no family, we didn't know what to do. We just kept it."

"I still cannot get over the idea that Leslie was thinking of us at the end of her life."

"Finally we opened it," said Mrs. Johnson. "We thought it might tell us something. But we recognized no one in the photograph except your daughter. We kept it here, as a reminder of the woman who had saved our Nissy. We've been praying all this time that somehow God would bring our paths across the people in these photographs so we could meet them and know why their pictures were there that night. I can hardly believe seeing the two of you here now. God was really listening to our prayers all those years!"

"You didn't read the correction in the paper about Luke?" asked Janet.

"No, what correction?"

"It was a week or two later. It just said that Leslie had a son, and that he was at the children's home."

"If only we had known!" said Mrs. Johnson. "We might have been able to do something for him."

As Janet continued to ponder the photograph of her family, Mrs. Johnson sat down and opened the book Luke had handed her a few moments before. In scanning through the handwritten pages, she began to see Vanessa's name on nearly every page. Soon she was seated and reading earnestly, with Janet bent down and reading over her shoulder. Both women had tears running down their cheeks. They were stunned with the unfolding story of the Christmas Eve dreams.

All this time, Luke had been trying to maneuver his wheelchair through the small room to the side of the bed. He turned and glanced at Carl.

Carl knew exactly what he meant. He stepped forward, took Luke's two hands, and pulled him to his feet. Grasping the bars at the edge of the bed, Luke shuffled his way awkwardly toward the head of the bed. Carl stood behind to steady him.

Luke lifted his right hand, extended it to the bed, and laid it gently on the back of Vanessa's hand where it lay outside the sheet. A faint smile spread across her face. Immediately the beeping of the heart monitor quickened its pace.

"Mom...Dad, look!" cried Vanessa's twelve year old sister. "Nissy's smiling!"

The others all hurried to the bedside. It was clear that a change had come to Vanessa's face.

"So many nights I've sat here with her hand in mine," said Mrs. Johnson, "praying that the Lord would bring her back to us, praying that he would come and visit this room with his healing touch. I believed, I really believed that he would. But she never responded to my touch. It's almost like...I wonder if she is having one of her dreams about Luke right now. I don't understand it. but the dreams and real life seem to mingle somehow."

All of a sudden the beeping monitor doubled its pace. The

smile disappeared from the face in the bed. It was replaced with a grimace of pain. Vanessa's features contorted and she began struggling to breathe.

"What's wrong...nurse!" cried Mr. Johnson running to the door. "Nurse!" he shouted.

Two nurses came running and hurried to the bedside.

"Dad, what's wrong?" said Vanessa's sister. "Is Nissy dying!"

"Stand back! Stand away from the bed," commanded one of the nurses. "Get away from her, boy!" she said to Luke when she saw him touching her. Roughly she shoved him aside.

Luke fell backward, but as always Carl was there to catch him.

Everyone waited silently around the room as the two nurses examined both the patient and the sudden wild monitors.

"Call Dr. Brimlow stat," said one. "Something's wrong. I don't know what's going on."

The younger of the two nurses ran from the room.

Luke! said a woman's voice. It was so soft he scarcely heard it.

He turned and glanced around the room.

Luke, came the voice again. All the others were anxiously watching the nurse. No one was paying any attention to him.

Believe with your heart, Luke. Frantically Luke searched the room again. This time he knew the voice. It was his mother's! The faint outline of a radiantly white human form stood by the door. She was smiling. Luke tried to take a step toward her. Slowly she shook her head and faded from sight.

Your time has come, Luke, now said a man's voice. Luke spun his head back to the bed. A Man was standing opposite him beside the nurse. No one else could see him.

Luke returned the gaze from the man's radiant eyes and he knew him. He had been with him and with Vanessa all along, preparing them to face this moment together. He was the Man of the Toys, the Steward of the Feast, the Soccer Referee, the Hospital Doctor, the Homeless Man, the Doll Maker, the Shepherd, and the Pastor from last night's party.

The Man smiled and then nodded, beckoning Luke

247

forward.

Still supported by Carl's strong hands, Luke inched back to the bedside. He took hold of the rails again to steady himself.

Believe, Luke, said the Man. *Focus on what you have to do…then believe.*

Luke felt a tingling sensation in his throat…an itch, a stinging, as something was struggling to free itself, to get out, to fly.

Believe, Luke!

Luke opened his mouth. Terror gripped him. Could he do it? Or would he sound like a babbling fool?

He took a breath, reached down and again took hold of Vanessa's hand. Focusing more willpower than he had ever had to summon, he placed his teeth to his lips.

"V…V-a…" he croaked. "V-a…V-a-n-a-s…"

Suddenly the word blurted from his mouth, soft but powerful, *"Vanessa!"*

Janet's head jerked toward him and she gasped with disbelief. Carl's eyes shot open. Had they just heard what they thought they heard?

Luke squeezed the limp white hand that he held. *"Vanessa,"* he repeated.

Suddenly he felt a movement in his hand, and a return of pressure. Gazing upon her face, he saw Vanessa's eyelids flutter. Her eyes raced back and forth beneath closed lids.

Her mother and father had seen the change. Now it was the nurse who was shoved aside.

"Nissy…Nissy!" cried Mrs. Johnson in an ecstasy of sudden hope.

Slowly the eyebrows flickered, and the lids slowly opened. Gasps and sobs and astonished exclamations filled the room.

But the newly opened eyes only saw one face gazing down into hers. A soft, peaceful, contented smile spread over Vanessa's lips.

"Luke," she whispered faintly. "You came!"

FIFTY-THREE

THE KEY

Dr. Brimlow hurried into the room at the very moment Vanessa opened her eyes.

Surveying the scene and greeted by the tumult and cries and exclamations, seeing the choked up father embracing the sobbing mother, hearing shrieking sister and brothers, and glancing toward the bed, he quickly apprehended the truth—that Eaglescliff's "coma girl" had come awake at last.

"Please…please, everyone!" he said, attempting to be heard over the commotion. "We must remain calm. Please, quiet down."

Urgently he pulled the mother and father aside. "I realize what this moment means to you," he said, "but for your daughter's sake, we mustn't overly excite her system. I think it best for the first few moments for you to take the younger children out of the room, and also these other people. She must remain calm. Who are all these people anyway? Who's the young man holding your daughter's hand?" he added.

"It's because of him that she is awake, Doctor," said Mrs. Johnson through her tears. "He is the one person who must *not* leave her."

"Very well, then," nodded the doctor. "But if you could take the others out to the waiting room. We want your daughter at peace as she returns to our world."

"Look at her face and eyes, Doctor," said Mr. Johnson. "I believe she is very much at peace."

Janet, too, amid her shock at hearing Luke's voice for the first time, had been staring at Vanessa's eyes and the wan smile on her lips. In a miraculous and mysterious way, it was like seeing a reflection of her own Leslie's eyes. She had come to this town seeking her daughter. She had found instead two young people who would not be alive today had Leslie not passed on her own life to them. Truly did her daughter live on through her son, and in this girl whose life she had saved. It was almost as if the moment Vanessa's eyes opened, Leslie herself had come back to life in Janet's heart.

Janet wept as she left the room with Carl and the Johnsons and the doctor and nurse. She had indeed found her daughter, for Leslie's *life* truly lived on.

Luke stood at the bedside heedless of the melee in the room around him. To realize, after all these years, that the angel-friend of his dreams was alive in real life too was the most stupendous gift he could imagine. His brain was struggling to grasp the fact that in the last few minutes, in this room, his two *lives* had merged into one.

Vanessa's waking was quiet and peaceful. The energy and vibrant life she had known during the years of her dream-wakings were gone. The physical life that had been drained from her during eleven years in a coma made even breathing almost more fatiguing than she could bear. She was vaguely aware of many people in the room, of sounds and cries of joy. But Luke's face staring down at her from above was the only reality she could cling to. Their shared dreams had been her *only* life for so long. She did not yet remember her childhood. She did not remember the accident. She knew only Luke's face, the one recurring constant from her dreams.

As Janet and the Johnsons filed out of the room, Carl took Janet aside.

"I should get back to the orphanage," he said. "They're going to need some explanation why we disappeared! But telephone when you and Luke are ready for me to come for you, or if there's any change."

Janet nodded. "Apologize to the children for me. Especially the younger ones. Tell them I'll be back as soon as I can."

Carl drove slowly back to the orphanage amazed at what he had just witnessed, and still puzzling over the strange key in his pocket that had been so carefully wrapped in green and had been given to him with no explanation. As he entered the lot and pulled the van into its usual space, he saw what appeared to be a familiar black car parked across the lot. It looked like his own '32 Ford Coupe!

He got out and slowly walked toward it. As he did, the driver's door opened and a man stepped out.

"Hello, Carl," he said.

"Mr. Sanders," replied Carl. "This is a surprise."

"You surely haven't forgotten that I bought this little beauty a few weeks ago," said Sanders, nodding toward the black hot rod.

"I thought I recognized it!" said Carl with a smile. "I really appreciate the good price you gave me."

"It's a classic after all."

"I see you've decided to keep it for yourself. You couldn't do better. It's a fantastic automobile."

"Actually no, that's not why I'm here. I am here to deliver it to you. It's a Christmas gift."

Carl stared back dumbfounded.

"Strangest thing I ever saw in twenty years," said Sanders. "A fellow came by the dealership yesterday and paid for the car in cash. He asked me to deliver it to you right here, today, at eleven o'clock. He said you would already have a key. He looked at me so intently — I didn't think to question him. I just did what he said.

Carl reached into his pocket and pulled out the mystery key. Why hadn't he recognized it? It was a shiny new key, but now he saw that the cut was identical to the key he had given Mr. Sanders.

"The title's in the glove box. A second key's in the ignition," said Sanders, " — the one you gave me. All I need is a ride back to town. You want to take the wheel? She's yours again now!"

In a silent stupor, Carl drove the car dealer back into Eaglescliff and dropped him off at his home.

"Merry Christmas, Carl," he said as he stepped out onto the snowy sidewalk.

"And to you, Mr. Sanders. I hardly know what to say. Thank you."

When he was alone, Carl sat a moment longer. Children were out up and down the street, bundled up against the cold,

251

building snowmen, throwing snowballs, playing with Christmas toys. One or two were out with new bikes, though it was a little slippery for biking. Several men were shoveling the snow from their driveways.

Carl did not know what to make of what had happened. At length he reached across the dashboard and opened the glove box. A folded sheet of paper was inside along with the car's documents.

He pulled out the sheet, unfolded it, and read:

Carl,

The love in your heart for all my children makes me very happy. Thank you for keeping Christmas in your heart every day. My eternal blessings rest on you and your sister.

Emmanuel.

FIFTY-FOUR

HAPPY BIRTHDAY!

"I am so tired, Luke," said Vanessa weakly when they were alone. "I have never felt like this. Is it Christmas Eve? Are we dreaming again? I didn't think I would see you again."

"We're not dreaming," said Luke. "It's really Christmas!"

"*Christmas,*" she repeated, as if the very idea of it was strange. "I don't think I've been awake on Christmas for a long time. But I am so tired. I feel like I need a nap."

"You can't go to sleep, Vanessa," said Luke. "You've been asleep for too long already."

"Have I really? Why am I so tired?"

"You haven't eaten for a long time. You need to stay awake and get strong again."

"Will you help me, Luke? I feel so weak and funny. I don't think I will know what to do."

"I will help you!" laughed Luke.

Suddenly he realized that he had been listening to the sound of his own voice! He was actually *talking*! His dream world, like Vanessa's, had become real!

"Merry Christmas, Luke…Merry Christmas, Vanessa," said a Voice.

Luke snapped his head around. The Man of the Dreams still stood on the opposite side of the bed. His eyes were dancing with love, and a great smile was spread over his face.

Vanessa had also heard the Voice. With difficulty she lifted her head slightly off its pillow, then turned toward it.

"You are the Shepherd!" she said, the smile on her face spreading wider. "I hoped I would see you again. Now you're here with Luke. Is it you who spoke to me and told me to wake up?"

"It is. I told you through Luke's voice."

It was Luke who spoke next.

"Are you...*God*?" he asked simply.

The Man walked around the bed and stood beside him. His only answer was a great radiant smile. It was enough. "The two of you have been wonderful Christmas angels," he said. "I gave you the chance to shine your love on others in your dreams, which were far more than dreams. You have made me very happy by spreading my love among those you have met, and with the young man and young woman you have become. The time has now come for you to *live* your dreams. I gave you your dreams so that you would come to know me through the many faces of my personality. But in this world I am known by another name. It is time for you to know me by the name that means *God with us*."

Luke stood listening in disbelief. Vanessa lay absorbing every word with blissful contentedness.

The Man with the dancing eyes continued. "Luke and Vanessa," he said, "the two of you have been faithful over what you were given to do. So from now on you will be my Christmas angels all the year long. I want you to keep my Spirit alive every day and with everyone you meet. They can find me and walk with me and live with me too, just as you have done."

The Shepherd called Emmanuel, stretched his hands out and touched Luke's leg. A tingling sensation exploded through his body, spreading as a million tiny painful pin pricks through his legs all the way to the floor.

"My love has the power to heal all things," he said. "Believe, Luke...*believe*."

Now he turned to the thin form on the bed. Again he reached out and this time took Vanessa's hand.

"Your eyes have opened, Daughter," he said. "Now come fully awake. Be healed and be strong. You have a life to live and work to do. To you also, I say...*believe*."

"You have been with me all along, haven't you?" said Vanessa.

The Shepherd smiled and nodded. "From before you were

254

born. All along I have been preparing you for the day of your waking."

"I'd forgotten, but now I remember hearing my mother praying all those nights. I remember her crying beside this bed. I remember wanting to tell her that I was fine. And now I remember — you were standing beside her."

"Though she did not know I was there, I was giving her strength to keep praying for you. Her prayers were helping to keep you strong."

"Will you tell her?"

"I think that will be for you to do."

As Luke and Vanessa beheld him, the Man from their dreams stepped back from the bedside. His form began to recede and grow faint. Again Luke took Vanessa's hand. Suddenly they knew that they would not see him again like this, their season of dreams was drawing to a close.

From across the room, His form was but faintly visible now. He looked upon them one last time, then lifted His eyes toward the heavens. "Thank you, Father," He said. "You have given me the greatest gift — seeing your Love reign in the hearts of your children."

At the bedside, and from the waiting room outside, and throughout the hospital, heads turned as a distant roll of thunder sounded. But the Man smiled and in the rumbling heard his Father say, "*Happy Birthday, Son.*"

Luke and Vanessa continued to gaze across the room. The Man disappeared from their sight. But they felt no loss, for they knew that He would always be with them.

Both had awakened into life.

FIFTY-FIVE

THE DREAM THAT WAS NOT A DREAM

August 2, 1952

Janet Holiday gave the stubborn black tie one last adjustment, then drew in a deep breath and stared earnestly into the face in front of her.

"I am so proud of you, Luke," she said, her voice soft and husky. "I am proud of the young man you have become. I know you are happy today, but I do not see how you could possibly be as happy as I am."

"Thank you, Grandma," said Luke with a loving smile. "We are both entitled to be happy. We have been through a lot together."

"I think I'm going to cry!"

"You are entitled to cry too."

"I just didn't want to *yet*! Because I know once the music starts..."

Luke opened his arms and tenderly drew Janet to him. At twenty-one, he was now several inches taller than she. Careful over his boutonnière and her corsage, she laid her head against his chest. How could either of them have dreamed that such a moment would ever come? The intertwined odyssey of their lives had been long, lonely, and full of heartache. It hardly seemed they had the right to be so happy. Yet maybe because of the fortitude with which they had endured that pain, they deserved it after all.

In the few seconds she stood contentedly in her grandson's embrace, Janet's thoughts flitted swiftly back over the past four and a half years. So much had happened since that wonderful Christmas morning when they had discovered

256

one another in Luke's room at the orphanage. How could she possibly have known when she awoke on that wintry morning that the day would also bring closure to her quest for the truth about her daughter? Or that she would discover that Luke's mother had died a hero, giving her life for the young woman—probably at that moment wearing as big a smile as her own—now waiting for this remarkable young man whose life in so many ways represented loves lost and loves found.

So many memories! thought Janet.

Yet for the two young people at the center of attention today, in spite of everything they had been through already, their life together was only beginning.

Both Janet and Luke found themselves, in but the span of a few moments, reliving the last four and a half years through their memory of all that had taken place. The subject of today's joyous celebration had come up for the first time not many days after that fateful Christmas...

Grandmother and grandson left Wyoming during the second week of January, 1948.

By then Karen Sanders had returned to Eaglescliff. She and Janet and BJ spent an afternoon together before Janet's departure. With many tearful interruptions, and accompanied by numerous questions of disbelief, Janet told Karen of the sequence of events that had led her to her grandson.

Despite the most earnest entreaties from everyone on the orphanage staff, as well as most of the children and students, Janet knew that she could not remain indefinitely in Eaglescliff. Not only did Dallas represent her life until four months before, the small Wyoming town held too many bittersweet memories of Leslie's tragic death. Luke, too, though he had never known any other life than at Eaglescliff, and though he had many friends at the orphanage, was eager to start a new life with his grandmother.

He had family again!

For Luke, Texas represented a future such as he had only been able to dream of, and with it a host of new opportunities that came with that dream. He would, of course, forever be linked to Eaglescliff by ties too strong to break. The only life he had known was there, his mother was buried there, and now he was leaving a big part of his heart behind in the small Wyoming town as well. He would be back. Luke knew that. But he also knew that he had to discover what the wider world held for him now that suddenly he had roots and a genealogy and a past. At this moment of his life, that past, and what it had to teach him of his future, lay in Dallas.

With both rejoicing and sadness, half the town, and all the orphanage, turned out in mid January to extend their final farewells as Luke and Janet boarded the Greyhound that would take them to Cheyenne, Denver, and on to Dallas. So many clustered around to shake hands with Luke one final time—Mr. Pratt, Rusty, Marco, Reuben, Stuart, Jeanie, Karen, BJ, even the Cracker, and of course Vanessa's parents and brothers and sister—that the bus was ten minutes late departing. Billy from The Telegram was busily snapping pictures for the front page story he planned to run in his next issue.

At long last, Janet boarded. Carl helped Luke up. While the driver stowed their suitcases and Luke's wheelchair in the luggage compartment below, Carl got Luke situated in the window seat next to Janet, then descended the steps back onto the sidewalk.

The crowd then watched, a sad silence descending upon it, as the bus inched away—Luke waving energetically with his face at the window—then picked up speed, moving south along Main Street, and finally disappeared from sight.

As the bus rumbled along the desolate highway south of Denver the next day, after a long and thoughtful silence Luke turned toward Janet with a serious expression on his face.

"Do you mind...ask you...ask a question, Grandma?" said Luke, struggling to get the sentence out. Speaking was still such a new sensation that each word took an effort. Yet every sound to pass his lips made the next sound easier. Everyone who knew him was amazed at how rapidly Luke's speech had already improved. Unfortunately the use of his legs did not progress so quickly. He remained mostly still confined to his wheelchair. So determined was Luke to learn to walk, however, that by early January he was able to move about clumsily with a walker for a few minutes at a time. With

Carl's help, he had resolutely practiced several times a day. Already his legs were noticeably stronger. Janet's first item of business when they reached Dallas was to get Luke into speech and physical therapy. Whether he would be able to walk or talk normally, it was too soon to tell. But if anyone could overcome such handicaps, she thought, Luke could.

"No, of course not, Luke," replied Janet to Luke's question.

"What do you think...do you..." Luke began again, summoning every ounce of energy to put into words the thoughts burning within him, "—would you approve...what would you think...I want to ask Vanessa...to marry me."

Janet's head shot around. She stared with wide eyes at Luke sitting in the bus beside her, wondering if she had heard him right.

"You want to ask Vanessa...to marry you?" she said. Astonishment was evident in her voice.

Luke nodded.

"I hardly know what to say," replied Janet slowly. "The person you probably need to be talking to is Vanessa's father."

"You're the only family I've got, Grandma...wanted to talk to you first."

"I appreciate that, Luke. It's just unexpected, that's all. Don't you think...I don't know—it seems a little soon to be thinking of marriage?"

"We've been waiting...all our lives."

"But Vanessa's still in the hospital. The two of you have only just met."

"I know...may look that way but...we know each other...better than you may think...known Vanessa most of my life...we grew up together."

"I see what you mean. But believe me, I know the difficulties of marrying too young. Don't you need to learn to be friends first?"

"We are friends...been friends for years....we're both...you know, Grandma...different for us...who knows how much time...what if...can't know how much time we might have left...want to spend it together."

The thought sobered Janet. She realized that he was right. This was unlike any relationship she had ever known, unlike any other relationship in the world.

Janet pondered Luke's words thoughtfully. She could tell from his expectant expression that he was waiting for an answer.

"You've taken me by surprise, Luke," she said after a moment. "I can tell that you have been thinking seriously about this. But it's new to me. I would like the chance to reflect on it for a while."

Luke nodded as he listened.

"I also think we need to see how Vanessa's recovery progresses," Janet added. "She will need a great deal of therapy to learn to walk again. We cannot know how long that might take. In the meantime, why don't you write to her? You and she can continue to get to know one another...in this world!"

"Could we...maybe invite the Johnsons...visit us in Dallas?" said Luke.

"I think that is a wonderful idea," replied Janet. "We will have to wait until Vanessa is out of the hospital and able to travel. But I understand what you have told me, Luke. I learned to trust your judgment and intuition even before I knew who you were. So I will trust your instincts about Vanessa, too. If this is to be, I will support you one hundred and ten percent. Whenever it takes place, what a wedding it will be—for two people who met under, shall we say, very unusual circumstances."

"Thank you, Grandma," said Luke, returning her smile. He pulled out his notebook and pen. "Maybe we could...invite them for Easter."

"If her recovery continues to progress, I think that would be great."

"Then I will do what you said...write to Vanessa...and tell her to hurry up and get strong!"

Janet laughed. "If she is even half as determined as you," she said, "I would not be surprised to find that visit taking place sooner than any of the rest of us expect."

It turned out that Vanessa was not just half as determined as Luke, but fully his equal in resolve and tenacity. Had she not been anxious on her own to get out of her hospital bed, Luke's almost daily letters detailing his own progress were all the motivation she needed. She drank juice and tea by the gallon, was soon eating with a ravenous appetite, and insisted on being helped out of bed several times a day to practice with a walker. A few falls to the floor of her room sent poor Mrs. Johnson's heart to her throat. By the time Luke had been in Dallas two weeks, however, and was busy with his own therapy, Vanessa was hobbling down the corridor of the hospital behind her walker with a dexterity that amazed and brought tears to the eyes of the nursing staff that had been caring for her for so long. None of them ever expected to see Vanessa out of her bed, much less clattering clumsily down the hall of the Carnegie Wing spreading hope and cheerfulness to everyone in the rooms as she passed.

Vanessa was released from the hospital in the second week of February. By the end of the month, though still using a walker, except for her atrophied legs her body had regained much of its strength. Her weight was up to 115 pounds. Though noting caution and restraint as befit his professional obligation, Dr. Brimlow declared her physically capable of a trip of a thousand miles and back in the Johnson family station wagon. The fact that Easter fell during the last week of March gave her another month to grow stronger yet.

As the Johnson visit to Dallas drew closer, the pace of letters between the two young people quickened. The efforts of both grew almost frantic to make as much last minute progress in their therapy as possible. By then Luke's legs were strong enough that he had mostly abandoned his walker, though still used a crutch to steady himself and keep his knees from getting wobbly.

The Johnsons arrived in Dallas on March 27, the day before Easter. Far from the letdown that might have been expected following such a build-up of anticipation, the reunion between the two dream angels was everything both had hoped for. Vanessa did not exactly fly out of the station wagon as it eased to a stop in Janet's driveway. Even as she fumbled to get the back door open and swing her awkward and uncooperative feet around and onto the ground, there stood Luke before her.

She gazed up, her heart too full even to blush. He stared down with an expression of contentment and peace. Vanessa smiled the most radiant smile Luke had ever seen. He stretched out his hand. Vanessa reached up and took it. Luke pulled her to her feet. Their eyes met.

"Hello, Vanessa," he said.

"Luke," she replied softly, "you are...so big."

"And you! Gosh—look at you! The last time I saw you, you were in bed. You look strong as a horse—but far prettier! You are just as beautiful as you were in my dreams. The dream you has become the real you!"

Vanessa could not help laughing—a high musical laugh that sent the chords of Luke's heart vibrating with the music of hope fulfilled beyond his wildest expectations.

"You are strong, too, Luke," she said. "Your voice, your legs, your arms—I felt it in your hand when you pulled me to my feet. My dream boy has become a man."

By now Vanessa's sister and two brothers had scrambled out the opposite side of the back seat, while Janet and Mrs. Johnson were renewing their acquaintance in one another's embrace. Both sensed something of what the future held, and knew that their lives would be forever intertwined.

The following afternoon, after a joyous Easter service together, the two families spent the afternoon getting to know each other more intimately at White Rock Lake. The only two who already seemed to know one another as if they had been friends all their lives, talking and laughing and reminiscing feverishly for the first time with their real voices, were Luke and Vanessa.

Midway through the afternoon, Luke asked to speak with Mr. Johnson alone. As she watched them walk slowly away, up a small incline toward a grove of birch and pine just beginning to show the green of the spring's new growth, Vanessa's heart swelled. She knew they were talking about her. It was a conversation she never heard, but a sight she would forever treasure in her memory.

They returned about thirty minutes later. Fran Johnson, Janet, and Vanessa were subdued as they watched them reemerge from the trees. Even the three younger Johnsons, sensing momentous tidings in the wind, grew quiet. Down the hill the two men came, Eric Johnson speaking quietly, Luke, limping noticeably with the aid of his single crutch, listening intently. The others waited as they approached.

"Luke and I have something to tell all of you," said Eric. "But first...Luke," he added, turning to the young man at his side, "I assume you will want to speak with Vanessa alone."

At the word alone, Vanessa's heart began beating so rapidly she thought it would fly out of her chest. Luke walked toward her where she sat at a picnic table, offered his free hand, helped her to her feet. A moment later the two walked away from the others together, Vanessa pushing her walker a little awkwardly over the dirt path, Luke with his crutch beside her.

The announcement, when twenty minutes later Mr. Johnson informed Janet and the rest of his family of the gist of his conversation with Luke—Vanessa beaming from ear to ear as she listened—surprised no one except one of the twins who had been paying more attention to the boats on the lake than the swirling romantic undercurrents of the day's events.

Anxious as is youth to cast caution to the wind and rush headlong into love, the wiser counsels of parents and grandmother prevailed upon these two young people. They recognized the wisdom of waiting until both were physically strong enough, if need be, to care for one another. They also wanted to wait until both had completed sufficient education as to give Luke an idea how he would, and a reasonable expectation of being able to, provide for a wife and family.

The next four years passed as slowly as time always does for those in love, and as rapidly as, in retrospect, it will seem to have flown by in the memory of future years. But time moves forward with inexorable predictability. A moment that is four years off comes as certainly as if it were next week. And at last the day of great preparation and anticipation drew near.

It would be the greatest celebration Eaglescliff, Wyoming had seen in years. The passage of four years, far from diminishing interest in the two local favorites, had heightened their status in the public consciousness to legendary proportions. Luke had of course been back to his hometown many times, not only to visit the Johnsons but to renew acquaintances at the orphanage. However, he had not been able to return for the past year and a half. His coming was therefore awaited with the eagerness of a conquering hero returning from foreign lands.

Billy Grimes, who took as much pride in what had transpired as anyone in the town, and with justifiable reason, had followed Luke's exploits through the years in the Telegram, including a front page article and photograph of Luke's graduation with high honors just last week from the University of North Texas, fourth in his class, with a degree in English Literature. During the same time, Vanessa, with more educational ground to make up, had zoomed through high school with an accelerated home-based curriculum, and two years of college level correspondence courses. She was eager to enroll in actual classes and complete her own degree at the earliest opportunity. Her dream was to become a nurse specializing in care for children with terminal illness and permanent disabilities.

The wedding ceremony was slated for All Saints Church in Eaglescliff, Wyoming on Saturday, August 2 of that same year. Even before it took place, it promised to become a thing of legend in that part of the country. Though Vanessa, her mother, and Janet all assumed that it would be a relatively small event, and only fifty invitations were sent out. News had been following the miracle couple for so long that the moment the date was announced word of the wedding spread like wildfire. People from throughout Wyoming began making plans to attend. Luke and Vanessa were not only the most well-known young man and woman in town, they were also the most loved.

Though most of those of Luke's age who had been with him at the orphanage were by now scattered far and wide, not one of them intended to miss this! As the throngs began to descend on Eaglescliff during the final days of July, it was hard to tell whether a wedding or an unofficial orphanage reunion drew them. By now Reuben Aruna was a rising young star in the art world. Many in town, especially the teachers of his early years, were as anxious to lay eyes on Mr. Pratt's one-time troublemaker as they were the former mute and wheelchair bound Luke Kirch.

It soon became obvious that the small church would not hold a fraction of the more than a thousand people—

invitation or no invitation—who planned to attend the wedding. Last minute scrambling by Karen Sanders, B.J. Roth, and Janet hastily shifted the venue for the reception from the church to Riverside Park. A host of volunteers throughout town was hurriedly enlisted to bake cookies and cakes and prepare snack trays and bring drinks and platters and punch bowls and paper cups and plates and plastic utensils. Meanwhile, Eric Johnson and Luke, with the help of Gary Dunn, Carl Elkin, and Mr. Pratt, ran wire and set up microphones to outfit the parking lot and area surrounding the church with loud speakers so that the music and vows could be heard by those gathered outside.

The big day finally came.

A great cheer went up from the waiting crowd when the bride arrived in her father's car. The hubbub rose yet higher as she alighted to the ground. They cleared a path for her as Vanessa made her way, on strong legs, into the church beside her proud father.

Behind Luke and Janet, a soft knock sounded on the door of the small room. Janet and Luke stepped away from one another's embrace. The door opened a few inches and the face of Annie Brodie appeared.

"It's one minute till two," she said. "Everyone's in place."

Beside her, Vanessa's mother now crowded into view. "It's time for our moment in the sun, Janet," she said. "They're waiting to walk the two of us down the aisle."

"I'll leave you," said Annie. "See you all afterward!"

"Annie," said Janet as her friend turned to go. "Thank you...thank you for everything!"

Annie smiled, then disappeared.

"You are so handsome, Luke," said Mrs. Johnson when the three were alone. "You have made my daughter very happy. We are all thrilled that you are part of our family."

"Thank you, Fran," replied Luke. "I will do my best to make her happy, and to make you proud of us both."

"You already have."

"We'll be going now," said Janet.

She gazed one last time into his eyes, then took both his

hands in hers and gave them a squeeze. "I love you, Luke."

"I love you too, Grandma."

Seconds later Luke was left alone. Outside, he knew the minister and Carl, his best man, along with Gary and John Brodie, Jr. in their matching black suits, were waiting for him.

He closed his eyes and drew in a deep breath.

"I guess this is it," he whispered. "Thank you, Lord."

A moment later he opened the door and walked out to join the others...and to await his bride.

EPILOGUE

Luke and Vanessa moved in with Janet for the first year of their marriage while Luke completed his Master's degree at North Texas. He was hired the following August to teach English Composition and Literature at Dallas's Cedar Valley College. The young couple bought a small home near the campus so that Luke would be able to walk to and from campus. He knew the importance of daily exercise to continue strengthening his knees and legs. Vanessa completed her Bachelor's degree the following year, and entered the nursing program at North Texas University.

Content for the next several years, Luke with his position at the junior college and Vanessa on the nursing staff at the Children's Medical Center, their lives changed abruptly when word reached them announcing the retirement of Mr. Pratt as Administrator of the Wyoming Children's Home in Eaglescliff. Both unexpectedly found themselves privately seized by the same thought. Luke's application for the position a month later was greeted by everyone at the orphanage with as much disbelief as rejoicing. The job was offered to him immediately.

Happiest of all about the turn of events were surely Eric and Fran Johnson.

Luke and Vanessa relocated to Eaglescliff the following June, the moment Luke's commitment for the term at Cedar Valley was completed. By then Vanessa had applied to and been hired by Roosevelt Hospital.

Two children were born to Luke and Vanessa—Jackson "Jack" Kirch brought the exuberance of an expanded family to their home a year after their arrival in Eaglescliff. His sister,

Leslie Janet Kirch, joined them two years later. Eaglescliff's most recognized couple also adopted six other children. With a quiver of grandchildren to add to her own joy, Janet sold her home in Dallas, moved to Eaglescliff, and returned to the teaching staff at the orphanage, taking her orders now from her own grandson.

The Kirches lived the rest of their lives in Eaglescliff. Within a few years Vanessa was in charge of the children's program at Roosevelt, skillfully harmonizing a career and a large family decades before that delicate balancing act came to dominate the headlines of the feminist movement. She was assisted immeasurably in fulfilling the many demands on her by a devoted mother and grandmother-in-law.

Luke and Vanessa's vision to help disadvantaged children never diminished. They worked tirelessly not only for the orphans at the Wyoming Children's Home and the Carnegie Wing at the hospital, but with orphanages and handicapped children all over the nation. Stories continued to be written on the miracle couple and their amazing story. Their unsought notoriety enabled Luke and Vanessa to establish the Angel Dreams Foundation, using donations resulting from publicity about their own story to help fund orphanages throughout the world.

The years flew by quickly. Their children grew and became men and women in their own right. The generations that had preceded them went to join those that had gone before. The years of their youth faded further into the past as they began marking the passage of their own lives not by years but by decades.

As was his custom at least once a day, Luke left the orphanage and walked slowly away from the rear of the red brick building toward the river. He tried to get away from the noise and hubbub, even if just for a few minutes, whenever he could to keep his focus and pray for the children who were in his charge. He was especially pensive on this particular day. A transition was coming. For some time he had sensed it drawing gradually closer. The result was that he had been prayerfully considering the inevitability of his own eventual retirement from the orphanage he loved with all his heart.

Evening approached. The children were at supper. This

was the first opportunity the busy day had presented him to slip away. He made his way toward the river, walking slowly though with vigor, having had no need of a cane for many years. His legs were strong and his hair was graying with the gray of wisdom. Luke's thoughts were full of gratitude for the journey on which his life had taken. He happened to have been on the fifth floor of the building that afternoon and had paid a visit to the room, vacant at the moment, that had once been his own home — the room where he had gradually learned to become a man. It was there he had experienced his Christmas dreams. He had been quietly thoughtful ever since.

As Luke retraced his steps ten or fifteen minutes later, a slender women in a nurse's uniform came into view walking toward him. He paused and waited.

"I had a feeling I might find you out here!" said Vanessa, greeting her husband with a smile.

"Hello, my dear," rejoined Luke, taking her in his arms. "Through for the day?"

"I am indeed, and on my way home. Care to join me?"

"I've got a couple things to wrap up in my office. Five minutes — if you don't mind waiting."

Vanessa stepped back, turned, and slipped her hand through Luke's arm. The two strolled along the quiet dirt road together toward the orphanage. The shadows of late afternoon gradually lengthened as the birds sang and locusts hummed, both warming up for their symphonies of evening. A green field of ripening corn stood tall on one side of them. On the other, across a fence of narrow wood slats, green pastureland extended for about a mile. Beyond it, against a cloudless blue sky, jagged peaks rose abruptly off the valley floor.

"You are quiet this evening," said Vanessa as they went.

"That mountain there always reminds me of my first angel dream," nodded Luke, "when I thought my mother was an angel." He smiled at the memory. "And the old building brought back many memories today as well," he added. "I will miss it."

As the sun dropped further in the sky, behind them they heard the sounds of laughter and running. They paused and turned to see a boy and a girl running toward them from out among the fields.

269

"Who are these two?" asked Vanessa. "I don't recognize them."

"Nor do I," replied Luke. "I have never seen them before. They must be from one of the neighboring farms."

"They remind me of us at that age—though we only shared that time in dreams. Funny, isn't it, how real it still is?"

Luke nodded. "As long ago as it is now, sometimes my memory of our dreams is more vivid than my recollection of much more recent events."

"Mine too!"

"I suppose that's a sign of old age—you remember childhood with increasing clarity, but can't remember what happened yesterday. *Are* we getting old, my dear?"

"Not a chance!" laughed Vanessa. "You will never be *old*, Luke."

"Do you ever wonder why we never had any more dreams?" asked Luke after a few seconds.

"Don't you think it is because God blessed us to live all of our lives as a dream," replied Vanessa at length. "*Afterward*, I mean—after you came to the hospital and I woke up. Our dream became real. We no longer needed the dreams. He gave us health. He gave us each other. He gave us our family. What more could we want?"

The boy and girl came toward them and stopped.

"Hi, Mister," said the boy.

"Hello, young man," said Luke, setting a gentle hand on the youngster's head.

"My name's Brad," replied the boy. "This is Maggie. She's my friend."

"I am glad to know you, Brad.—And how are you, Maggie?" Luke added.

The girl stared up at him but said nothing.

"She doesn't talk," said the boy. "To anyone but me, I mean. She says I'm her only friend. And the man."

"What man?" asked Luke.

"The man that comes to her in her dreams."

Vanessa's eyes shot open at the boy's words.

"Do you see the man too?" asked Luke.

"Not yet. But Maggie says I will."

"How does she know?"

"I don't know."

The girl turned toward her brother, cupped a hand over her mouth, and spoke something neither of the other two heard into his ear. Luke and Vanessa waited patiently. A moment later the girl stepped away.

"Maggie says to tell you," said little Brad, "that the man said that the time is coming for his angels to come home."

A chill swept through the two older listeners.

Again Maggie leaned forward and whispered into her brother's ear.

"She said that your mothers are waiting to see you again," he said, "though it might be a long time." He began laughing. "That's funny," he added. "Old people don't have mothers!"

"So you think we are old, do you, Brad?" chuckled Luke.

"Yes, Mister. You are the oldest man I know."

Luke roared with laughter.

It fell quiet again as the sound of Luke's laughter died away. Maggie was staring intently into Vanessa's face. She looked as if she was trying to speak. Vanessa stooped to one knee, then drew her face close to the girl's. Maggie reached toward her with two small pudgy hands, laid them on the sides of her cheeks, then turned Vanessa's head and pulled it toward her. She set her lips to Vanessa's ear.

"The Man said that he loves you," she whispered.

Another involuntary shiver swept through Vanessa's body. Her eyes darted up toward Luke. "Him too?" she said.

"Him too," answered the girl into Vanessa's ear. "We have to go now," she added matter of factly. "I hope to see you again. Bye."

With the words she stepped back from where Vanessa knelt, spun around, and ran back in the direction from which they had come. The boy sprinted after her. Moments later the two young dream angels had disappeared in the direction of the river.

Vanessa stood and turned to face Luke. "That was amazing," she said. "She spoke to me."

"Perhaps the spell is broken," said Luke.

"She said...I can hardly believe it—she said the Man of her dreams had a message for us."

"What message?"

"That he loves us."

Vanessa shook her head in awe. A smile slowly came to her lips.

"How strange..." she said softly. "How wonderfully strange. All of a sudden we're seeing things from the other side of the dream."

Luke smiled. "It would seem that two new angels have been found to replace us. Apparently the dream program is still alive and well."

"From what little Maggie said, I find myself wondering if ours may not be altogether through yet either!"

"What a delight it would be to see our old friend again," said Luke. "I wonder how He would appear to us now."

"Probably as the One we have known on this side—in our hearts—all these years."

They continued on back toward the orphanage. No more words were spoken between them.

Their hearts were too full for words.

Continue the dream...

For more about Chris Schneider...

> Chris is the Sports Director for CBS Radio in Dallas. He is available for radio and television interviews, and for seminars, including: "Angels, The Greatness Formula," and "Running the Race to Win."
>
> Book Chris for inspirational speaking engagements, and contact him at:
> www.RadioActiveSpeaking.com.
>
> "Like" Chris on Facebook at:
> www.facebook.com/Godaminute
>
> And follow Chris on Twitter at:
> ChrisSchneider@WarriorOfGrace

For more about Michael Phillips and his writings...

> "Like" Michael Phillips on Facebook at:
> michaelphillipschristianauthor@facebook.com
>
> Contact Michael Phillips through the website:
> www.FatherOfTheInklings.com.
>
> And don't miss Michael Phillips' other "angel" titles:
> *Angel Harp*
> *Angels Watching Over Me*

274

Peabody Public Library
Columbia City, IN

CPSIA information can be obtained at www.ICGtesting.com
Printed in the USA
LVOW05s1043021114

411661LV00013B/500/P

Peabody Public Library
Columbia City, IN